THE LONELY ELEPHANT OF DUMMUKONDA

The Lonely Elephant of Dummukonda

And Other Animal Stories from India

Samuel Schmitthenner

Quiet Waters Publications
Bolivar, Missouri
2009

Copyright © 2009 by Samuel Schmitthenner. All rights reserved. Printed in the United States of America. No part of this book may be used or reproduced in any manner whatsoever without written permission, except in the case of brief quotations embodied in critical articles and reviews.

For information contact:
    Quiet Waters Publications
    P.O. Box 34, Bolivar MO 65613-0034.
    E-mail: QWP@usa.net.

For prices and order information visit:
    http://www.quietwaterspub.com

Cover design by Kaitlyn Ramsey
Other photographs provided by the author

ISBN: 978-1-931475-43-3
Library of Congress Control Number: 2009933475

Table of Contents

ONE The Lonely Elephant of Dummukonda   16

TWO The Raging Tiger of Lakshmipuram   38

THREE The Demon Monkey of Vadarevu   49

FOUR The Hungry Leopard of Tadavaripallem   59

FIVE Nandeeshwara Rao the Heroic and Holy Bull of Blessing   73

SIX The Remarkable Bison Herds of Manjampatti   91

SEVEN The Screaming Serpent Eagle and the Necklace   100

EPILOGUE   115

ACKNOWLEDGEMENTS

The Lonely Elephant of Dummukonda is now the fourth of my books published by Quiet Waters Publications. The others are: *Ramblings with Ruth*, *The Diary of Dr. Aberly—India Years*, and *Between the Lines of the Bible*. I am so happy and grateful to Stephen Trobisch, the publisher, for the encouragement he and his staff have given to me to make this possible. There is more to writing a book than just a good imagination or the ability to put thoughts into writing. Writing should be clear and meaningful, and should reflect the faith, personality and perspectives gained from experiences of life. I believe that Stephen Trobisch has helped this to happen. His guidance has been good for me. Thank you so much, Stephen!

After I finished the first draft of *Ramblings*, finding a publisher took longer than writing the book.

Several of my learned missionary friends had written very good articles and books and sent them to our church publishing institutions. They were told, "We do not publish that kind of book any more." I experienced the same rejection from five church publishing houses and was in despair and about to give up. Then I met Dr. Maria Earling who teaches Global Missions in Lutheran Theological Seminary, Gettysburg, Pennsylvania. She showed me the book *Miracle at Sea* by Eleanor Anderson, published by Quiet Waters Publications. I sent my manuscript to them and it was accepted in a few days. That gave a boost to my life in retirement and has been a blessing to me and many others. Thank you, Dr. Earling, for your guidance and encouragement.

Again, I thank my children, nieces, nephews, cousins and my grandchildren for listening to these stories and insisting that I must write them down. I have many more to tell and share. At present a novel and a children's storybook are in the works, and I go from one to the other depending on whether I feel like talking to children or adults. My family encourages me to keep going.

My neighbors, David Crowner, and Robert Karsteter were my patient, careful, faithful and prompt proof readers. Thank you so much, David and Bob.

One day my son Peter, a teacher in the humanities department of Virginia Tech., came for a working visit. We spent the morning checking spellings of Indian names and Telugu words and made many improvements. Then I requested Peter to write the foreword for this book. He was part of The Vadarevu monkey story, and has been to the places where these stories took place: Kondaveedu Fort, Kotappakonda Hill and its temple, Tadavaripallem where the hungry leopard was shot, and the Manjampattti-Kukhal bison mountains. That, along with his good knowledge of Telugu and the culture of the Andhra people, made him the right person for this task. Thank you, Peter Babu.

One day as I was working on this story I received a card from my good photographer friend, Dorothy Blauvelt Ralson. Enclosed were four photos of my last book signing. My first thought was, "Good, now I have the photo I need for the back cover of *The Lonely Elephant*." I accepted her gift with much joy. Dorothy has a joyful spirit and loves to be helpful in spite of life's difficulties.

The other photos of animals were sent to me by my friend Ben Johnson, who spent his early years in India and went to Kodaikanal School. Years later, after he retired from teaching physics in America, he taught physics in Kodaikanal School. His sister, Marian Johnson Karl, took the picture of the tiger while they saw it in the wilds of North India. Marian was in my grade school class in Kodai before the start of World War II. Thank you, friends, for all the pictures you have taken and shared.

Thank you, Marie Crouse, for being one of my first test readers. You have always been interested in my stories, asked questions and made most helpful suggestions. Marie never hesitated to point out where I could make a phrase or story more expressive and understandable.

Lastly, I thank Becky Brown, librarian of Gettysburg Adam's County. For each of my books she has written an article for the Gettysburg Times before the publishing and book signing events. She has promised to do this again when this book becomes available.

I have been blessed by my whole family and many friends and cannot imagine how I could publish anything without their loving encouragement.

FOREWORD

It is an honor and it gives me great pleasure to write some thoughts about this extraordinary collection of animal stories by my father, which pertain to his missionary career in India (1952-1981). My siblings and I, our children, members of our extended family, fellow "mish" kids, and countless others have had the pleasure of hearing Dad tell these stories, though he has never rendered them the same. Thus for a good storyteller like my Dad, it is difficult fixing these stories in written form, something my siblings and I have been prompting him to do for years. Indeed these written stories can never replace the oral renditions upon which they are based; however, for those who have heard Dad's stories, this book will evoke fond memories; and for others who have never heard his stories, they will be treated to a gifted storyteller in this book.

As an historian, what strikes me most about this collection of stories are the various histories they contain. At a basic level is family history. No better is this presented than in the first story, *The Lonely Elephant of Dummukonda* (my personal favorite among Dad's stories). This story begins when my grandparents were missionaries in India. Through the story we learn about August and Marian (Dad's parents) and their growing sons (my uncles Jerry and Fritz, and Dad; aunt Molly had not entered the picture yet). My siblings and I also enter into this and other stories. In regard to another story, *The Demon Monkey of Vadarevu*, my siblings and I will never forget hearing the temple priest say, "The damn monkey is biting everyone! You [Dad] must kill it."

The stories also capture pieces of the history of Christian missions in south India. We learn of the changing nature of relationships between missionaries and Indians from the time of my grandfather to Dad's final years in India. The stories detail Dad's field experiences in rural areas and the close understanding and connections he develops with rural inhabitants, including *adivasis* ('original dwellers,' often referred to as 'tribals'). For me Dad always defied the stereotypical "fire and brimstone" missionary by his close attention to studying and understanding the local language and cultures, and in how he has utmost respect for the majority non-Christian populations who surrounded him during his years in India. These stories certainly exemplify this quality of many missionaries. And, of course, we learn how missionaries mixed "business" with the pleasurable pursuits of camping, hiking, and hunting.

Being set in India, these stories obviously capture different aspects of the history of India. Several stories, most particularly *Nandeshwara Rao: the Heroic and Holy Bull of Blessing*, tell of a mythic past and typify traditions of storytelling that continue in present-day India. In several of the stories, the great Indian epics are often referenced, as for instance Valmiki, the alleged author of the Ramayana (in *The Lonely Elephant*), and Hanuman, the monkey-god servant of Lord Rama (in *The Demon Monkey*). This Indian tradition of storytelling even takes on a Christian message in *The Screaming Serpent Eagle and the Necklace*, a story which epitomizes the indigenization of Christianity in India. The stories also capture the twentieth century history of India as the country transitioned from a colonial subject state to an independent country. As noted above, we learn of the changing nature of relations between missionaries and Indians during this century. The stories describe Indian traditions and lifestyles that are slowly disappearing as India becomes increasingly modernized, as for example the native medicinal cures described in *Nandeeshwara Rao*. While perhaps these descriptions have a nostalgic tone, through them Dad seems to suggest that there is benefit holding on to certain traditions.

I would like to characterize this collection of stories as falling somewhere in between the famed hunting stories of Jim Corbett and the Panchatantra, an ancient Indian text of animal stories comparable to Aesops Fables. Like Corbett, Dad tells a good hunting story, though perhaps more believable than Corbett. Unlike Corbett, however, the animals in Dad's stories aren't always the victims of a rifle, unless they act immorally. Like in the Panchatantra, animals who act morally in Dad's stories, especially in their service to humans, allegorize what should be the ethical human behavior. What else could one expect from a preacher-storyteller!

I am delighted that Dad will leave a printed legacy of his wonderful stories that generations to come can learn from and enjoy.

Peter Schmitthenner
Son of Samuel and
History Professor at Virginia Tech

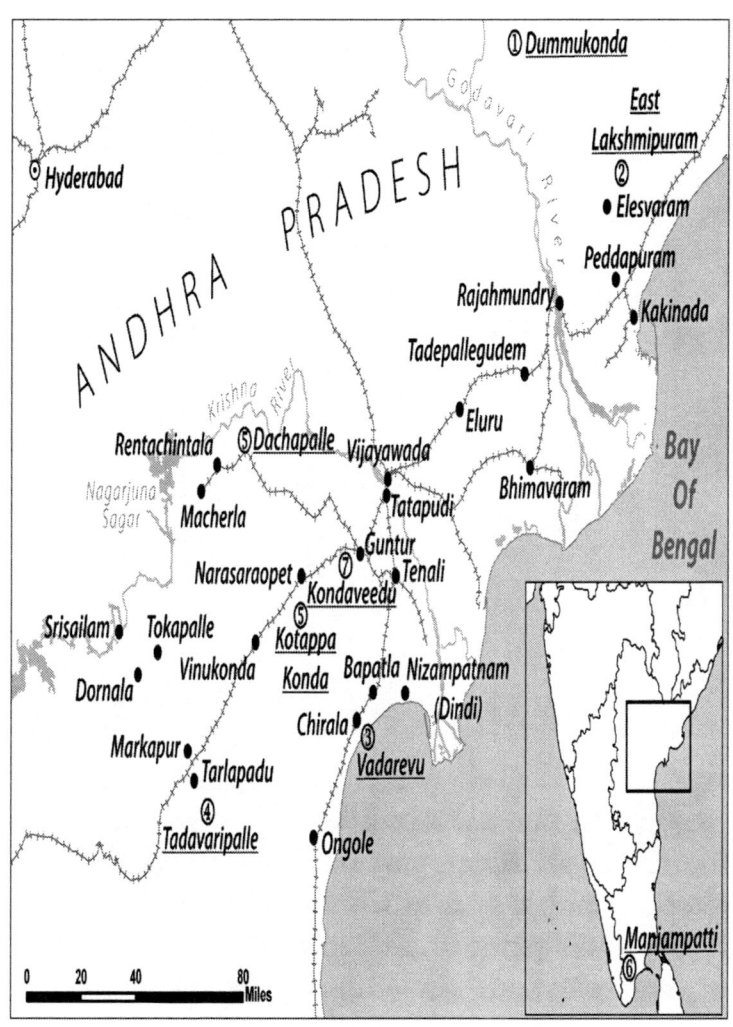

Map of Andhra Pradesh

The numbers indicate the locations of the seven stories

ONE
THE LONELY ELEPHANT OF DUMMUKONDA

Aenugu Raja's English name was Elephant King. He worked in the teakwood forests on the banks of the Godavari River, not far from Bhadrachelam in the Andhra area of southern India. He had been given this name shortly after being captured in a great elephant drive in which his father, mother, sister and brother had been driven into a strongly built log enclosure, along with 12 other elephants, in the year 1924. This happened in the Tamil area of southern India in the Mudumalai National Forest, where there are still herds of wild elephants.

It takes months to train a captured wild elephant. The very best, most experienced *mahouts*—that means elephant riders—are able to do this with the help of the tame, trained and experienced elephants. Every year the trained elephants and mahouts take part in these highly dramatic and dangerous capture and training events. Since Raja was a young four-year-old elephant, it took less time to train him. He was trained by a mahout named Valmiki. He was named after the ancient tribal hunter "from the hills" who met Rama and became his servant. Valmiki then wrote the epic story of the life of King and Lord Rama. That story, called the *Ramayana*, was written down in Sanskrit more than 2000 years ago. It is perhaps the greatest, most beloved epic in Hindu literature.

The Valmiki of our story believed that kindness and good care were better tools for training than force or punishment. He made sure the allowance he was given for feeding the elephant was used faithfully to provide the best for Raja. Not only did he find the best grass or hay for his elephant, he also bought bellum (unrefined brown cane sugar), onions and extra salt for Raja each day. When they returned to their camp, Raja would have his onion as the reward for a good day's work. He would crunch it, then blow a blast of onion breath toward any elephant or person who was nearby. "Ha! Smell my onion breath," he'd say in *elephanti*. Valmiki taught him all of the commands that mahouts use to steer an elephant, have it go faster or slow down, to be careful: "Here is a bad mud hole!" "There is danger here—stand quiet!" "Put this rope around the log!" "Tighten the rope!" "Kick the log so it rolls into the river!" "Tear off that limb—it's in our way!" "Work is finished, head for home!" and dozens of other commands. Once an elephant knows and obeys all the required commands, he is ready to become a working elephant of the forest department. Raja responded to kindness. Fully grown and in full health great strength, he was ready for a work assignment. Valmiki reported to the chief forester, an Englishman named Mr. Smythe, that Raja was ready to be a full-time work elephant.

"By Jove, what a magnificent beast!" said Mr. Smythe in English. He then switched to Tamil. "Valmiki, we are going to ship ten of these newly trained elephants to the Andhra area, where there are great forests of teak. How would you like to go with them? You must care for them during the journey. Then, if you like, you could stay and be the mahout for Aenugu Raja after the elephants are delivered. Do you know any Telugu?"

"Yes, Sir, I lived in Andhra for two years when I went to the 6th and 7th standard. Yes, I would be happy to be with Raja as long as I live." (Elephants live as long as people, 60 to 80 years of age. At the time, Valmiki was 45 years old and Raja was about five years old).

Valmiki and the elephants traveled by trains, changing three times before they arrived in the town of Bhadrachallem. At the station they were met and given a warm welcome by forest department personnel and nine experienced mahouts. After feeding themselves and the elephants, the mahouts loaded each elephant with supplies. They began their journey as an elephant train, traveling for several days until they reached the great teak forests and joined the elephant work camp. The resident elephants were glad to meet new friends; there was much trunk-touching, grunting, snorting, trumpeting, spraying each other and the mahouts with water when all bathed in the river. It was a gigantic, noisy elephant celebration!

Soon the new elephants were put to work. Every mahout was amazed to see how effortlessly Raja skidded out the largest and heaviest teak logs and the skillful way he could tighten and then loosen the ropes. They watched him rolling logs into the beautiful Godavari River.

("Why did they put the logs into the river," you ask?) Well, there were no truck roads or railroads within 50 miles. The easiest way to take the logs to the markets was to tie the logs into rafts and float them down the Godavari River 100 miles or more to Rajahmundry. In that city were lumber yards, saw mills, and a railway station on the Madras-Calcutta rail line. This valuable teak wood could be shipped by the river to any place in India or the world.

The river crew would take each log and lash it onto a log raft. When several such rafts were ready the boatmen pushed off for the five to eight or more days' journey, depending on the current of the river and the prevailing winds. In the middle of each raft there was a wooden platform where the men would stay, cook, eat and sleep as they floated down the river to the city. Each of the crew had a long, strong, seasoned bamboo pole. With these they could push the clumsy raft to the deepest part of the river, where the current was strong, or bring it to the shore to camp.

Valmiki was happy to be in the forest taking care of Raja and working with him as a team. The two were the best elephant-mahout team in the whole camp, and everyone was friendly with them. Each day Valmiki found the best grass and provided special treats for his friend. In the month of May, the hottest time of the year, the wild mangos ripened. All the mahouts went with their elephants to where the huge mango trees were. Every time the wind blew, the small ripe mangoes would fall. The mahouts gathered them in bags, but the elephants just reached up with their trunks and picked them off the branches. Ah, what a feast!

Life was good; work was hard. Now and then the tree sawyers would move the camp to a new area, seeking a fresh supply of good quality, larger trees.

When the *tamarind* fruit was ripe, the same kind of joyful gathering and tasting was celebrated, only the mahouts kept most of the fruit for cooking.

Tamarind means "date of India." When ripe for picking, packing and storing it has a sweet-sour taste. When I was a boy we ate it green and raw. When the stiff skin is taken off, the tamarind are pressed together in special bamboo baskets and can be kept for a year. The hill tribal people made a lot of money picking, cleaning, packing and selling the tamarind, and they use it to make pepper water which makes rice and curry so tasty.

After three good years of health and work, with Aenegu Raju, Valmiki began to feel very weak and dizzy. After just four days he died suddenly while he was working with Raja. The whole camp was shocked and very sad. Raja was filled with grief by this tragic and sudden death of his best human friend. He kept moaning elephant moans and weeping huge tears. *Ayyoo* (too bad), how lonely he felt! Valmiki had been father and family to him.

Now life would become even more difficult for Raja. A new mahout was assigned to care for and drive him. The mahout's name was Neechudu, which means "dirty fellow." He was a drunkard. Each day after work he would head for the liquor shop to spend the money he was given to take care of Raja, on drinking locally made brandy and on rich food for himself. Raja had to eat leaves off trees while he worked and during break time. Neechudu never gave him any salt and, of course, never any onions or bellum. In the evening Neecha (his nick-name) would come to see that Raja was securely tied to a tree, and sometimes he would beat the elephant with a stick, but noble Raja pretended nothing hurt him and stood there taking all this senseless punishment. Night by night the beatings became worse.

One night Neecha drank more than usual. He came and cursed Raja and then lifted his bamboo staff to beat him. Then he looked down at Raja's feet. (Reader, do you know the elephant's most tender place? Its toe nails!) Neechudu began to club Raja's toe nails. What horrible pain! Raja did not cry out. Neecha continued beating Raja's toes until Raja could stand it no longer. He quickly swung around, grabbed Neecha with his trunk, and threw him against a tree. Neecha fell to the base of the tree, unconscious and bleeding. Was he dead?

Immediately Raja was filled with fear. Once during his training, one of the elephants went mad and killed his mahout. In a few minutes, Mr. Smythe had come with a strange-looking, short iron tube with a handle and pointed it at the killer elephant. There was a terrible, booming explosion, and the elephant dropped dead with a hole in its side. "Oh, now the forest ranger will come and kill me, I must run away!" thought Raja. He used all his strength to break the rope holding him to the tree. He ran to the river, went down the slope and entered the water. First Raja waded, but then the river became deep, and there was a current. He swam with all his might for almost half a mile, then could once again touch ground and wade to the shore on the northeast side of the river. He was safe for now.

Raja rested till early morning and then kept traveling further and further to the north, going into the higher hills. After two days of fear and constant walking, Raja felt he was safe. He had not yet seen any humans in this dense jungle. He started to walk slowly, browsing, taking branches and leaves in his trunk and putting them into his mouth. Then he noticed a wonderful smell coming up from the valley below. Someone was cooking onions! He carefully and quietly (yes, elephants, though heavy, can walk very softly if they want to) walked down to the valley and there he saw some cleared fields where rice and beans were growing. "Umm, good food!" he thought. At the end of the valley there were some small thatched huts. A few people were walking and sitting near their homes.

Raja walked into the open and went straight toward the hut where he smelled onions cooking. The children saw him coming and screamed out a warning to their parents. Now, I must explain that in Andhra State there have been no wild elephants for hundreds of years. These village people had never seen an elephant. They were terrified. They gathered their children together and fled into the forest. Then the braver ones stopped, turned around and hid behind trees to see what the elephant would do.

Raja tried to get his head through the small doorway. His head got stuck. He gave a mighty push upward and the door came loose, and so did the bamboo and palm leaf thatch roof of the hut. Some of the roof came down around Raja's head, so he looked like an elephant wearing a huge straw hat. The hiding residents who saw it were terrified, but they had to laugh at this ridiculous sight. Raja took his time. He found the onion sack and slowly ate six or seven, and after each one he breathed out a huge amount of onion breath, "fouooughhh, fouooughhh," all over the little village. (Guess what he found next?) Salt! He put some in his mouth with his trunk and was so happy to taste salt again. He had suffered from not having enough salt. Then he finished off his adventure, eating all the bellum he could find in the hut.

Raja walked back the way he had come and went down to the stream, found a deep spot where he could sit down and soak, and then took a shower. Now for the first time in many days he felt better. He was free from torment, and he knew where he could find onions and his other favorite things. Going up the other side of the stream, he came upon an orchard of *kamala* fruit trees. (*Kamala pandu* means ripe tangerine fruit.) These tasted soooo good. He picked the golden fruit and ate about 20 before he was satisfied. What a great place this was!

After a couple of days, Raja found another little settlement of seven houses. There the people had built a small dam across the nearby stream and dug an irrigation canal to water their rice fields.

The rice was ready for harvest. To Raja it looked like a feast. He waded into the field and ate rice stalks and crunched up the solid grains. Then he went to one of the houses, and the residents fled. Again he wrecked a house, dug out the onions, salt and bellum he wanted, and ate the rice they had been cooking. He liked this new way of life, and every few days he hit another village and grazed off the bananas and *kamala* (lotus fruit tangerines, some of the world's best).

Meanwhile, the terrorized villagers had made every effort to get help from the forest and police departments of the East Godavari District. A number of them walked 20 to 30 miles to the village of Guterdu, where there was a school and a forest department office. They told their stories of woe to the teacher, who then drafted a letter describing all of the destruction the elephant had done to eight villages, and the damage to their rice and orchard crops. This information was sent by telegraph to the Superintendent of Police at Kakinada, the headquarters of East Godavari District. Three days later, a select band of four of the men and the school teacher came from Guterdu to plead for help. The police chief invited them into his office and ordered tea. After introductions their leader said, "Sir, a mad elephant is destroying villages in the highland valleys of our district. Sometimes he wears a hut roof as a headdress. This is a demon. We fear to stay in our villages. Up until now twelve of our homes have been destroyed, our supplies of onions, salt and bellum are all gone, and our kamala orchards are being ruined. You must help us by coming and shooting down this terrible beast before any of us is killed. We have had to leave there for safety; now all of our crops will be destroyed. Sir, kindly have mercy."

The British District Superintendent of Police (DSP) stood up, looked them in the eye and gave a solemn promise, "The beast shall be destroyed! You have my oath!"

As soon as they had left he wrote out a letter and sent it by constable to the missionary who lived near the hills and took care of many small congregations of Christians in the highlands of East Godavari District. He was a good hiker and an experienced hunter. He loved the hill people and could talk to them in their particular dialect of high toned hill Telugu. His name was August Frederick Schmitthener, my father. Augie, my dad, and my mother, Marian, lived in Yeleswaram and the edge of the forested hill country. They had three boys Jerry, Fritz and me, Samuel.

The letter from the Police officer was very brief:

> Dear Rev. August Schmitthenner.
> We are having a serious Problem in the hill country west of Guterdu. We need your help. I would urge you to please come to my office tomorrow as this is a most urgent matter.
>
> Yours faithfully,
> Thomas Owen

The next morning my dad left on his motorcycle and made the 40-mile journey from Yeleswaram to Kakinada in about two hours.

The policeman on guard waved Augie to the police headquarters, and one of the staff took him immediately to see Captain Thomas Owen, Esq., the resident DSP. Augie was warmly greeted, and Mr. Owen sat down with Augie and told him the whole story. Mr. Owen had telegraphed to the various elephant work camps and thereby learned from the superintendent of the Bhadrachallem teak lumbering camp that their favorite elephant, Raja, had hurt his mahout by hurling him against a tree. Then Raja had run away. There was an enquiry, and most of the blame was placed on the mahout, the drunkard, Neecha. "Rev. Schmitthenner," Mr. Owen explained, "there are no wild elephants in the Andhra area, only in Mysore and in the jungles of the Tamil area of South India and Travancore. So this so-called mad elephant knows the ways of people and will try to depend on the villagers for his needs—onions, salt, bellum, sorghum, rice and fruit. The Konda Reddies, Konda Kapulu, Koya Dorralu and Valmeekulu (names of regional tribes) need our special attention. We protect them from the merchants of the plains. No outsiders can buy land from these tribal people. They use the land carefully and are very good at hill farming and orchard agriculture. I am requesting you hunt down and shoot the marauding Raja. I know of your love and interest in the hill tribal people and know that they will help you in this venture."

Dad was very hesitant about this proposal. He said, "I only have a small bore rifle and a shot gun. Neither of those would do the job. I have no experience hunting elephants."

Thomas Owen replied, "Not to worry, Rev. Schmitthenner, I will give you my double-barreled, high-powered rifle. That's what my friends in Africa use. Here are some good maps I have made up showing each village that has been damaged by the elephant Raja, and also where we have police or forest department offices with telegraph equipment. We can keep in touch with each other."

Reluctantly, my dad agreed to go on the mission for the sake of his beloved hill tribe friends. Then he got on his motorbike and headed home with the elephant gun slung from his shoulder.

Dad was very quiet during dinner and would not answer our questions about this "urgent matter" the police had talked about with him. After our late supper, he told us boys to read our favorite books—there would be no story tonight. Dad was in a serious mood.

Sometime later that evening, my brothers and I could hear Mother and Dad arguing with each other. That was a rare occasion. And it kept up, on and on. Mom was crying. Jerry had his ear up against the door and motioned for Fritz and me to be quiet.

"Wow," Jerry whispered, "The superintendent of police wants dad to shoot a wild elephant that has been troubling villages in the hill country way up by Guterdu. He has given him a double-barreled rifle—an elephant gun. But Mom doesn't want him to go. She said, 'I am not ready to be a widow and raise these boys alone.' She's crying. I think Dad isn't going. Ayyoo, that's too bad."

Jerry was right. The next morning both Mom and Dad looked tired and unhappy. Dad announced that he was going back to Kakinada to see the District Superintendent of Police and return the gun. We boys thought Dad should have gone ahead with the elephant hunt and we were disappointed. Years later we looked at it differently.

Several days later, the DSP drove in his car with some well trained police, armed with rifles. He drove to Rampachodavaram, and from there hiked for three days with a company of porters who carried food for the journey, a tent, camp cots and chairs, and his heavy rifle. At each village settlement they inquired about the mad elephant.

They sent messengers to every village within 50 miles of Guterdu. After five days an exhausted messenger returned, reporting that the elephant had raided Nulakamaddi, a village of 12 houses about 15 miles away. Immediately Thomas Owen set out with the armed constables and a guide who knew a shortcut to Nulakamaddi. It was dark by the time they arrived, so they camped for the night. Early the next morning, after tea and biscuits, Thomas Owen and his men set out with several brave men from the village. They found the elephant tracks and followed the swath the elephant had made through the tall grass, and the tree branches he had broken while feeding on leaves. The elephant had not gone very far. There he was in a grove of coffee trees, browsing on the ripe red coffee berries.

Thomas Owen tried to stalk closer to the elephant, but he stepped on a dry stick and broke it, making a loud snapping sound. Raja heard the noise, turned quickly, and saw Thomas standing 60 feet away holding a stick with a metal tube—the same kind that Raja had seen being used to kill an elephant at Mudumulai in Tamilnadu. He lost his temper, stuck out his ears, and charged full speed at Thomas, trumpeting as loud as he could *butterblastboom*! Thomas was unnerved and could not hold his heavy rifle steady. He shot once, hitting Raja in the wide part of his left ear flap. The infuriated Raja kept trumpeting and charging. Thomas could not get off another shot. Just before the elephant reached him, Thomas jumped out of the way, dropping his rifle. He ran off, following his constables. Raja turned around and charged again, but after a few steps saw the stick with a metal tube and ran to it, picked it up with his trunk, and banged it against a stone till the stock was splintered and the barrel twisted and bent. Then he looked around. The men had gone.

Now a new period of Raja's life began. He would never forget the kindness of Valmiki and the fun of working with good team elephants and men at the logging camp. But he would also remember forever the cruelty of Neechudu and seeing another elephant shot. He would not forget this man who shot at him, giving him a pain every time he moved his ear. He decided to go into the highest hills, 2000 feet higher than Nullakamaddi, and to avoid even the forest people. He would learn to do without onions, bellum and the produce of the village gardens and orchards. Again he walked and climbed for two days, until he found the highest peak in the land. Up on top of these mountains it was very strange—there were trees only where there was a stream. The rest of it was grassland, deep, luxurious sun-dried grass that tasted good like hay. On another hillside he saw a herd of 20 bison (gaur or wild oxen) grazing peacefully with their young calves. They would be no problem. In fact, they would be helpful. He followed the herd for three days and discovered where they licked salty rocks or dirt. That's how all wild animals get their salt.

Now and then in the hot summer, some villagers would come to this high range to collect certain plants or hunt for deer. Sometimes these men would start fires and watch the grasslands burn. Then the bison, deer and Raja would gather in the forested stream valleys, which never were burned. He avoided people for the rest of his life. Every time he heard or smelled them, he headed quickly away. The birds got used to him and perched on his back. He had plenty of fodder and water, sweet mangos in the stream valleys, and small but tasty hill guavas. Raja wandered for many miles all around and up and down this mountain range of Dummukonda. He was content, but lonely.

This might seem as a good place to end the story. But to my amazement, I re-established contact with this magnificent elephant many years later, after Ruth and I went to India in 1952. We were appointed to go to Yeleswaram to live and minister in the area, and we lived in the same house where our family had lived until Mom and Dad left India in 1945. We moved to Yeleswaram with Bill and baby Hans, and later Chris and Peter were born, so Yeleswaram was their first home. In the big office closet I found an account of my dad's, which detailed his going to the region above Addatigala, then walking to Ramavaram and climbing Dummukonda.

I wanted to see this great hill country, so I went there with fellow missionaries Joel Mayer and Bill Coleman. We recruited three men from Nullakamuddi to be our guides. We climbed to the top of Dummukonda, which is more than 4000 feet in elevation. We camped up there and shot a barking deer, and later a bison that was coming towards us from only 30 feet away.

I went there once again with Elmer Burrall, but due to a late start we could not get to the top before dark. So we made a campfire and put up a small tent. As we ate supper, we smelled something foul. Elmer whispered that it was a leopard. We grabbed our weapons and shone our hunting lights, picking up the eyes of the sneaky leopard. It kept circling our camp, then finally went away. We decided to take turns on guard duty, one sleeping and the other shining the lights.

Another time I went with fellow missionary Hank Leutkehoelter, and several hunters from Nullakamuddi. We camped, then Hank, a guide and I followed our stream for several miles until it cascaded 200 feet over the beautiful Dummadara waterfall. On our way back to camp from our higher ridge, we heard a tiger roaring and could see the hunters and our cook, Mark, running away from the camp. We ran to join our men. They had actually seen the huge tiger and knew their bows and arrows were not enough for that big beast. Emboldened by my rifle, two hunters came with me to the campsite to take on the tiger, but it had gone.

I went several more times with other friends. We always climbed there late in April when it was so hot on the plains.

In winter of 1969 Ruth and I returned with our family. The grass was too high, the trail overgrown. Insects of various kinds plagued us, and we were too cold at night. It was miserable.

Early before dawn I woke up Bill to go hunting. I posted him at the top of a forested valley, then I went around and down as low as possible and began to "beat" upward through the jungle toward Bill's position. I slowly zigzagged making a moderate amount of noise and was able to chase two barking deer toward Bill. Unfortunately, he did not get to have a clear shot at either, but he was glad to see them for an instant.

When we returned to camp it was pretty obvious that all the rest wanted to go home as soon as possible and feared spending another night on the mountain, so we packed up and left. We were exhausted when we reached our car at Ramavaram, and then spent the rest of the day and half the night driving back to Guntur.

On my last journey to Dummukonda, taken with Fred Lueders and Ed Nabert, I went out early the first morning with Laksmanudu, a hunter from Nullakamuddi. He suggested I ascend a high ridge and sit in a certain place where the forest thinned out into grassland. He would follow up the little stream and zigzag through the forest till he could see me. He was sure there was a deer or two or a pig in there. I could hear him, occasionally chopping with his machete, making enough noise to move the animals up that valley. Then there was silence. What was taking him so long?

He finally appeared and waved to me with a big grin on his face. He had a bundle of something wrapped up in wild banana leaves and vines.

"Look what I found," he shouted with glee. Then he untied the vine and showed me. There, wrapped up in banana leaves were two huge, week-old elephant droppings. Each was about half as big as a soccer ball. (How did I know it was a week old? Hunters get to be pretty good at judging the age of turds. By examining the contents, you can find out what the animal has been eating and how healthy it is. In other words, I am an animal turd expert.)

I was amazed to see evidence that there were wild elephants at Dummukonda. "Lakshman," I asked, "how is it possible? There are no wild elephants in this state."

He replied, "There is only one. Raja used to be a logging elephant working in Bhadrachallem; he wounded his mahout and crossed the Godavari, and he roams around this highland. Once an Englishman tried to shoot Raja. As Raja charged him, the Englishman shot Raja in the ear flap. Then the Englishman jumped and ran for his life while Raja destroyed his rifle. Only a few of us mountain people have seen the elephant. Since he was shot in the ear he avoids people, and never comes near a village, fields or orchards. But we see broken branches in the forest, areas where he had eaten huge amounts of grass, and these *perda bantulu* (balls of dung). Oh how happy my village will be! We make medicines out of this dung, mixing it with lime, tea and bellum. We also mix it with fresh cow dung and use it on boils, broken bones, and for massaging old people who have pains. It is good, healing medicine."

Then I remembered Jerry listening at the door, hearing about Raja and how the Superintendent of Police had asked Dad to shoot the 'mad' elephant. A year later Dad had told us that story. Now, after almost 40 years had gone by, Lakshman's story brought back these memories, I was glad Dad hadn't killed Raja.

Ten years later, I went to visit our congregation in Yarlagadda at Ramavaram. After our communion service I walked through their rice fields till I could get a clear view of Dummukonda. Coming toward me was an old man who looked familiar. It was Lakshmanudu, of Nullakamaddi, my old friend, guide and village medicine man. I was shocked at how he had aged. Well, of course I asked about Raja. He looked sad and said, "Oh, he died this year in the high grasslands of Dummukonda. Three of our village men went up there to harvest wild curry leaves. They saw hundreds of vultures on the ridge above our campsite, feasting on more meat than they had ever eaten. The three men took Raja's tusks and later sold them to an ivory carver. Then they returned to Nullakamaddi to share the news of Raja's death. From that day on, the stories about his life became part of the folktales of the Konda people of the Eastern Ghats of Andhra Pradesh and of the Schmitthenner family.

Thus ends the tale of Raja, the lonely elephant of Dummukonda. He died in 1980 at the age of

60 years. He had been so lonely. If elephants are allowed into paradise, no doubt he is there staying with Valmiki, eating good rice, onions, salt and bellum, and enjoying the companionship of other faithful elephants. Now he is free from trouble and happy. Can't you picture him standing in the shallows of the River of Life, giving joyful showers with his trunk to angels, saints and elephants?

TWO
THE RAGING TIGER OF LAKSHMIPURAM

One night, long after midnight, the peacefully sleeping residents in the small Indian village of East Lakshmipuram were harshly wakened by the roars of an enraged tiger very close to the village. They were terrified. Frightened children who had never heard such a fearful, blood-curdling and angry roar began to cry. No one in the village had a gun of any kind. A few had spears and bows and arrows, which they had obtained from a nearby hill tribe village, but they were not very skilled in using them. What could they possibly do on this dark night? What if the tiger entered the village? The families huddled together in fear for five hours until dawn finally came. What a fearful night!

The recognized village leader was K. Lazarus, catechist and acting minister of the Christian congregation to which most of these villagers belonged. He was a dedicated servant of the Lord, deeply loved by all in the village, and the one they would come to for advice, marriage arrangements and settling disputes between neighbors. Lazarus had an eighth grade education and two years of Bible training at Luthergiri Seminary in Rajahmundry, Andhra Pradesh. Along with his wife and family, he had been living and serving in East Lakshmipuram for 15 years when I first met him.

At first light people came to see Lazarus. He gathered them into the small thatched village church and had a simple prayer of thanksgiving that no one in the village had been hurt. Then the bravest men of the village, armed with bows and arrows and several spears, set out with Lazarus to see what kind of signs the tiger had left around the village. A short distance away vultures were beginning to circle, so the men headed in that direction.

What an amazing sight they saw! The tiger had killed a big, humped Brahmani bull and carried it over 200 feet, taking the shortest path to the jungle where it could hide the beast from vultures and feast on it for a few days. It had followed a foot path going between two tall *Palmyra* trees.

Tigers carry their prey by holding the dead animal by the neck in their mouth, lifting the animal and carrying most of its weight. A large animal like a bull will have legs dragging in the dirt, so it is easy to follow a tiger "drag" mark. While going through the narrow gap between the Palmyra trees, the tiger and bull had become stuck. The tiger then gave its first angry roar. It let go of the bull, went around to the front, grabbed the bull by the head and tried to pull the bull between the trees. The harder the tiger pulled, the more tightly wedged the bull became. What terrible frustration! Yes, even huge, fierce tigers sometimes do stupid things. After that, the tiger had kept up roaring for a long time, terrifying the villagers. Then the tiger ate from the rear part of the bull about 80 pounds of meat, and went back into the thick Nagulakonda Forest to find a secluded and quiet place to sleep during the day. He would be back to eat a full meal soon after it grew dark again.

The villagers were amazed by the huge bull stuck between the trees. It was starting to bloat, so they also could not move it. Soon the whole village had gathered there to view this astounding sight.

Lazarus took charge. He set guards to stay and keep the vultures away from the bull. He sent two men to the nearby village of Gontivanipalem, where the owner of the free ranging "sacred" bull lived. He was Narayana Rao, the *karanam*—the government officer in charge of land survey, property rights and deeds—for these two villages. They informed him that his favorite, sacred bull had been killed by a tiger and asked him to come and discuss what should be done.

Gontivanipallem is a wealthy village at the base of a 1000 foot mountain, Devarakonda. There live people of higher castes: *Brahmins*, merchants, farmer castes, carpenters and other tradesmen castes.

Lakshmipuram, in contrast, is a small and poor village on the northeast side of the large irrigation reservoir called Timmaraju tank. In years when there are heavy monsoon rains and the tank is at the highest level, with both overflows roaring with floodwater, the rising lake backs up into the village, flooding the streets and sometimes even the houses with several feet of water. The villagers are all *Dalits* or *Harijans*, the lowest in the caste system, mostly poor and exploited. They cannot buy new house sites on higher ground. They do not want to move out, either, because they have plenty of farm labor to do: plowing up the muddy rice fields, working for the wealthy farmers of the *Kapu* (farmer) caste, planting the rice, watching the crops during the night to protect them from ravages of wild pigs and various kinds of deer, weeding, and working from dawn till dusk during the harvest season. In their spare time they help the farmers and land owners look after their livestock, cut good grass in the forested hilltops, and bring firewood from the Nagulakonda Forest. In the dry months they pick tamarind fruit, climb the palmyra trees and cut the leaves to replace the thatch on their houses.

They take the old dried out palmyra stem stacks that ring around the trees. These are pounded to get out the strong palmyra fiber, which is exported for making brushes and brooms.

The meaning of *Nagulakonda* is King Cobra Mountain. From the air this range of hills looks like a snake twisting for more than 80 miles from the Timmaraju tank, going north almost all the way to Vishakapatnam, the most important naval base of India. The rare king cobra is found in this snaking range of hills. All the drainage from west of this range flows into Timmaraju tank, the second largest artificial lake in coastal Andhra. Nagulakonda Reserve Forest abounds in game, especially sambur, spotted deer, barking deer, pigs, leopards, and tigers. The forest contains lots of bamboo, valuable hardwood including rosewood, and tamarind trees which provide fruitpicking and processing work for the people of Lakshmipuram.

Though poor and always working hard to make ends meet, these faithful people gather for worship every Sunday morning and try to take a full day of rest to renew their strength and faith. Now they had a new problem which they shared with their rich Brahmin neighbor – a raging tiger that was beginning to kill cattle. What could they do?

Narayana Rao arrived at the scene of disaster and wept when he saw his sacred bull dead and wedged between the two trees. Lazarus expressed the sorrow of all the villagers. Then he asked the karanam what should be done. With sadness in his voice Narayana Rao said, "The tiger must be killed or he will continue to kill the cattle of these villages. Doesn't your missionary Schmitthenner have a rifle? You should go to Yeleswaram and ask him to come immediately to shoot this cursed beast. Meanwhile I will send a good carpenter to build a *machaan* (hunting stand) in that tamarind tree. It would be only a 40 foot shot from the machaan to where the bull is. Yes, surely the tiger will return tonight to feast again on his great prize. If he could not carry it to the jungle, he will come each night to eat. His greed will be his undoing!"

Lazarus cycled eight miles to Yeleswaram to the missionary house and asked the office clerk to see Pastor Schmitthenner. Prasada Rao said, "Oh, I am so sorry. He has gone to Guntur by train for church meetings and will not be back for three days."

"Ayyoo," said Lazarus. He went to visit the elders of Yeleswaram and told them the sad tale about the tiger killing Narayana Rao's sacred bull. They knew Narayana Rao and all expressed their concern.

"There is a hunter in the village here named Nagabushanam," an elder said. "He has much experience and has shot panthers and wild cats and also many deer. I am sure he can help you." He sent a boy to fetch Nagabushanam with instructions to bring his gun. Soon the boy came, bringing his shotgun with him. He said he could easily shoot a tiger. He had both buckshot and solid ball shot, which he had used to kill panthers. He said he might have to stay for two days. His fee would be 200 Rupees a day and 300 more as a bonus when the tiger was killed. Back in 1954 that was a good amount. He also expected free meals of goat or chicken curry and rice, and coffee and tea when requested. He should also be given the skin.

Knowing that Narayana Rao was wealthy and would gladly pay for this service to the whole area, Lazarus promised this would be done. He then rented another cycle for Nagabushsanam . Nagabuushanam packed a bag including shotgun shells, a three cell flashlight with new batteries, and several blankets. He tied these and his gun to the cycle frame, and the two men set out for Lakshmipuram.

They arrived at 2 p.m. Lazarus' wife had prepared a good chicken curry meal, and Nagabushanam ate as if he had been hungry for many days and soon fell asleep. Lazarus woke him up at 4 p.m. and took him out to see the bull between the trees and the machaan the carpenter had made, using a rope bed as flooring and securing it with nails and ropes. Nagabushanam climbed the ladder, sighted his gun at the target area and said it was an excellent arrangement. However, when he saw the size of the bull the tiger had killed and carried for a considerable distance he began to have worries. He asked, "How high is the machaan?"

"Eighteen feet," replied the carpenter.

"*Saray,*" Nagabashanan said, meaning "okay!" Yet he was worried. He walked back to Lazarus' home and then suddenly demanded, "I must have a bottle of brandy before I go up into the machaan this evening."

Lazarus had none in his home and believed in temperance. "I don't have any and I cannot buy it," he said. "I believe it is wrong. All the brandy in this village is home brew; sometimes it poisons people. Please do not do this!" But Nagabushanam insisted that unless he had brandy he could not face the tiger and demanded 20 Rupees in advance. With much reluctance Lazarus gave him the money. Nagabushanam went around the village until he found some brandy, bought a bottle and then went with many of the young people of the village to climb up into the machaan with a blanket, a shotgun, and a light. Quickly all of the villagers went home to have their evening meal and hoping and praying that Nagabushanam would kill the raging tiger.

After a simple vegetarian curry and rice supper, the families settled down. The children went to sleep. It had been an exciting day and they were worn out. But none of the grownups could sleep. They were waiting to hear gun shots, sure that the tiger would come to take its dinner.

As it grew dark and the night advanced Nagabushanam grew more and more frightened. To bolster his courage he drank more brandy. First he felt warm and brave and ready to fight the tiger, even barehanded. "Bring on the tiger!" he said to himself. Then he thought even more courage would be good, so he finished off the bottle. He began feeling sleepy and nodded off. He nearly fell out of the machaan, and woke up with a start. Then he heard close by the growling of a tiger. He began to sweat with fear! He raised his loaded shotgun, felt his flashlight which was clamped to the gun, pointed it toward the bull and waited. Then he heard the greedy tiger eating, tearing off chunks of meat, growling with joy. Nagabushanam turned on the light. He saw the huge tiger. Suddenly the tiger gave a terrible roar that seemed to shake the machaan. Nagabushanam began to tremble violently. He was sure the tiger would jump up and catch him. He lost control and had a wet loincloth (as they put it so mildly in India). His hands were shaking as he fired off one barrel and immediately the other, missing both shots. The tiger began to roar again and again, then it settled down and finished eating all it could. Next it circled the village again, roaring in triumph. Nobody could do it harm!

Back in the village they had heard the roaring and the shots followed by more roaring as if the tiger was as healthy and angry as ever. What had happened to Nagabushanam? They all knew he had been drinking. Was he dead? In the dark with the tiger on the prowl, no one had the courage or foolishness to go to the site. It was another long night of suspense, fear, crying children, and lost sleep.

Early in the morning the young brave men with their few weapons went with Lazarus and Narayana Rao to see what had happened to the hunter. They found him in a deep sleep, snoring in the machaan. His shotgun and flashlight were on the ground. They examined the bull and saw where the tiger had eaten. They woke Nagabushanam, "Come down, rascal, drunkard, stupid, donkey (the worst insult in India), idiot-fool!" yelled Narayana Rao with fierce anger. "You have put the whole region into danger. Lazarus, take him back to Yeleswaram to return the cycle." Do not pay him anything." Then all the young men were enraged and wanted to beat up Nagabushanam, but both Lazarus and Narayana Rao prevented them. Lazarus told them, "Learn from this, see how foolish and harmful it is to get drunk, especially when others, your family, the village and helpless people are depending on you. Learn from this and let this poor, miserable man go!"

As Lazarus left the scene, Narayana Rao instructed the villagers to remove the bull and have it cremated. By great effort they managed to extract it from the two trees. Everyone helped to gather firewood, and soon the priest of the Gontivanipallem temple came. They cremated the bull as the priest chanted poems about Siva's bull, the Lord's vehicle and his sacred friend, Nandi.

Strangely, the tiger never returned to bother the villages in that area. Perhaps it did not like the sound of the shotgun or the light flashing into its eyes, or the strong smell of brandy. So the villagers dwelt in peace, and they had another story to tell to their children and grandchildren.

THREE
THE DEMON MONKEY
OF VADAREVU

One of the most delightful spots on earth is the beach at Vadarevu, on the east coast of southern India. Vadarevu is the name of a large village on the Bay of Bengal. Someone with great imagination named this place *Vadarevu*, which means "place where ships land." The bay is so shallow that not even a motorboat can put into this harbor. There are no docks. Fishermen who live in their own little village nearby go out at the dawn of each day in their ancient catamarans made by lashing two shaped tree trunks together with rope, with strong wooden sides tied to the logs. There is a center hole in which a mast is fit after the cataraman has been pushed through the surf. (Our word *cataraman* comes from Tamil, a South Indian language. It means tied tree trunks.)

About 300 yards south of the village lies the Andhra Evangelical Lutheran Church retreat center, a large, beautiful site filled with casurina trees, which thrive on the sandy, somewhat salty soil. There is a guesthouse with two apartments, each with a kitchen and a bathroom. A large veranda facing the ocean and a wide breezeway between the apartments provides enough space for 100 or more to sit on mats and worship during retreat time. There are also five small block houses where families can stay, a long open dining hall where up to 100 people can eat at one time, and storehouse where tents, camping equipment and large pots and pans for mass cooking are stored.

The peak season for mission and church retreats is from after Christmas until the end of March. This was the ideal season, as it was cool. The temperatures would drop to 60° at night and not go above 85° during the day, and there was always a breeze offshore during the night and early morning, and onshore later in the morning when the sand heated up and the hot air ascended over the land, sucking in the cooler ocean air. After March, the sand becomes uncomfortably hot.

At this retreat center we had retreats for pastors of the whole church, pastors' family retreats for the three synods nearest Vadarevu, retreats for Bible-women and evangelists and new Christians, and the annual missionary retreat from Dec. 27

to January 3 of each year. I have attended all of these retreats and found them to be uplifting to the spirit, a great time of fellowship, physically reviving and days of great fun.

Sometimes early morning prayers would be held on a wooded knoll overlooking the bay, and as we sang we would watch the sun rise over the Bay of Bengal. It was as if we were seeing the dawn of creation where earth, sky and sea met in perfect harmony and there was Light!

Now and then, when our children were down from boarding school, our family would reserve the guesthouse for our family camp. We spent a lot of time at the beach. Since the bay was shallow, we could walk out 30 or more yards through the gentle waves and then body surf into shore when larger waves came along. This was a safe beach without undertow. Even in winter the water was warm enough for swimming, even at night. Swimming at night was a beautiful adventure, as the water was filled with tiny phosphorescent creatures. When these creatures were disturbed by churning water, they all lit up, making us look and feel as though we were in the midst of lit Christmas trees.

Our family became friends with many in the fishing village. We would see them pushing their catamarans through the surf very early in the morning in order to catch the offshore breeze, which would take them three or four miles offshore to where the fishing was best. Most of them would return in the evening before sunset.

Often we'd go to meet the incoming fishermen and bargain with them for shrimp, sea bass, herring, ocean catfish or crabs. Mostly regular buyers were there to meet the boats, but out of courtesy and respect they would allow us to buy small amounts of the catch. Often the fishermen would save part of the catch for their own families. Some varieties they kept to make dried salt fish, which they could sell for a good price. The fishermen's catamarans were often met by wives and children. In that case the wife would handle the bargaining. The fishwives were loud, energetic and strident—let's say more ef*fish*ient at bargaining than their husbands.

We would buy our fish for the evening meal, take it to the retreat center and let the faithful caretaker clean it. I asked him what he would do with our catch. He said, "I will pilate it than pry in peanut oil." It took me awhile and some watching before I realized he meant *fillet*. Telugu people do not have the "f" sound in their language, so they pronounce: fish "pish," figs "pigs", and fry as "pry."

The main village of Vadarevu had a bazaar, several coffee shops, restaurants, some offices, two constables, a dispensary with a resident compounder (pharmacist), and middle class, sturdy homes for the fish agents and merchants. It also had electric current.

The most important man in the village was the karanam, a Brahmin named Venkateswara Swami, who was responsible for keeping village records and copies of deeds of property. In Vadarevu he was also the natural leader of the village. People with problems would go to him. We dealt with him also. One of our missionaries worked with him to get a legal site and deed for the roadway going from the village to the retreat center. Venkateswara Swami was friendly and helpful.

One afternoon after our family had enjoyed three days at the beach, we loaded up all of our things in our trusty jeep station wagon and set out on the road to the village. As we approached the junction we saw a group of the townspeople blocking the road. What could this be? I stopped and got out of the car. Venkateswara Swami and other elders approached me. They were agitated. The karanam was the first to speak, which he did in a loud voice so that all could hear.

> "Sir, we are glad you can be with us and help us today. There is a dangerous monkey that is causing much suffering to the people of this village. You see, we have always had this tribe of monkeys living in the village. They are very clever. They compete with the village dogs in taking every scrap of food. They steal fruit from our orange, papaya, banana and mango trees—even green fruit. They climb over our houses, and if anyone leaves a window open a monkey will enter the house to steal whatever food it can find. Monkeys are a pest to the hotel and coffee shop owners and customers. They are so

skilled at suddenly reaching through a window to snatch *idlies* and *pakordies* (different kinds of rice and lentil cakes) and other good things right off the banana leaves of the coffee shop patrons. But all these years we put up with this because, to us, monkeys are sacred. You must know how the deity Hunaman was a devotee to Lord Rama and helped him in many ways. We worship both Rama and Hunaman. For the monkeys to steal and find food from us is acceptable; it is the *leila* or play of the gods. But now we have this crazy and cruel monkey problem."

I asked, "What has this terrible monkey done?"

Haridas, headmaster of the village elementary school replied,

"The wicked monkey is biting everyone it can. This is the largest and fiercest of the male monkeys and the tribe leader. Two months ago, suddenly it became very mean and ferocious. When women come to draw water from the well, it jumps on them, scratches and bites them. Also, without warning it will swing down from a tree where it has been hiding to jump in the midst of children playing, biting and wounding them. We have seen our children running home, screaming and bleeding. Women can no longer go to the village well alone. Children are afraid to leave their homes. This evil ape is bold. It often breaks into the huts of the poor people, stealing, threatening and causing so much fear and suffering. You must help us get rid of this animal. We have no weapons in this village, no guns, not even spears. This is why we need your help. Do you not have a rifle in your car?"

I had brought along a .22 rifle, and we had had target practice in a deserted place among the sand dunes, so they all knew I had a rifle. "Yes, I have a rifle." I knew what they were going to ask next and I began to sweat from apprehension.

"Then shoot this monkey for us!" demanded Venkateswara Swami.

I remembered how years before one of our impetuous young missionaries had shot several monkeys who had been stealing vegetables from his garden. This had sparked a riot, during which the village priests stirred the people to march against the missionary. Only police intervention prevented them from harming the missionary and his family. It made it necessary for him to move to another area. He had learned a hard lesson: you must learn not only the language, but also the culture and religion of the people among whom you live and serve. Arrogance, blatant disregard for their religion and their feelings, or ignorance of beliefs and culture can do immeasurable harm to the work and ministry of a missionary, and detract from the witness of the church in that area.

I answered carefully, "I am sorry, but I cannot shoot the monkey. I am from America and am a missionary here to serve your people. To shoot and kill an animal that is sacred to Hindus and represents your god Hunaman would not be acceptable. It would stir up the people, and it would make it difficult for us to maintain the work of the church retreat center. Please excuse me from doing this. I cannot do this deed that goes against your religion."

By this time more people had gathered, including a number of women. One of them began to scream at me,

"Don't you care about our children and the women of the village who are being attacked and wounded? We would never blame you or allow anyone to come against you for shooting this terrible beast! Have mercy on our village, especially our children! I thought you missionaries were here to help people!"

I glanced at my good wife, Ruth and she gave me a nod and that look of hers which made it clear she thought I should listen to the woman.

Then the karanam, Venkateswara Swami spoke as their leader,

"Sir, this is not Hunaman the monkey god. This is a *rakshasi*, a demon, that has taken the disguise of a monkey to deceive us and cause suffering. God only incarnates himself to help people who are being persecuted. This is undoubtedly a rakshasi that will continue to do great harm and could even kill a child if you do not help us. I swear three times by this ground (*Ee bhumi ke todu, mumartiki chepputunnanu*) that we will never come against or blame you, but will only thank you for this deed. You must shoot the monkey! Here is our priest, Bhagavan, listen to him!"

Bhagavan was attired in his priestly shawl, sacred thread, with three holy ash marks on his forehead, signifying his god was Lord Siva. He spoke with a quiet voice,

"Sir, we all request you to do this. It is the unanimous decision of the village council. As priest, I also believe this is a rakshasi that is doing much cruel harm to the innocent people of our village and, if unchecked, this could become a mighty evil force that would create much wider evil and harm. The damn monkey is biting everyone. Kindly do the needful and shoot the monkey so that children can play safely and the people live and work without fear."

That ended the argument. I unpacked the car enough to find my .22 rifle, loaded up and waited while some of the young men searched through the village for the monkey. I asked the karanam to give me a reliable guide who could identify the monkey with certainty.

Soon one of the young men returned, saying, "the rakshasi monkey is in a casurina tree near the village well. I told everyone to go into their homes or clear off the street."

He led me and my guide to the place. We were accompanied by the karanam, several of the village elders and my boys. As soon as the monkey saw us it began to snarl. I was surprised at how large it was—no doubt one of the biggest and certainly the meanest rhesus monkey I had ever seen. It grasped the branch above where it had been sitting to pull itself up. That gave me a clear shot at its heart. It took the hit, but clung to the branch as its life ebbed away and then, after a minute or two, fell to the ground. Immediately seven or eight dogs pounced on it and tore it apart. Venkateswara Swami told me the monkey had jumped on many of the dogs and bitten them also, so now they had their revenge.

The whole village cheered and thanked me. A man appeared from nowhere bearing two flower garlands. One was given to Ruth by the lady who had pleaded for their children, and the other was placed around my neck by the thankful karanam, who then gave a little speech while the villagers cheered.

By the time we left the village and got to the main road at Chirala, it was time for supper. We stopped at our favorite restaurant-hotel, Raja Villas. We had our choice between shrimp, crab, catfish head or herring curry, and between 5 small dishes of curried vegetables, lime pickle, yogurt and buttermilk spiced with onions and ginger. It was a good way to end our adventure with the demon rakshasi monkey of Vadarevu.

FOUR
THE HUNGRY LEOPARD
OF TADAVARIPALLEM

A fierce and clever leopard had been terrorizing the villagers of Tadavaripallem and their livestock. Almost every night the leopard would sneak into the village after it became dark and quiet, find a sleeping animal, kill it and quickly carry it away before the householder knew what was going on. If there was moonlight the panther would come very late at night, or make a raid early if the moon rose late. None of the villagers had weapons that could deal with a leopard. After this terror had continued for several months, the village *munsif* (headman) sent for help to the headmaster of Tarlapadu High School, six miles away.

Tadavaripallem and Tarlapadu are in the western inland portion of Ongole District, Andhra Pradesh. Ongole, the district headquarters, is on the Bay of Bengal. Tarlapadu is about 80 miles to the West and located on the railway going from Guntur to Hubli on the West Coast. It is a dry, rocky area with lots of scrub jungle, fields for dry crops in the valleys and much grassland shared by sheep, goats and *jinka* (black buck antelope).

The headmaster of the Lutheran Tarlapadu High School wrote a letter explaining the dire circumstances and daily fear of all the residents of this village, which was just six miles from the high school. He gave me the toll: 15 dogs, 9 piglets, and 37 goats. A total of 61 animals had been lost in the past ten weeks. The headmaster asked, if I would please come and shoot the panther.

Just five days after I had received his letter, a retreat was scheduled for all the gospel workers at a traveler's guesthouse twelve miles from Tarlapadu. We would be going through the Tadavaripallem village on our way to the retreat location. We had booked the guest house, built on the edge of scrub jungle at an important junction where the road coming east from Cumbum divides. One branch went to Podili and the other to Ongole. This guesthouse was not used much because it was not near any town. Now, when government officers are on tour they prefer stay in comfortable hotels. The old guesthouse was well-built, with teak roof beams and with stone and cement walls. There were three very large rooms and several small rooms, a kitchen with lots of cooking space and a good well with steps descending to the water level. This is called a *digudu baavi* (a climb-down well), and is most helpful to travelers who have no bucket or rope with them. There were few comforts there—no beds and only two tables with four or five chairs. There were no inside toilets. Outside there was only one, and it was in bad shape. So the guesthouse was rugged, but it had plenty of space for the 60 people we expected to join the retreat. We would all be sleeping on the floor on mats. Above the main room there were the wooden remains of a *punkah*. During the British Raj, such government buildings had a ten-foot long fabric attached to a wooden board. A rope stretched from the middle of the punkah above the doorway going outside, and one of the servants would pull the rope back and forth to fan everyone eating underneath it.

My friend Ed Nabert, trusty driver Solomon and I drove more than 120 miles west from Guntur to Tarlapadu. We arrived a day early with the hope that we could hunt for the leopard. The headmaster came along with us to the village. The people there, especially the shepherds were happy to see us. They had been making plans. They showed us two places where the leopard usually entered the village. The first was where it crossed a stream. It always stopped to drink there, and there were many sets of tracks in the sand. The other spot was a path that a few feet down the way became a street. This path was lined with trees. One of the elder villagers was the munsif. He said, "We will put up two *machaans* (platforms), from which you can shoot the leopard—one in that tree overlooking the path for you," and he pointed at me. "The other will be in the tree nearest the stream where the panther usually takes a drink." We agreed it was a good plan. Quickly they brought two ladders and two small rope beds five feet long and about two and a half feet wide. They turned my bed upside down and tied each leg to a nearby branch, making sure the bed was level. They chopped off two branches that were in the way of my view. Then they tied up another machaan in the tree where Ed would spend the night. The final deed they did for the good cause was to bring a goat and tie it to a stake near my machaan. (Oh, you want to know why only one goat? Well, they knew that the panther might come for a refreshing drink where Ed was sitting in the machaan. So why not give the hunter on the path equal status by offering the leopard something to eat. This was all their idea. We were here to serve them.)

Ed and I made up peanut butter sandwiches and put a banana, an orange and some cookies in each lunch box. We packed these along with our flashlights, clamps, coffee thermoses, and ammunition. I climbed up into my machaan with my rifle slung over my shoulder, then dropped a rope and pulled up my bag of provisions. It was beginning to get dark. I checked the flashlight, clamped it onto the rifle and loaded up. Only then did I start in with a peanut butter sandwich. Meanwhile, the head man and his son tied the goat to a nearby shrub 10 yards away, put a fish hook through its ear and brought the string up to me, tying it to the bedpost. I did not want to do that, though I knew the goat might be killed anyway. This fish hook trick was cruel. They told me to pull on the hook line every half hour after 10 pm, saying, "That will make it bleat! The panther will hear it from a long way and come."

Then they said, "We do not like sacrificing a goat, but remember, we have lost over 61 animals to this hungry leopard. This goat will be sacrificed for the good of the whole village."

Bidding me goodnight, they left me sitting on the bed, eating a cookie. Then the darkness deepened; there was no light between me and the darkness. Then I looked up to see all the stars, and I thanked the Lord for creating the heavens and giving us the stars, which do help a lot when the moon does not rise.

After an hour I ate another peanut butter sandwich. It sort of stuck in my throat, so I reached for my coffee flask. As I turned the cap it made a loud screeching, "keek, keek, keeek," so I stopped and then started coughing because of stuff in my throat. I tried the thermos again, making more noise, and at last got my cup of coffee. I wondered, "Did the leopard hear me? Will it come? Not if it heard this screeching!"

Two hours later I was still waiting. I was scratching myself, and felt some insect bites—then more painful, itchy bites, and I realized that the bed must be full of bedbugs. They hide in every crack in the wooden frame. "This is going to be a miserable night!" I thought. "Nothing like being a great white hunter." To distract myself I pulled the hook line and the goat began to bleat loudly. I settled down, watched the stars and noticed the path being right in line with the Southern Cross.

Then I heard a sound. Something was coming toward the goat, stepping on the dry leaves now and then. It was the dry season, during which there was no rain for four months, so there was a carpet of dry leaves all over the area. I thought, "If I turn on my light, it will freeze and I can shoot it before it gets the goat." But before I could shine the light, the animal turned and came toward me. It was under me, and I couldn't shine the light below the machaan. The leopard circled behind the tree. Then I heard claws scratching and digging into the bark as it climbed up the tree. My heart was beating rapidly, and I was scared out of my wits. Yes, I knew that leopards could climb trees. In desperation, I twisted around so I could aim at the back of the tree. Ready to shoot, I turned on the flashlight. There, just six feet away was the biggest wood rat I have ever seen. Whewwwww! It scurried down the tree and ran off. My shirt was wet from sweat, and I began to shiver and thought, "This is getting to be ridiculous." I finished off the coffee, ate a banana, and then got back to concentrating on the leopard.

I pulled the hook line every half hour or so. Each time the goat yelled "ma-a-a ma-a-a ma-a-a!" I looked for familiar stars, the Seven Sisters, Orion and Cassiopeia's Chair. Then I saw a satellite climbing in its perfect orbit from one end of the heavens to another. Was it Russian or American? I thought about the Cold War. In the distance, about five miles away, I could see the lights of an occasional truck coming down the Cumbum-Ongole road next to fields of pearl millet, chilies, and lentils. At night the *jinka* (black buck antelope) roamed these fields and grazed without the villagers shouting at them, as they did by day. There were also several packs of wolves in the area. Wolves do not raid the villages, as leopards do. They are content to catch rabbits, occasional jinka or a stray goat.

I now felt peaceful and began to enjoy the silence, the wonder of the stars and the cool summer night. I began to hope the leopard would not come and kill the goat. I stopped the occasional pulling of the fish line, content to contemplate my happy life in India. Today the retreat would begin and I had the opening Bible study. It was prepared, but I would be pretty sleepy by then. I went over the study in my mind. Then I noticed the beginning dawn. How beautiful it was before the sun appeared! After the sun rose, some of the village people came to get me and Ed. No, we had not seen anything. There were no new tracks at the drinking place and the goat was still alive. The village teacher came by and invited us to breakfast—Indian-style coffee (half milk, coffee essence, bellum) and *upma* from *sugi* wheat (like cream of wheat) browned with onions, black mustard seed, and cashew nuts. It was delicious!

As we ate, the munsif and other shepherds came and pleaded with us, "Please stay with us and try again tonight." We said we were sorry, but Ed had to leave by train that morning and return to Guntur, and I was the opening speaker at the retreat.

"We'll try to come as soon as we can," we assured them. "Thank you for all your preparations and for breakfast."

Then trusty driver, Solomon, and I drove Ed to Tarlapadu station and left him waiting for his train from Hubli on the West Coast. As we drove through Tardavaripalli, we waved to our friends. They signaled us to stop and informed us news had just arrived that the leopard had raided another village near the Gundlakamma river three miles away. That is why it had not come for us.

We went on to the gospel workers' retreat. (That sounds like the end of the story to me. What do you think? No?)

The retreat began well. Sixty elders did come, as expected. We had much enthusiasm to learn, and I was glad I was awake enough to deliver the opening message and Bible study. We had other speakers, discussion about how to approach Hindus and how best to teach—by stories, by example, by ministry of care to the sick, by prayer.

We had a good opening meal eating huge amounts of rice. At this rate we would need another bag. The cooks gave me a list of stuff to get from Tarlapadu that evening. Even if the bazaar was closed I could get it from the high school. I had an afternoon nap while others spoke and had devotions, and then awoke to the sound of the others singing hymns.

It began to rain at about 3 pm, and we were glad for the good shelter of the old guesthouse.

As soon as the food was ready that night, Solomon and I ate and then climbed into the jeep to go to Tarlapadu. We had to get supplies and also pick up Dr. N. Isaac, a devoted church man, scholar in archeology and head of the History Department of Andhra Christian College. He was from a remote village in Tarlapadu Field and was greatly loved and respected, especially in the area.

Salomon and I had driven about three miles when we saw some animal far in front of us. We slowed down, and as we grew closer we could see it was a leopard. I loaded my rifle and checked the light clamp, making sure it was tight. Then I whispered to Solomon, "When it goes to the side of the road as we get closer, just stop." It went to the right side. So did Solomon, but he was too far on the right side, almost up against the bushes. I quietly got out of the car and shone my light, but all I could see were bushes and rain drops reflecting the light off the leaves. I walked slowly beyond the jeep for a while, but I could not see any eyes watching us. Then I heard Solomon excitedly saying, "Look! It is up there ahead of us, walking down the road." So I got back in the jeep.

"Solomon, this time stop in the middle of the road. We'll have a better chance of seeing it."

"Yes, Sar," he said.

I remembered a magazine article I had read saying that when it rains, leopards and tigers prefer a good trail or road, where it is not muddy or slippery. We drove until the leopard crossed the road to the left. We stopped in the middle of the road, and I was just getting out of the jeep to shine my light, when a bus came around the curve, heading straight toward us. The driver jammed on the brakes, stopped just in time and yelled at us to get out of the way.

"Side EE!" An angry Solomon began to yell at the bus driver about a leopard and how the bus had spoiled everything. Their enraged shouting match was, in a way, ridiculous! I said to Solomon, "back up to the side and let them go." The bus passed us with the blaring of its horn and suddenly all was quiet.

I poured a cup of coffee, and as I drank it, I ate a couple of dates and said to Solomon, "You know, Solomon, we are only about two and half miles from Tadavaripallem. I think the leopard is going there. Let's wait five minutes more, and then we will start out. The rain is almost over. When we see the leopard again I will sit on the roof of the jeep. I gave him several signals I would make with my feet.

After going about a quarter of a mile, we saw the leopard ahead of us on the road, no doubt thinking about the goats of Tadavaripalle. Solomon stopped, and I climbed up on the roof, placing my feet in the middle of the windshield. As we slowly approached the leopard, it crossed to the left and went off the road. I wagged my feet. Solomon brought the jeep to a gentle stop. I put my 30-06 rifle to my shoulder and shone the light to the left. The leopard was on a little ridge of stone, 30 feet away and broadside to me, with its snarling face turned towards me. I aimed behind the shoulder and pulled the trigger. The leopard collapsed and lay there, apparently dead. I got down from the roof and said, "Thanks Solomon. Now we will wait some time and then pelt it with stones. I drank some coffee. Then, with my gun ready sighted on the leopard, we approached. We could see it was certainly dead. Nothing moved; a stone Solomon threw thumped off of its chest.

Then I noticed that the leopard was female, and her nipples were swollen. No wonder she was such a persistent hunter; she had to be well fed each day in order to nurse and feed the cubs. How many did she have? Were they old enough to live without her? Probably not.

We put her in the back of the jeep station wagon and drove the several miles to the village. They were so happy to see us and hear the good news. When they heard she was a female, they immediately said, "Oh yes, that is why she was so hungry and clever. Thank you so much, Sir for helping us. We know this is the one!"

We drove to Tarlapadu Station. The train had arrived but Dr. Isaac was not on it. The station master handed me a telegram: "Sorry emergency situation not coming tonight coming tomorrow first train. N. Isaac."

We went to visit the headmaster. He was so happy and wanted us to show the leopard to all the boarding students, which we did. We borrowed the extra bag of rice and supplies we needed from the boarding school kitchen, and returned to the retreat. The last prayer meeting had just ended. Our leopard tale made quite a stir.

Even though I was dead tired, I knew the leopard had to be skinned that night, so I did it with the help of a village elder who was an old hand at skinning animals. The only time I took over was to skin the paws in such a way as to keep the claws, and skin out the head so it could be mounted. I had done this twice before following a good set of directions, so knew how to do that. I kept the skull with the beautiful cruel teeth. We had several stout fellows drag the carcass a hundred yards away from the buildings to the edge of the jungle. Then I folded the skin, took a hot pour bath, and went to sleep on my thin cotton mattress as soon as my head hit the pillow.

The next morning we watched the vultures gather, and within an hour of the first vulture's arrival the carcass was reduced to a skeleton.

During the morning retreat three men from Tadavaripallem, including the munsif, came to visit us, bringing a goat with them.

"We want the gospel workers gathered here to have a good retreat meal tonight. Here take our goat. Instead of sacrificing a goat to get the leopard, we can now have a thanksgiving meal of the goat with all of you."

I thought we should pay them for the goat and was about to say something when I saw the look in the elder's eye.

"This is how we show our thanks. This is our part of the retreat, and we are honored to share this with you," he said.

I kept quiet. When the poor give with thanksgiving we should learn from them!

That's the end, right? Well, almost, but not quite.

About three months later when I visited Tarlapadu, the munsif of Tadavaripallem came to visit me again. He said, "We really felt sorry for the cubs of the mother leopard. We contacted other nearby villages, and all of us searched for a cave or den where the cubs might be. We wanted to save them, feed them and sell them to a zoo, but we never saw or heard them and believe they must have died. I wanted you to know that we really tried hard to find them."

I thanked him for that. What kind, caring people!

Now, that's the end!

FIVE

NANDEESHWARA RAO THE HEROIC AND HOLY BULL OF BLESSING

Preface

About one hundred and fifty years ago, a most unusual and heroic event took place in the Palnad area of the Telugu. I have never heard that this event was ever written down. It was a folktale that now only a few older people in that region remember hearing. One of them was my friend

Kotiah, the faithful mission driver of Rentachintala Lutheran Hospital, who was later designated as the church president's driver. He worked for me from 1973-1981, then retired. Kotiah related this story to me before he passed away. I hope that it will be remembered, so I have included it as part of this book and dedicate this story to P. Kotiah, church driver.

Story

Kommatothi Subbarao came from a long line of cattle-breeders and dairymen. The pride and joy of his family was his bull, Nandeeshwara Rao, meaning "The Lord, Nandi." He was named for the holy bull, Nandi, the vehicle of Lord Siva. This Brahmini bull, big and strong, was independent and had the run of the village. Nandi's near deity position gave him the privilege of grazing through the bazaar of Dachapalle and the nearby village of Nadikudi, deliberately sampling the vegetables, grain, and fruit in the open stalls by the road. After all, he was holy in the eyes of the people. And so they tried to tolerate this loss with amusement and hope that it might bring them blessing and good *karma* for the future.

Nandi exercised the same prerogatives in the fields. He wandered here and there by himself, grazing and sampling the crops as he pleased.

Nandi sometimes wandered far and was skillful in investigating new places and finding the best grazing areas. In the evening he would turn toward home, where he was assured a generous meal of bran and special feed.

One night Nandi did not come home. He always had returned at dusk for feeding because his owner fed him very well. As Nandi was a prize bull and used for breeding purposes, his owners let him just wander around. He never charged at or hurt anybody. For some reason most of the bulls in India are gentle, whereas the bulls in America are not—I don't know why. Anyway, Nandi did not come home that night.

Subbarao was worried, so early the next morning he organized his servants and friends to help him in search of his precious bull.

Kommathoti Subbarao and his wife *Girija*— which means one born in the hills, an alternate name for Siva's consort—lived in the village of Dachapalle, in the *Palnad Taluk* (administrative region) of Guntur District.

The Palnad is full of limestone ledges, and the fields between the limestone shelves are wonderfully rich and fertile. Farmers are able to raise good crops as long as there is enough water. The crops most people ate were *zonna* (sorghum*), ragi* (horse-tailed millet*), tsadza* (pearl millet) and rice, where irrigation was available. These crops and the plant stalks are full of calcium, so it is a great place to raise cattle. *Paalu* also means milk, so the

Palnad is the land of milk, and *Paalrai*—white limestone—also contains the word for milk.

Limestone has brought prosperity to this region, with its quarries, stone cutting and polishing, and burning of slaked lime, and within the past one hundred years this region has supplied all the stone needed for two large cement factories.

The search party went over all the fields between Dachapalle and the Krishna River, then began looking in the rocky and uneven scrub jungle that could not be farmed. One of the men then spotted vultures circling over an area of scrub jungle to the east of the river. The youngest and fittest ran toward that site. As the others followed they came to a clearing at the edge of the jungle and there saw a most amazing spectacle. None of them could have ever imagined anything like this.

There was the bull lying on the ground, with a huge tiger lying on top of it. Pools of blood were everywhere, and the grass and weeds were trampled and the small trees broken. The evening before the tiger must have jumped on the bull to start this terrible fight. Somehow Nandi had thrown the tiger off. Then they circled each other, and the tiger had sprung again, getting a good hold of Nandi—but the strong bull had crushed him against a tree. The tiger had lost its hold and was again separated from Nandi. It had circled around and around Nandi, looking for another opportunity. Several more times it had attacked, but could not maintain its grip on the fierce bull.

Finally the tiger, with a roar and a rush, had sprung again. Just as the tiger sprang, Nandi, who had very sharp horns, bucked his head and was lucky enough to hook the tiger squarely in the throat, penetrating a major blood vessel. The doomed tiger had then bled to death. During its dying fury it, clawed deeply into the bull's body inflicting wounds of terrible punishment. Then it died on top of the bull. Nandi was helpless; his horn was still in the tiger's throat, and he was too weak from loss of blood and exhaustion to shake it free.

Subbarao anxiously asked, "Is Nandi alive?" Nandi was still alive but was helpless and extremely weak. The rescue men lifted the dead tiger off the bull and immediately gathered round to examine and touch the bull. They called him *Nandeeshwara Rao*—the bull of Siva—and came to worship him. Subbarao suddenly realized what a lucky and fortunate a man he was. Here was his magnificent treasure, a bull holy by its breed, but also now proven to be blessed and holy enough to have killed a fierce tiger.

Subbarao said, "Two of you elders must go to the village and announce what has happened, and I want you to meet us with a band and we will have a parade. Bring an old, long bed on which to carry the tiger. We will cut two straight trees and use extra cloth *panchas* (men's sarong-like garments) to put under Nandi and fasten the cloth to poles to help him to stand and slowly walk. Also, bring some food for Nandeeshwara

Rao. Bring water for Nandi to drink and for cleansing his wounds.

"Also, declare throughout the village that tonight we will have a dinner for the whole village. Hurry with your mission, as all must be ready tonight for the big *panduga* (celebration).

"Hire two Brahmin cooks to prepare vegetarian meals for the upper caste people and have Muslim cooks make *mutton biriani* for all the rest. By a miracle our sacred bull is alive. We must all praise God and rejoice!"

Next Subbarao examined Nandi's wounds and was horrified to see how deep and dirty they were. He sent word to the native doctor, who knew *ayurvedic* medicine, an ancient Indian system of medicines and herbal remedies. He also sent word for the senior member of the cobbler caste, who was his friend, saying, "We will need his services."

One of the men had seen Pentayya, the cobbler, walking in a nearby field. (This man's name means cow dung. The farmers take it as a compliment because the word also means fertilizer or strength.) Immediately they called Pentayya to come to their aid. He had been going to repair a leather bucket used for well irrigation, so he had his leather sewing kit with him. He said to Subbarao and the others, "These wounds must first be cleaned with good water and herbs." They sent for buckets of water. Meanwhile a runner came from the village saying the ayurvedic doctor was on his way. The Brahmin doctor first cleansed the wounds, then poured in some healing balms and ground-up plants and medicines. Then the cobbler sewed up the leatherly skin of each wound. This is very hard to do because the bovine skin is so thick. Finally the task was completed. The bull had been resting peacefully after eating the offered feed and drinking water.

Consider the wonder of this scene: the only one who could sew up the skin of the sacred Nandeeshwara Rao was from the outcaste Dalit community, who in those days was considered to be untouchable. As a Dalit, he was not allowed to learn to read, write, attend school or to wear the clothes that higher caste gentlemen wore. Yet, there the Brahmin doctor, a member of the highest caste, was working beside him to restore the health of this precious deity bull.

The strongest men worked to get Nandi to his feet. They slipped strips of cloth and panchas under the belly of the bull, tied them to two bamboo poles and then together lifted Nandi to his feet. The magnificent bull snorted and gave a bellow of delight. Slowly they began the long journey to the village. After several hours they heard a band playing as the villagers approached.

Subbarao arranged the procession. First came the vanquished tiger stretched out on the bed frame carried on poles by twelve men. This was the first time any of the children had seen a tiger, and they were frightened. The town jester walked along with the tiger explaining to the children how fierce the tiger was, how it had killed hundreds of animals, how it could eat 70 or more pounds of meat each day, and that it was the strongest animal in the world. Then he would hold up a claw of the tiger and roar, pretending he was going to scratch one of the nearest boys with the claw. The boys would jump away, screaming as every one else laughed.

The welcoming party and the search party joined and slowly made their way to the village of Dachapelle. The wounded bull walked very slowly. The parading party kept announcing, "The bull, Siva's Nandi, sacred bull, has killed the tiger, outside in open combat. This is a marvelous deed!"

Late in the afternoon they finally reached Subbarao's home. Then all helped Nandi lie down and rest, the pieces of cloth still under him so they could help him stand up the next morning. Subbarao thanked all who had helped on that day, then invited the whole village to share in a feast. The cooks had been working in two different locations, and the village air was loaded with the pleasant smells of curry powder, garlic, ginger, roast curried mutton and good, spicy rice. The vegetarian cooks had made pumpkin curry, eggplant and pea curry and vegetable sambar, including okra and the delicious ridge gourd. *Dahl* (lentils) with pots of *ghee* (clarified butter) were prepared in abundance.

The villagers all sat down in long rows according to caste and family, on mats each family had brought. A row is called *pankthi*; hence, when a whole village or congregation sits in rows, it is called *pankthi bhojanam* (line meal).

The meal was served with generosity and grace by Subbarao and his family members, relatives, and servants. They were happy to wait and serve and show their love for their villagers and for each other.

In the midst of the meal, Subbarao rose up and spoke loudly so that all could hear,

"We know that today we have viewed a miracle, and Nandi has proven Siva's power is fully with him. If the elders of the village and the priests agree, I would like to build a temple to our Lord Siva near my house. I plan to have the temple built so that the entrance to Nandi's stall will face the entrance of the new temple. Whenever Nandi is at home for the night he will be facing the *lingam* (cylindrical stone symbol of Siva) in Siva's temple. In this way our beloved Nandi will always be adoring the god that saved him and made him his own."

To this the whole audience shouted, "*Aounew, manchi uddeshamu!*" meaning, "Yes! A grand idea!"

Then Subbarao added, "The whole village is safer with Nandi living here, and he has saved us from untold loss and danger by killing this vicious tiger. We praise God for him, *Stotaram* (praise)." All responded, "Stotaram!"

With high spirits they all finished the delicious meal. Then several of the elders thanked Subbarao for making such good arrangements and promised to help him in every way. "We are proud to have a godly man of great imagination and generosity in our village and pray that you and your family and cattle may be blessed."

All the time they had been eating and rejoicing, the cobbler and his men were skinning out the tiger most carefully with only oil lamps for light. Afterwards they bathed near their homes, and then ate the delicious mutton biriani the Muslim cooks had prepared. They were the last to eat, but the Muslim cooks had patiently waited, and they served the cobbler and his men with kindness.

It took a long time for Nandi's wounds to heal. He spent much time in the stall resting and had all of his feed bought to him. People from other towns and villages came each day to view this magnificent and holy bull, and of course they wanted something to remember him by. They were to pay for a basket of the dung that comes from this holy bull.

Dung is used in many ways. First, it is used as plaster and flooring—a solution of water, cow dung, and clay is stirred up and used to smear on the once dirt-floors of village homes. When it dries it has a pleasant smell and is a good, clean surface. The same dung application is used in doorways and outside courtyards, which are swept and cleaned daily, so the area in front of a house where children play and old people sit and talk or read can be kept clear and clean. Dung is also used in heavier proportion for plastering walls of village homes. When it dries it is often painted with whitewash. This keeps the home warm in the winter and cooler in the summer.

Pilgrims paid Subbarao for the dung and smeared their huts with the sacred product. They believed that rich blessings and the presence of divinity was brought into their own homes. Of course, they also used cow and bull dung for cooking fuel. After the harvest season there is a lot of chaff on the roads and threshing floors of each village. This is mixed with cow dung and then plastered onto walls and tree trunks, where the cakes will dry out and season. This provides excellent fuel for cooking.

Now, young readers, please don't make all those faces and make nasty remarks about my Indian friends' habits. Do you know what the pioneer settlers in America used for cooking food as their wagon trains traveled across the prairie? They used what the history books call "buffalo chips." Guess what that means? It means they used the dried-out dung of the huge wild buffalo herds. So many peoples, including our ancestors, have been doing this for a long time.

As soon as Nandeeshwara Rao regained his strength, Subbarao made arrangements to purchase the finest cow in the area, and after nine months of waiting, a heifer sired by Nandi was delivered and treated like a holy child. The mother was called *Parvathi avvu* (the goddess cow). The heifer was named the *Kamadeenu* (holy mother cow that supplies milk and dairy products in abundance) by the people of the area. Their milk, butter, ghee, yogurt and buttermilk became famous. The ghee was deemed precious, a must to pour over hot steaming rice to purify it before eating. Ghee also was and still is used as holy oil for worshiping the Lord in temples because the gods are known to love the smell of burning ghee.

There was great demand for Nandi to breed with many more cows. All this the divine Nandeeshwara Rao did with strength, patience and willingness, of course. In turn each one of the cows bearing calves was considered special, and the calves Nandi sired were considered sacred. The town became famous for its exceptional ghee and yogurt which people came from afar to purchase.

It must be noted that not all of this abundance was sold. Subbarao's compassionate family gave some of their milk to sick and poor people who had a need and yearning for divine milk.

But the most sought-after product was an ancient ayurvedic tonic that enhanced health, especially for the elderly. The tonic was called *pancha gavyamu* (the five products of the cow: milk, yogurt, ghee, dung and urine). To have all five of these products as holy as possible the dung and urine had to come from Nandi himself, and the other three products from one of his offspring. Slowly this tonic trade developed, as did Subbarao's dairy, and in time he became very prosperous.

Again Nandi had the run of the village and bazaar, but now when he went out into the fields he was followed by boys collected his dung in baskets, chattering and telling stories. They made up more stories about him killing the tiger and his ability to frighten off panthers and bears. Each morning the boys competed with the herdsmen for the privilege of smearing vermilion dye mixed with oil onto his famous horns. Nandi missed the days when he had wandered around alone; however, he was content with company and with the excellent food he would be given everyday if his grazing opportunities were insufficient.

This story could end here. However, the story of Nandeeswara Rao continues.

Two years later, after Nandi had regained his full strength, Subbarao decided to take him on a pilgrimage to Kotappakonda, the mountain where there was a special temple to Siva and his consort, Gollamma. According to legend, Gollamma had been a girl from a village near the mountain. Siva had appeared to her in the form of a *sanyasi* (wandering holy man), whom she met while taking care of her father's cattle on Kotappakonda.

It had been a tradition for hundreds of years for faithful worshippers of Siva to gather at Saivite temples the night before *Maha Siva Ratri* (Siva's Great Night) and stay up all night listening to stories of the gods, worshiping at the temple, bathing in the holy waters of the temple pond, talking to holy sanyasis and giving them gifts, and watching dramas or shadow and puppet shows of Siva's great adventures and deeds.

Subbarao and his family prepared to attend this great Saivite festival. He knew they would have to take all of their own food supplies and some firewood, as well as the sun-dried cow chips (of which they had many). They could rely on wells from the villages they passed through, as there was plenty of water in the area. The family packed all of their supplies onto bullock carts. Then very important decisions had to be made. Who would stay behind to safeguard the property, including the cattle, who did not come with the pilgrims, and watch over their fields? Subbarao's eldest son, Prasad, now 20 years old, decided to stay behind because his wife was heavy with their first child and could not make the journey. He lined up the help of others with personal business to attend to at home. Many villagers decided to join Subbarao and his wife Girija on the pilgrimage. Leading the procession would be Nandeeshwara Rao. With him would come three of his holy cows (*Kamadeenu*), three bulls that he had sired and four more cows so there would be a sufficient milk supply and yogurt and ghee to sell. They also took a three-weeks' supply of ghee. The village band gave them a festive sendoff. The distance from Dachapalle to Kotappakonda is about 45 miles. The highways are safe, and during this festival they were patrolled by the prince's soldiers and guards. It took four days to reach Kotappakonda. Subbarao had wisely sent his most trusted servant ahead many days before to arrange a good camping lot, centrally located in the pilgrimage area. There they had built a hut for Subbarao and Girija.

As they drew closer to the holy place, the road became more and more crowded with elaborately decorated bullock carts. These were drawn by beautifully groomed yokes of prized oxen with horns painted blue and red and shoulders and foreheads smeared with vermillion powder. Many of the carts were bearing *prabhas*. These were twelve to sixteen-foot high panel-like shields made of bamboo frames and covered with tapestry or cloth painted with pictures of gods. Each individual prabha was kept from toppling over by guy ropes held by six to eight men.

On the last morning of the journey, they passed through Narasaraopet, a town just seven miles from the temple. Excited children and youngsters were running everywhere, heedless to the traffic and danger. How beautiful it was there at the foot of the mountain at the temple tank (artificial lake). Between the groves of casuarina trees there was a newly constructed community of thatch-roofed shops and temporary shelters. By that evening more than 200,000 people would be at the campground. Cloth merchants were already selling their wares. There were temporary "meals hotels" and coffee and tea shops selling snacks. Every possible item from the Narasaraopet Bazaar could be found at the festival at a special price. People of every religion attended this festival because it was not only a religious festival. It was held in the spring to invoke a good harvest and good weather, falling early in the Lenten season as a lunar holiday. There were marvelous shopping and entertainment opportunities, puppets and shadow plays and storytellers. Clever entrepreneurs arranged for dancing girls to perform on flatbed bullock carts. Many bands played. And there was a circus! The people had no trouble staying awake during Siva's Great Night.

Large numbers of pilgrims encircled the campground of Subbarao and his faithful Nandeeshwara Rao. A storyteller from their own town was telling the glorious tale of Nandi's triumph over the Tiger. Two merchants who came with Subbarao were busy selling ghee and yogurt produced by the Kamadeenus. The doctor friend, of course, had come along with them, and he was selling the special ayurvedic medicine, pancha gavyamu. By the next morning all of the ayurvedic medicine, the ghee and the yogurt were gone. People were coming around asking for milk for their coffee, so the herdsmen were busy milking their sacred cows. The men were admiring the sacred bull Nandi from a distance, listening to the storyteller, who was hoarse from telling the story so often. After eating a morning's breakfast of coffee and curd rice (black mustard seed, onions, yogurt and leftover rice), most of the people in the camp rested and fell fast asleep. At that time the soldiers and guards patrolled the whole area.

Subbarao and his *Satimani* (jewel of a wife) were delighted. He said to her, "Later, my dear, we will renew our marriage vows and pray for our children. We will do that tomorrow. Today we need to take rest."

The next morning they rose early while most in the camp slept. Subbarao wore a clean new dhoti and his wife encased herself in a brand silk sari. They went to the lake below the temple, down the steps and into the water until they were shoulder-deep. Then they climbed up to the first temple, their wet clothes clinging to their bodies. Subbarao and his wife entered the temple and were met by a priest, who told them the story of the temple. They gave an offering to the priest, which included two bunches of bananas and a coconut. He blessed their offering, broke the coconut and let the water pour over the idol in the temple. Then he blessed the couple, and gave back to them one of the two banana bunches and half of the coconut. This is called *prasadam*, which means part of the blessed gift is returned to the giver. Subbarao put the prasadam in a shoulder bag. He and his wife descended from the temple to the plain. Then Subbarao searched for a rock that weighed at least seven pounds. He tied his turban in such a way that he could carry the rock on top of his head. Girija, his wife, tied her sari to his pancha, and they walked together seven miles around the holy mountain, renewing their marriage vows. They were reminded that during their marriage service they had walked together seven times around the marriage fire as they made their vows. This symbolized their promise to the whole holy mountain, a promise he carried with him, to be true to his wife and she to him.

They stayed one more night at Kotappakonda. That night Girija conceived again. She had given birth to Prasad, her eldest son when she was just sixteen years old. Now, at 36 she would be blessed with another child. (In those days higher caste women married at age 14 or 15.)

The next day the tired but happy Dachapalle family and friends resumed their journey home. The children and those who had come for the first time were thrilled with this great experience. The cattle all made it safely home. No one was hurt or became sick. Each family rejoiced and felt more prepared and assured that they would live their life with God's blessings.

As soon as the returning pilgrims had settled in their homes Prasad came and showed them his first child, a girl, who was born the morning after Maha Siva Ratri. What a happy family!

SIX
THE REMARKABLE BISON HERDS OF MANJAMPATTI

When I was a lad in Kodaikanal School in southern India, the month that we most enjoyed was May. The school would close the first Saturday in May with the school play. For three weeks we had vacation. Our parents would always come up for the month of May and part of June to enjoy their vacation with their children. The cool weather in the 7,000 foot high Palni Hills was a delightful climate for hiking, camping, tennis, golfing or boating on Kodai Lake.

My first experience going to Kukkal was in my junior year of high school. We had big, terrifying pictures in our minds of the *leech shola* (forest). Hiking from the village of Kukkal two and a half miles uphill with the fear of leeches in our hearts made us strain our lungs and legs to get out of there as soon as possible. After arriving at the top of the ridge, we came to a beautiful grassland area where the only trees were Rhododendron. These are fire-resistant and have survived scores of grass fires.

From there our party had a gorgeous view of Kukkal Cave, one and a half miles away and the distant Manjampatti valley with two prominent, sheer rock domes on the other side of the valley in the state of Kerala. This region was and is really wild. We had been warned to be most careful when hiking in this grassland. As we looked down on the whole area, we could see rainforests in every one of the gullies where there was a stream with enough moisture to nourish the trees through the droughts from December to May.

Suddenly one of my friends spotted a herd of bison coming up out of one of these rainforests, quite close to Kukkal Cave. There were about 15 in the herd, including three calves.

The Indian Bison is really a wild cow. It looks exactly like an ordinary cow, but bigger and black with white stockings up to the knees. It is the wild ox referred to in the Bible. A male wild ox stands seven feet high at the shoulder. They are not shaggy, but have skin like an ordinary ox, and they are very athletic. We saw them running up a steep hillside effortlessly. After having our lunch, we discussed whether or not to go down to the cave. Though we wanted to go, we realized we did not have time to make it back before dark to the spot six miles from Kukhal village where we had left our car and faithful driver.

I would not see bison again for eight years. Immediately after graduation in May of 1944 I set forth on my wartime journey to America. There I studied for seven years at Gettysburg College and Lutheran Theological Seminary, got married in 1950 and graduated in 1951. We were called to be missionaries, and in 1952 I was able to vacation in my beloved Kodai Hills again.

My wife and I went to Kodaikanal in April 1952 with our son Bill, who was one year old. By this time Ruth was carrying another child, who would be called Hans. She wanted to hike with us but could not go on a hike as long as Kukkal. So we hiked together to Pillar Rocks Cave, Ten Mile Round, Green Hut, and Berrijam Lake (one way uses seven miles—we got a ride back).

Later on in the year we stayed on in Kodai for two more months with our Telugu teacher, who had come with us from Andhra. During that time one of the staff members, Steve Root, asked if I would like to go with him to Manjampatti on a hunting trip. Two of the schoolboys would go with us—one was Chuck Gosselink, Ruth's brother, and his friend John DeVries. Steve was the only one with a hunting license or rifle.

We took the school car to Manavanur and left it there in care of the driver who had relatives in the village. Then we hiked five miles to a small village, Killanavai. There we picked up our guide Perumal, who had gone ahead of us to recruit three of the hill tribe men to help carry our supplies down the very steep trail to Manjampatti, which was about eight more miles of hiking.

At that time there were no roads through Manjampathi valley. From the village of Poondi in the Palni hills, not far from Manavanour, a large stream flows down through terraces of irrigated fields and a series of waterfalls into Manjampatti Valley. Other streams join it to form the Palar River.

We found a good camping spot near to the river where we could put up our tents and build our fireplaces. By the time we made camp, gathered firewood and filled our water containers it was too late to go out hunting.

The next morning Steve woke us all up when it was still dark and offered us coffee, dates and bread. "This is to sustain us for the morning hunt. It's not breakfast; that comes later."

We went out slowly, quietly and carefully, going upstream against the wind. Within a quarter of a mile we heard the noise of splashing animals just as it was becoming light. There were six adult elephants and two elephant calves having a wonderful time bathing in the river. We carefully approached them, being as quiet as we could, and just watched for about 20 minutes. Then we went west of the river and found ourselves climbing up old rice terraces. These had been laboriously carved out of the hillside, but were now overgrown with trees and bushes.

"Steve, what happened here?" I asked. "Perfecting these terraces must have taken years of work by a large number of people."

"Malaria," Steve replied. Then, lowering his voice, he said, "Let's be real quiet. I hope we will soon meet some bison. They have very keen hearing and smell, but not good sight. We are walking against the wind, so they will not smell us." We went slowly, carefully and silently.

We heard a slight noise off to the right, and Steve motioned us to be quiet. The mist was shifting, and gradually a herd of about 20 spotted deer (axis deer) came into sight. Steve slowly lifted up his rifle and shot the biggest buck I had ever seen.

Perumal and one of the porters came to join us when they heard the shot. They were ecstatic. They quickly chopped down a small tree, made a pole out of it, and tied the deer to it. We took turns carrying it back to the camp. "No bison for this morning," said Steve, "but I did have to get that deer; it was so beautiful." Perumal cooked breakfast while Steve and the other men skinned and butchered the deer. After breakfast Steve salted down the deer hide. Then, while the porters and Perumal had their breakfast, we discussed our tactics and schedule. We decided to send two of the men with as much venison as they could carry to meet the driver and have him take it to Kodaikanal so it would not spoil. We would eat the rest. The men said, "First of all, we will eat a meal of rice and venison before we go up that hill." By eleven o'clock we had a wonderful meal of rice and venison curry with enough leftovers to last us for another day. The two men took off, and we noticed that each of them had several extra packs of meat that they would give to their families and the village elders of Kalanavai.

During the afternoon we rested up, swam in the river and loafed until about four o'clock. Then we started off to find the bison. Steve said, "It's too wasteful to shoot a bison down here. You can't carry even ten percent of the meat up to where it can be used, and the thick skin is remarkably heavy. So we'll try to avoid shooting one." We went slowly, against the wind, mounting some more terraces. Then we saw a herd peacefully grazing. We knew Steve was being very careful because he was the only one who had a gun, and there were five of us including Perumal.

There were 16 bison in this herd, with several huge bulls seven feet high at the shoulder and weighing much more than half a ton. There were also several calves grazing at the edge of the herd. Steve whispered to us to get behind a tree or a rock and just stay put. One of the calves was very curious and came quite close to us. Then we heard a funny sound. What was that? We realized it was a big bull urinating with quite a splash.

Shortly thereafter that curious calf came close enough to touch us, and it suddenly smelled us. With a startled cry it ran back to its mother, and the whole herd stampeded the other way.

"Whew, that was a close one," said Steve. Steve had already been in Manjampatti a number of times, as he had been teaching at Kodai for many years. He told us that these herds of Manjampatti belong to two states, Tamilnad and Kerela. Their boundaries joined in this beautiful forest. The Palar River was the border. During the monsoon season the bison would range in the higher hills of the Palni range. Sometimes herds would come together, and he had seen herds of over 70 bison. There was a rumor that there were some albino bison somewhere in the valley. Albino calves had been seen but no one had seen any adults. This special herd of 70 or more would sometimes go as high as Kukkal Cave.

We then examined the area where the herd had been grazing. There was a lot of buffalo dung and some pools of urine. It was astonishing how big an impression that stream can leave in the ground.

The next day we saw a lot more game—more elephants, more deer and several more bison herds. We did not hear or see any predators. We asked Steve, "Do tigers ever kill bison?"

"Very rarely," he answered. "The herd has a way of protecting itself. The large bulls stand on the outside with the cows and calves on the inside whenever danger threatens, except of course when they stampede."

We certainly enjoyed that first hunt with Steve. That was one of the experiences that led me to buy a rifle and start hunting in the Kodai hills. Normally we could go on only one hunting trip a year there, considering it took five days out of our vacation of five weeks.

I did have the joy of taking each of our children down into Manjampatti for a hunting trip. We would exercise a lot to get in shape for this special hunt, which included the twelve mile descent of 5,000 feet and the much harder task of climbing out of the valley with full packs, sometimes laden with meat. When camping with the children, we never saw the albino bison.

Twenty years later after my children had all graduated from Kodai, I took one more hike down into Manjampatti after staying in Kukkal Cave overnight. Early in the morning, we saw a herd of bison, and there on the edge of the herd were two albino calves. Earlier that month I had read an article in *Hornbill*, a Bombay conservation magazine, about the albino bison of Manjamphatti.

Just this year I received the wonderful news that a national park, including the Manjamphatti and Kukkal areas, is being planned by the government of India. This will be one of the few places in southern India where bison, elephants, deer and other interesting animals will be safe. I hope many people will enjoy their adventures in these parks and that they might occasionally see albino bison, too. I pray that this new national park will be a great blessing to the people of southern India and to all who go there.

SEVEN
THE SCREAMING SERPENT EAGLE AND THE NECKLACE

Preface

This story is not my own. I heard this Telugu language story more than a dozen times during the 30 years that I lived and worked in India as a missionary. It is a kind of folktale. I inquired several times and was told it has never been written down, and each time I heard it, the story was slightly different. Twice it was used to illustrate hard work and honesty, for which Christians and their children should strive. I have told this story in Sunday Schools, in camps and to various groups of children in India and in America, and to my own children, nieces and nephews. The kids like it.

Here I have adapted it to fit into the Kingdom of Kondaveedu. The walls of that great mountain fort still survive, along with legends of how the Muslims conquered that Reddi Fort. My family lived near the Kondaveedu for 18 years during our work in Guntur District of Andhra Pradesh.

Story

More than three hundred and 50 years ago there was a rather poor, hardworking, frugal and faithful family living in the village of Gollapallem in the Telugu speaking area of Andhra in southern India.

The two children, *Deva Das* (Servant of God) and *Paranjyothi* (Heavenly Light), were both fortunate enough to attend a school at Gollapallem that had been started by French Catholic missionaries during the time when the French had a good relationship with the Nizam of Hyderabad.

The Nizam was, at that time, the richest man in the world. He had control of the diamond trade, and through that gained control of the pearl trade as well. He ruled over most of Andhra with the backing of the French. It may be noted that his bodyguards were fierce Muslims from Muscat in Oman, from where all of the pearls came. There was also a colony of Hyderabadi Muslims in Muscat, Oman.

The mother of Deva Das and Paranjyothi was named Annamma (*Annam* means food or rice. *Annapurna*, the famous peak in the Himalayas, is named after the Goddess of rice). Annamma always made sure there was enough to eat in the home, and she handled all housekeeping problems with great care and skill. Her husband *Satyam* (Truth) often talked lovingly to his children and encouraged them to be honest in all matters and obedient to their parents.

Annamma taught her children that on the way home from school they should look for anything that could be used in the home. She said even a torn cloth might be useful for patching or cleaning. If they found a bit of string now and then, they could put it all together and get a roll of string eventually. Twigs, branches fallen in a storm and cow dung could all be collected on the way home and used later on as fuel. So the girl, Paranjyothi, always had a basket along to collect cow dung and kindling.

About a dozen miles away from Gollapallem there was a prince living in the fort palace of *Kondaveedu* (streets in the hills). The prince was a vassal and a relative to the Nizam of Hyderabad. He had a daughter *Aneesa* (Ruth), who was lively and joyful and had many friends among the girls whose parents were connected with the family or the work of the Prince. Azeese loved this daughter very much, as did his dear wife, Miriam. On Aneesa's eleventh birthday, Azeese gave her a beautiful necklace.

Aneesa was so proud of this necklace that she wore it all day long, even though it was quite heavy. She thanked her beloved parents many times. All of her friends and the court said it was the most beautiful necklace they had ever seen. It contained diamonds, pearls, emeralds, rubies, jade, amethyst and topaz.

A few months later the princess held a party for many of her friends, and she was playing with them in the afternoon on the palace terrace. As they were running around chasing each other, she found that the necklace got in her way. She took it off and put it on a table. Unknown to her and the girls, a serpent eagle was circling in the sky over the palace. With its incredibly long range of eyesight, it spied a colorful ring of beauty on the table. If eagles' mouths could water, then this one's mouth would have started a rain shower. It had never seen such a beautiful snake before. The *Pakshi Raju* (king of birds) took one more circle, lowering itself into position, and began its power dive. Suddenly all the girls heard the terrifying rush of wings. Then the eagle gave a scream of triumph as it snatched the necklace in its claws.

The princess and all the girls screamed in terror. Servants came running. Then they called for Miriam, and a messenger ran to get the prince. The prince came immediately with his wife to find their daughter sobbing hysterically. All of the friends were in shock. Nobody knew what to do. There wasn't anything anyone could do.

That same day, the two children from Gollapallem went to school as usual. On the way home they looked for rope, old bricks, string, firewood, cloth or cow dung, yet they found nothing useful to take home. Paranjyothi asked her brother, "What is wrong today? There is nothing we can use, and we are almost home." Then, at the side of the road, Deva Das saw something green. It was the tail of a snake.

"There is a snake there," he said. "I can see its tail. I could kill it and take it home."

His sister said, "Don't try—it might be poisonous."

Deva Das walked behind the snake's tail until he could see the whole thing in the ditch. "This snake has been injured," he said, "and seems to be dead. Its head is smashed." He picked it up by the tail. It stank. Nevertheless he thought his father could use it. "You know, Paranjyothi, father will skin this out and give it to a cobbler, who could make a belt out of this.

His sister agreed, "Good idea." So, according to his instructions from his beloved mother, Deva Das took the four-foot-long smelly snake home.

When he entered the house with the stinking snake, Annapurna was wide eyed. When she sniffed it, she said "Ayyoo, Deva Das, this smells rotten. I don't think it would be useful to your father."

He answered, "Oh Mother, can't the cobbler tan it?"

"No, it's too far gone," she answered. Feeling quite upset, Deva Das flung the snake into the backyard.

Meanwhile, the serpent eagle was having trouble with the necklace. It perched at the top of Kondaveedu peak, trying to eat the serpent it had caught. It was harder than any of the reptiles it had caught, including the iguanas. It was hurting its beak when it realized the whole thing was made of stone—to him it was worthless! The king of birds took off, enraged, not realizing it was still holding the necklace. It flew a few miles further. Coming to Gollapallem village, it soared over the village several times in ever-narrowing circles. Then, to its delight, it spotted something it could eat and swooped down into the heart of the village.

Annamma and her daughter Paranjyothi were cleaning rice and pounding spices for a curry on the back porch of their hut. They suddenly heard a mighty rush of wings. The eagle screamed for joy as it dropped the necklace and caught hold of the dead, rotting serpent, and it flew up into the hills by the village. As the eagle soared away, it could smell that this was a fleshy, dead serpent—

a real treat because it was soft and tenderly rotten. It flew to a nearby ridge on the holy mountain Kotappakonda, lighted in the top of the tallest tree, and ate the whole snake. His heart was content and all his anger had turned to peace.

Deva Das had heard his mother and sister cry out in response to the eagle's scream. He came running out of the house to see the eagle, and then he noticed the beautiful necklace. Mother, daughter, and son immediately brought it into the house, where no one else could see it. Annamma embraced her son. "Oh Deva Das, because you always listen to me, we now have suddenly become rich and blessed."

Now, do you think this is the end of the story? Answer yes or no.

The answer is no, the story does continue.

The whole family was excited, but immediately Annamma warned that they must be very cautious, "Don't tell anyone about this and we will wait until father comes home. He will certainly know what to do."

When Satyam returned home that evening from a full day's work in the fields, he noticed how excited and happy his wife and children were. "What is going on?" he asked. "You all look like you have a great secret and you want to tease me with this secret." Then he smiled.

Annamma said, "Deva Das, you tell him what you found on the way back from school, and tell him the whole story."

Her husband said, "Can't we eat first? I'm famished."

"All right" she said, "Chicken Curry – a great treat – is ready."

Satyam and his two children sat on mats on the ground while Annamma put out banana leaves and served the curry with rice. There was also yogurt served afterward and, of course, half a banana for each person. Deva Das ate as fast as he could because he wanted to get on with his story. Even before he washed his hands, he began telling about finding the serpent on the way home. He described its beauty and the bad smell, and filled in every detail while his father became more and more inquisitive.

After the three had eaten Annamma sat down and ate; this was the custom—the wife is the cook and server. Meanwhile, the storyteller was at work. His sister was giggling, and his mother Annamma was making all kinds of faces saying, "Is it really so? Really? My goodness!" This encouraged Deva Das to tell the story even more dramatically. He got to the point where, rejected by his mother, he had tossed the snake out into the backyard.

Then Paranjyothi interrupted him with a loud voice. "It's my turn to tell because you didn't see it happen!" Then she related how the screaming eagle had dropped something in their yard and grabbed the rotten snake in its talons as it soared back up.

Then the mother said, "It's my turn. I'll show you, my dear husband, what the eagle dropped." She went into the next room and came back with the necklace around her neck. "How do you like my new jewelry?" Satyam was astounded. His wife said to him, "Now we are rich. We can buy the land you now till as a tenant farmer and we can have a better house, some fruit trees protected with a wall, our own well and garden, and have our own water buffalo for milk. Oh life is going to be so good!"

But in the midst of all this happiness Satyam frowned and he said, "Wait, wait, don't make any plans like this. We must be very careful. This precious jewel necklace is not ours. The serpent eagle must have brought it from the palace. How this happened we cannot say, but where else could such a costly necklace be found? Tomorrow we will get up early, bathe and put on our finest clothes, and we will go to visit Prince Azeese at the palace."

The children looked at each other with dismay, and one said to the other, "Then we will not be rich."

Annamma said, "It is better to be honest than rich. We should be happy that your father, named Satyam, wants to stand for the truth."

The children realized in their hearts that this was good. Annamma put the necklace on her daughter's neck and she said, "Let *our* princess wear this garland at least for one night."

The children went to sleep, and Deva Das dreamed of a new water buffalo and how nice it would be to have their own milk, cream and yogurt. His sister dreamed of dancing with the necklace on and wearing a beautiful sari.

Early the next morning the family shared the leftover curd rice and a cup of coffee. Even the children drank the coffee because it was mostly milk. Then they started off at six o'clock in the cool morning wearing their best clothes.

They were all used to walking; every day Annamma would walk to the village well, a half mile away, two or three times, carrying water for the household. Satyam walked a mile to his field and back every day. The children walked almost a mile each way every day to their school.

By ten o'clock they had reached the Fort Kota, which protected a village below the Kondaveedu hill, and the gateway to the steps leading to Kondaveedu Palace. At the gateway they were stopped by guards, and it took all of Satyam's patience and wisdom to convince the guards that they must have an audience with the prince himself, or at least the guardian of the palace. This was for the welfare and happiness of the prince. They searched Satyam and his son for weapons. Annamma was wearing the necklace, but it was underneath her sari.

Annamma knew that in front of Muslim men she should be quiet, very shy, and should not interfere at all. Her daughter behaved the same way. Finally, after an hour of questioning, they were permitted to climb up to the palace accompanied by one of the guards. They did not arrive at the palace until noon. The guard who was with them introduced them to the chief palace guard.

Again Satyam had to convince a military man that he must have an audience with the prince himself. So he said this strange thing to them, "If I am given audience with the prince, I will make this a most happy and joyful day for him and his family. I honor prince Azeese. Also, I know that he has lost something precious, and I know where it is."

He said this very quietly to the chief guard only. The guard was tremendously surprised and was eager to help his master. He ran to the dining hall and whispered this to the prince as he was finishing his meal. The prince called for water and a basin. He washed his hands at the table. Even in those days the prince ate with his hands; it is the only proper way to eat curry. Then he got up and hurried down to the palace gateway. There he saw this neat, modest and happy family. He asked Satyam, "What good news do you have for me? How will you make this the happiest of days?"

Satyam asked him, "Did you lose something very precious made of jewels yesterday, or perhaps the day before?"

The prince was astounded. He said, "Yes we did." By this time Annamma had taken the necklace off, and it was covered with a piece of cloth. She handed the wrapped necklace to the prince saying, "*Salaam alekum.*"

The prince stared at the family and said, "Alekum Salaam." Then he unwrapped the cloth and saw the necklace. Never had he been so happy. Meanwhile, his inquisitive daughter and wife had followed him down the steps, and they took in this whole scene. "Daddy," screamed Aneesa, "They found my necklace! Oh, how wonderful!" Aneesa was happy. Her father put her necklace on her, and she began to dance. Her mother Miriam just clapped her hands and then gave a hug to her daughter and to Annamma and Paranjyothi. Then, of course, they wanted to know how the necklace had been found.

Salyam said, "Our son should tell you this story." And so Deva Das began the story,

"Mother always taught us to bring whatever we could back to the home when we returned from school. We would always try to bring something useful like string, rope, a brick, some wood, kindling, cow dung or old piece of cloth—whatever might be useful in our home. We did this everyday, but one day we found nothing. Then, when we were disappointed and almost the whole way home, I saw a snake almost four feet long. I thought father could have a belt made from the snake which was beautiful, yet smelly." He screwed up his nose, and the princess laughed and clapped. Deva Das continued, "My mother told me it was too rotten, and so I threw it into the backyard."

Then Paranjyothi spoke up. "I must continue this story. My mother and I were grinding spices on the back porch, and as we heard a scream from an eagle as it swooped down, letting go of the necklace and grabbing the snake as it soared up to the mountain of Kotappakonda."

Then Annamma finished the story,
"We brought the necklace into the house, thinking we would become very rich. But in the evening my truthful husband Satyam came home. All his life he has tried to live the meaning of his name, Satyam – truth. So he insisted we should try to find the owner of this necklace. And he rightly discerned that this royal family in the palace must be the owner of these precious jewels."

Miriam was impressed; she spoke softly to her prince husband, "In all the kingdom have you ever met a citizen who was so faithful and truthful?"

The prince replied, "no." The guards, hearing this, agreed with the prince. The prince invited the family into the palace. The princess took Paranjyothi to meet her friends and decided that she would never take her necklace off outside again. The captain of the guard took Deva Das on a tour through the palace and to the stables where they kept the horses. The prince's wife Miriam showed Annamma around the inside of the palace: the bedroom, the kitchens, all the household matters. The prince sat with the faithful citizen, Satyam, and discussed how best the king could show his thanks in a way that would be good for the family, and they came up with a plan.

The king asked Satyam kindly if he would like to be in charge of palace supply purchasing. This meant that every part of palace life which required anything—from milk to food, lamp oil, bedding, curtains, rugs and all kinds of supplies needed for the household—would be managed by Satyam. Requests would come to him from throughout the palace. The prince knew he would save thousands of Rupees because Satyam was honest. The prince also said he would immediately give them a good house with a *patta* (deed) near the palace grounds. Since he knew that Satyam was a farmer, the prince said, "I will give you ten acres and you will have a tenant farmer work the land for you. This will be your land by deed of the prince, registered with the emperor. It will be the inheritance you will pass on to your children."

Then the prince said that he would like very much to have Satyam's wife Annamma take care of the smaller children in the palace, gathering them together all day like a kindergarten to enjoy one another's company. And Miriam expressed hoped she would tell these children stories and teach them good habits.

This, my children is a happy ending of the screaming serpent eagle story. In India when children are told stories with a moral, the stories always end like this,

"Children, the moral of this story is: always listen to the teachings of your father and mother, and obey, live truthfully, serve faithfully, and you and your family will be blessed."

May it also be thus with you, and may you have peace.

EPILOGUE

I dedicate this story book as a memorial to my beloved father, Pastor August Frederick Schmitthenner, and to my mother, Marian Eyster Schmitthenner. Dedications are usually very short. This one requires more explanation because my life with my parents greatly influenced my love for stories. Their life together is quite a story that has generated more stories.

Both of my parents were called to serve as missionaries in the Lutheran Church in the Telugu area of southern India along the Bay of Bengal. In October, 1921 they traveled on separate ships to England. Mother was traveling with another new missionary woman, and Dad was with a returning missionary family.

Schmitthenner Family in 1938

They first met on the boat that took them from Liverpool to Bombay. They arrived in Rajahmundry on November 20, 1921. A year later, November 30, 1922, August and Marian were married. During their first term in India they had three boys, Jerry, Fritz, and me, Sammy, the youngest. Mother was disappointed that I was a boy. She wept, for she naturally had hoped and believed that she would have a daughter. The afternoon when I was born, my oldest brother Jerry came to visit and asked for his new brother's name. Still grieving, Mother told him she had chosen only the name Rebecca, so I still had no name. Jerry said, "Why don't you call him Samuel after the picture in my room of the boy Samuel praying 'Speak Lord, for your servant heareth'?" So that's the name they gave me.

Dad was a fantastic storyteller. Along with my brothers, I listened to stories almost every evening that Father was home, even before I could understand them. I would fall asleep while Jerry and Fritz, fascinated by his voice and wit, kept listening. These night stories were long, serial, epic-like stories. I remember one about a Hindu shepherd boy who overheard nearby camping Muslim spies planning to invade the kingdom of Humpi. That story went on for months. Dad had been to Humpi with two of his buddies and heard many stories, which he adapted and changed.

Another epic that continued for months featured the adventures of John McCalister, a boy on a special mission to recover precious treasure in the land of the seven blue moons in China. Dad also told true stories about his adventures while visiting the hill tribal villages and about hunts he had been on. Saturday and Sunday evenings he often told Bible stories with great expression, changing his voice when he took the part of each different character. This way we learned many Bible stories even before we learned to read.

There were tales of the tribal rebellion against the British in the hills of Godavari, which had happened, few years before our family moved into the area. My dad heard eyewitness accounts from some of the village elders. Father spent much time touring in the tribal hill country, sometimes on a motorbike, sometimes by car. In the rainy season he walked or rode an ordinary bike. He lived in a tent, transporting his camping equipment in a bullock cart. He gathered stories from the village people and his co-workers. We insisted that he tell these short stories for several nights after he returned and then it was back to the epic stories.

After her marriage, Mother did not have a church assignment. She stopped taking language classes and concentrated on raising her children, nourishing us with her wonderful cooking and tender love and sharing in our activities as much as possible.

On evenings when Dad was away, which was quite often, Mother would read us stories like *Tales of Pooh* and *Mother Goose*, Robert Louis Stevenson, The Rover Boys and Hans Christian Anderson. Our fellow missionary families worked out a system of handing children's books from one family to another according to the ages of the children. We had no radios in our part of India until the middle of World War II. So we listened to and read stories more than most children would have.

My brothers went off to boarding school at Kodaikanal, 700 miles away from home, from the time they were in 2nd grade, so I had my parents all to myself for months at a time. Then my little sister Katherine was born when I was five. Nearly five years later she died from malaria when my brothers were home for Christmas vacation in 1937. That was the saddest time for all.

In May of 1938 we went to America by a small passenger liner, making several stops in the Mediterranean. Dad filled us in with stories about the Arabs, Egyptians, Pirates and Frenchmen.

After we reached America Dad began another kind of tale, "made-to-order stories." Each of us three boys could give him two or three people or animals or objects, and he would just spin out a yarn that used each of these articles and characters. These were fascinating and fun.

We stayed with Mom and Dad in New York for one year, going to a school in Hempstead, Long Island. Dad spent most of the year visiting congregations in New York and Pennsylvania, sharing great stories of his mission ministry. Then we enjoyed a full summer at our mountain lake, where my father's relatives had shared property since 1870. We had a full share of stories. But none of these stories were ever written down.

My little sister Molly Ann was born in August, 1938. This helped the whole family, but especially Mother, to be comforted after Katherine's death. We returned to India in September that year, hearing more stories along the way.

We did not have much time with our parents once we began boarding school at the age seven. School was from January 15 to the beginning of May. Then we had three weeks of vacation. There were mission cottages near the school, high in the cool 7000 ft. Palni Hills. Mother would come up by Palm Sunday and take us out of boarding from Holy Week until the middle of June. Dad would come up in May and stay for five weeks. For our three weeks' vacation and weekends we would go hiking and camping with Dad and we heard campfire stories. We spent a lot of time playing tennis and going on bike rides. We'd have picnics, including the great Lutheran picnic, and school picnics, and we enjoyed boating on Kodai Lake.

The time we did share together was meaningful, quality time, and we enjoyed being with our parents. Then there was the long four-month stretch, from June until the middle of October, when we were separated from our parents. But we wrote to them every Sunday afternoon. That was mandatory!

My brothers graduated and left for America to attend Gettysburg College, Jerry in 1940 and Fritz in 1943. When America entered World War II, Jerry was drafted into the army and was sent to finish college and medical school. Fritz became an infantryman. In July of 1944, at age 16, I travelled by Navy transport across the Pacific to Chambersburg, Pennsylvania, to stay with Mother's sisters. They made a home for me while I attended Gettysburg College. Mother, Dad and Molly Ann joined us in August 1945. We rented a house in Chambersburg, and Dad began a touring of churches ministry that went on for months.

In May 1946, as the college year drew to a close, we made our plans to stay all summer at our Bella Sylva log cabin home in the Endless Mountains. It was primitive and isolated there, without phone, electric current or running water. That's the way we liked it. It was a place of beauty and peace.

Dad and I went up to open the cabin and make many repairs and paint some of the rooms. After a week of working together, sharing stories and jokes, Dad had to go off to Chicago for an important, mandatory mission meeting. He drove to Tunkhannock, and took the Blue Diamond Express to Chicago.

Three days later while I was working on the road and spattered with mud my older cousin John came walking down the road toward me, looking so sad. He said, "Sam, it's bad news. Your father was killed yesterday in the Lasalle Hotel fire along with 70 or more others. Your mother got in touch with me, and I am going to take you home." John helped me close up the cabin, and then drove me to Chambersburg. Dad died on June 5, 1946. My brother Jerry had not yet arrived, and Fritz was serving in Korea, so I was the one who had to help Mother make decisions. The pastor and people of First Lutheran Church Chambersburg were most comforting and helpful.

Several weeks later Fritz came home from Korea and was soon a civilian. We all agreed we should keep to our plan to spend the summer at Bella Sylva. Here we would have plenty of room for visitors. We would just stay put and let friends come and see us. Many of our mission friends on furlough did just that, and we had a summer of good grieving, prayers, walks, blueberries, fishing, renewal of friendships, picnicking, fellowship, comfort and healing.

Mother wondered what she should do and where she should be. As an answer to that prayer, the mission board contacted her late in August. They called her to return to India to serve in Kodaikanal School as housemother for elementary school boys. This was for Mother a most appropriate and ideal call for which she had just the right training and experience.

Mother and Molly left for India October, 1946. They received a warm welcome. She knew how to handle boys! She delighted the boys with her winning ways, wonderful snacks, fair discipline and in knowing what they needed.

In my first month of seminary studies, in September, 1948, I was called into the President's office. Dr. Wentz looked very troubled. He informed me that my mother had been mortally wounded falling down the stone steps by her dormitory. She had died the next day, September 18, 1948 and was buried the day after in Kodaikanal Cemetery. An hour before her final operation she had written asking Pastor Ted and Dorothy Wood, close family friends, to care for Molly if anything should ever happen to her. The Woods had three girls, Betty Lou, the oldest, Shirley, seven years older than Molly, who was the one to bring the most comfort to Molly, and Pat, Molly's age and her best friend. Molly became a part of their loving and blessed family. She also remained a part of our family and spent time with us whenever it could be arranged. However, at that time in 1948, my brothers and I were all unmarried students in different places. We knew nothing about raising girls. So we believe Mother's plan proved to be by divine guidance.

The dedication to my parents includes acknowledgement to the blessed community of faithful friends in India and America who were part of their life, faith and ministry.

With love,
Samuel W. Schmitthenner

QUIET WATERS PUBLICATIONS

P.O. Box 34, Bolivar MO 65613-0034
http://www.quietwaterspub.com
Email: QWP@usa.net

Other titles by Samuel Schmitthenner:

Ramblings with Ruth

LOVE BLOSSOMED as high school sweethearts hiked on mountain trails in South India. Rambles during courtship years in Iowa and Pennsylvania led to marriage in 1950. Walking together, Ruth and Samuel ministered to Telugu people in India, then elsewhere. Their story portrays a calling to faith, love, and sharing in the Lord's service among God's people.
ISBN 1-931475-22-9

Between the Lines Of the Bible

Some people tell stories. Some people have stories to tell. With Samuel Schmitthenner, we have someone who is able to tell a story well, and it is a story he is called to tell. One can tell that he has lived with these biblical stories, and one gets the sense that these are stories that he has told many times until they have been finely honed into the form we now find in this collection. Sparkling

with humorous asides or perceptive details, these stories give us the chance to hear Samuel's voice.
ISBN 978-1-931475-36-5

The Diary of Rev. Dr. John Aberly

REV. DR. JOHN ABERLY was born on September 18, 1867 in Albrightsville, western Pennsylvania. He studied at Gettysburg College and for one year in the Lutheran Theological Seminary. He and Alice Strauss of Gilberts, Pennsylvania were married August 3, 1889. They were called to serve the Lord as missionaries, and in November, 1889 they left for India and served there until 1923. Dr. Aberly and his "dear wife" Alice worked as a team among the Telugu people of Guntur District. They cared for and helped educate two generations of Telugu Church leaders, pastors, Bible trained teachers, and gospel workers. Alice worked with boarding school children, women of the congregation, church music, and gave most gracious hospitality to many visitors. Dr. Aberly, though heavily burdened with parish work, administration of schools, and Bible teaching, edited various church periodicals in Telugu, commentaries for seven books of the Bible, and a complete Telugu Bible Dictionary which took 20 years to complete. His prodigious scholarly Telugu literary works and great teaching ability were, and still are, a gift to the Telugu Church.
ISBN 1-931475-27-X

Breinigsville, PA USA
13 April 2011
259742BV00001B/26/P

Let the Games begin!

UNMASKED

MAGAN VERNON

Text copyright© 2017 by Magan Vernon

All rights reserved

www.maganvernon.com

This book is a work of fiction. Names, characters, places, and incidents are either products of the author's imagination or used fictitiously. Any resemblance to actual events, locales, or persons, living or dead, is entirely coincidental. All rights reserved. No part of this publication can be reproduced or transmitted in any form by or any means, electronic or mechanical, without permission in writing from the author.

For information visit www.maganvernon.com

Summary: Can a hotshot snowboarder de-ice the ice queen?

At twenty-six, Blake Tremblay is one of the oldest snowboarders in the game. His sights are set on the gold medal, and he knows it's now or never.

Kelly Johnson has spent her entire life skating and winning. She's had no time for friends or an active social life, earning her the nickname "Ice Queen" – in and out of the rink.

Blake makes a bet without knowing all the terms. His ego won't let him back out, even though his target is none other than the American Ice Queen herself.

What are the odds the dreadlocked playboy can warm the frosty figure skater when the real games are unmasked?

Let The Games Begin.

First Edition, November 2017

More from the author:

Website: www.maganvernon.com

Goodreads: www.goodreads.com/maganvernon

Facebook Page: www.facebook.com/authormaganvernon

Twitter: www.twitter.com/maganvernon

Newsletter: http://eepurl.com/qIJA5

#FEELTHEVERN (Reader Group): http://on.fb.me/1lVsZEo

UNMASKED

Dedicated to Stale Sandbech

This book would have been done a lot sooner if I would have stopped watching your Instagram videos.

CHAPTER 1

Blake

"Don't screw up in preliminaries and get sent home on day one," Dad muttered, running his hand through his graying beard. I was surprised he didn't get it colored before The Games and try to keep up with appearances and all that. Actually, I was even more surprised him, and Mom didn't try and make a comeback. "Sixty-year-old skiing duo makes triumphant comeback in 2018 winter Games."

"Very supportive, Clint," Mom nudged his shoulder.

My parents were gold medalist Olympic skiers who raised me in British Columbia where I grew up skiing and snowboarding at the largest ski resort in North America. I grew up hanging around other gold medalists and spent the first fifteen years of my life, traveling around the world on whatever skiing excursion or competition they were on.

Hell, I thought they'd never retire, and I'd have to eventually compete with them in The Games. That is if I stuck to skiing and didn't pick up a board.

I wasn't one of those privileged ski brats, far from it. Even now, as I sat in the airport, waiting for the chartered flight with the other Canadian athletes to leave for Peyong Chang. , I stood out. Not just because I was sitting with two highly regarded Olympians, but with my long bright blonde dreadlocks and the red and white tracksuit provided by the Canadian Olympic committee, I was hard to miss in the sea of perfectly coifed brown hair. At twenty-six I was one of the oldest guys on the team and the newest member after screwing up each time I tried out for the team since I was fifteen. My parents never let me live that down, obviously.

"Well, I'm favored to win after my showing at Nats, so the worst that could happen is I choke, or maybe that American will get busted for pot again and then I'll be a crowd favorite if I get some good stoner jokes in," I joked, trying to add some humor to the situation that was getting more awkward by the minute.

Mom and Dad were flying separate to The Games but somehow felt the need to make their flight at the same time as mine and sit awkwardly at the coffee shop, drinking the tea that Mom complained was "American-tasting." I didn't know exactly what that meant. I'd traveled to America plenty of times, now gaining friends and teammates in California. Sure, they weren't as polite as Canadians and didn't have as many Tim Horton's, but their food or drinks didn't seem too different.

UNMASKED

"You know, I should probably head to the wing my teammates are at. Get in some bonding time before we take off," I said, standing up.

Mom and Dad looked at each other before they stood up as well. Dad gave me a brisk handshake then Mom hugged me, her brown bun almost hitting my chin. At five-foot-ten I wasn't a very tall guy, but it helped working the slopes. The taller guys were all arms and legs, which were good for skiers, but with snowboarding, I think I fared better being closer to the snow.

"We'll see you in Pyeongchang. Remember, you're welcome to our villa anytime if you're tired of sharing that place with Erik and Liam," Mom offered with a tight-lipped smile.

Dad smirked, putting his hand on my mom's shoulder. Mom was petite, but Dad wasn't a big guy either. Professionally skiing wasn't meant for the bulky and my parents still trained like crazy, even though they were years out of The Games. They both looked like little dolls standing there in their matching sweaters, and plastic smiles. It would be nice to get away from their scrutiny, even if they were still looking on from the sidelines.

"Blake will be fine, Maggie. You remember how much fun we had fun at our first Games in Austria," Dad said as Mom's face fell.

"Just be careful, okay? You're there for The Games. Not anything else. The celebration can wait until you get home," Mom added, widening her big blue eyes.

I smiled, giving her another hug. "I promise, Mom."

I'd heard a lot of rumors about the Olympic village and that condoms were handed out like candy. I had a lot of fun in Canada with women, but this was going to be a whole new plethora of women. Being away with my parents for two weeks, and hopefully, some medals could help me in that respect. As long as my parents didn't show up when I was meeting a girl and decide to invite her for tea or whatever else they did meddling in their grown up son's life. Damn it was time I moved out of their place. Hopefully, The Games were good to me and I could finally afford it.

I grabbed my carry on and headed in the direction of the chartered flights, happy to finally be out of their watchful eye.

At my age, I should have moved on with my life, hell, maybe even left Canada for the US and gotten a job in Silicon Valley. But after growing up staring at my parents' multiple medals on our living room wall, I couldn't stop chasing the dream and the only way to achieve it was with my parent's connections. I sucked at skiing, but on the board, I felt alive. Felt at home in the community of snowboarders who weren't as uptight as the ski bunnies that turned their noses up at me until they found out who my parents were.

As soon as I got to the chartered waiting area of the airport, I was greeted by a sea of red tracksuits. We had hundreds of Canadians going to The Games this year, but like a giant beacon, my buddy, and skiing legend, Liam spotted me, standing up and running over with a huge grin on his face that brought out his face full of freckles.

"Ey, Blake, think the rumors are true about the Olympic village? All of these world-class athletes with pent up sexual energy just going at it like Moose in heat?" Liam asked with a laugh.

This was Liam's first Olympics, like mine, but he was eight years my junior. In age and maturity. If the rumors were true about the village, the Olympic committee would have bowls of condoms and protein bars waiting for us. Which meant a few of my roommates would probably be spending more time in the village than our place we rented near the mountain.

"If you want to try your luck with the girl's hockey team, be my guest, but I won't come pull a hockey stick out of your ass if one of them gets too rough." I laughed.

"Ha, ha, real funny. I'm sure all you have to do is walk up to any of these snow bunnies, bat those big blue eyes of yours, toss those blonde dreads and tell them you're the Canadian national champion for snowboarding with Olympic legacy parents. Their panties will drop faster than you can say 'ey,'" Liam added.

I shrugged and smirked. "Maybe a little more like 'Ey, I like your panties,' then they'll drop."

So I had a way with women. Maybe too much. That almost got me in trouble when I got involved with a Canadian figure skater named Alexis who also happened to be going to The Games. I didn't spot her in the crowd of athletes yet, but I was pretty sure her death glare was on me, so I tried to keep my head down.

Liam laughed and shook his head. "You really think you're that good? Bag a few Canadian mountain women, and some American tourists, sure, but these are world class athletes."

The flight attendant announced we were boarding, so I grabbed my bag, thankful for the interruption. I didn't exactly want to discuss my sexual prowess with a guy who didn't have a filter. Some other athletes were already sneering at us as if we didn't already stand out with my dreads and his fiery red ponytail

I put my hands up, walking in step with Liam toward the boarding area. "I just agree with you."

I may not have been like the over muscled guys the girls went for at the gym, but that didn't stop the girls from checking out my full sleeves, and none of them complained about my long, lean physique. It worked the slopes and their bodies quite nicely.

Liam crossed his arms over his chest, the material of his puffy coat making a sound like a bag of deflated marshmallows. "Okay, smartass, let's bet on it then. I pick the girl, and if you can have her out of her panties by the closing ceremony, I'll give you my earnings from my gold medal."

I shook my head. "This is a really stupid conversation."

"Only because you don't think you'll win," Liam joked as we walked down the aisle and found our seats.

"Are we talking about the old man choking on the giant slalom?" Our buddy Erik, a slopestyle skier, took the third seat next to us, tossing his duffle bag under the seat. Erik was the tallest of all of us with his short black hair and million-dollar smile; he looked like a golden boy that any girl would bring home to their parents. Though, he was probably the craziest of all of us and wouldn't be surprised if he snuck alcohol or something harder on the plane.

Liam laughed, shaking his head. "Naw, not talking about the old man breaking a knee on the giant slalom, yet. Just talking about Blake using his good looks to get some tail in Pyeongchang."

Erik smiled. "Yeah, he does have that brooding, bad boy snowboarder thing going on. That'll probably get the American girls at least. Maybe even some of the Brits."

"This is ridiculous, guys. Wake me up when we get to Korea, okay?" I asked, sliding my headphones out of my bag and hoped that was the end of the conversation.

I thought after the very long flight to Korea that Erik and Liam would have dropped the discussion about bagging girls in the Olympic village, but I shouldn't have doubted their horniness. They were only a few years younger than me, but I felt like I was around a bunch of horny teenagers.

Even after the Uber ride to the village, I thought maybe the guys would forget about it. We still had to go to the cabin we rented that was closer to the slopes, but they wanted to check out the village first. I had bad jet lag, and all I wanted to do was sleep and not have this stupid conversation.

Liam stopped in front of one of the looming buildings. There were hundreds of athletes from all over the world milling around and barely even took a second glance at the two Canadians in front of me talking about how to say 'fuck' in different languages.

Liam then turned to face me. "Okay, let's make this interesting since we seem to be boring you old man."

I smirked. "Yeah? Gonna find some sheep or something?"

Liam frowned and shook his head before crossing his arms over his chest. "We both know we're going to get gold in our events. Even if we mess up royally, we'll get on the podium. If you don't really think you can live up to your hype, then we'll head to our place and get ready for the opening ceremonies tomorrow, and then you can go and have tea with your mommy and daddy or whatever else they want you to do at their beck and call."

I stiffened, scowling as he talked about my parents. "Get on with whatever lame ass thing you're going to suggest."

Liam smirked. "If you wanna make The Games interesting, and maybe go around the world in the sack, then put your medals and money where your snowboard is."

I raised an eyebrow. "Are you talking about my actual board or my dick?"

Liam rolled his eyes and put his hand out. "Are you going to take the bet or not? Our medals on the line, if you screw any girl, I pick in the village."

Mulling the idea over in my head, I thought about the pros and cons briefly. On the one hand, I could lose twenty-five grand if I really couldn't score with the athlete he picked. On the other hand, I never backed down from a challenge, and I knew Liam would give me shit forever if I did. As long as I just got this over with, Erik and Liam would shut up and maybe talk about something else. Then I could sleep and deal with brunch with my parents or whatever else I'd have to deal with before opening ceremonies and then they tried to tell me how to snowboard even though I don't think either of them had ever been on a board in their lives.

I put my hand out. "All right, buddy, if it'll get you to shut up, you gotta bet. Now, who's the lucky lady?"

Liam smirked and nodded his head behind me. When Erik saw where he was looking, his eyes widened. "It's like she just skated right into your lap."

I winced and turned slowly to see American pairs skating legends Kelly Johnson and her partner Logan Smith walking toward the dorm. Kelly got the nickname 'Elsa' for her cold demeanor. She was the youngest ever female Olympian to compete at the Vancouver Games and was back to get another gold around her neck. When I was with Alexis, she always talked shit about the American princess. They'd been rivals as far back as I could remember. If nothing else, at least flirting with the skater would piss off Alexis, which was at least half a win.

Kelly wasn't ugly either. Quite the opposite actually with her long blonde hair and bright green eyes. And, if I was honest, the dancer's body that filled out her American warm up suit wasn't bad either.

I turned back to Liam. "You're not serious, are you? I said women, I can't just take down Logan Smith, even though I'm sure he can give you a nice Double Axel if you'd like one."

Liam punched my shoulder. "You know who I'm talking about, dumbass. Get the Ice Queen to melt her cold, dead heart, and her panties and that medal money is yours."

Putting on my game face, I nodded. "You're on."

I didn't even wait for a reply and turned around, putting on my best smile as I walked toward Kelly.

"Hey, you're Kelly Johnson, figure skater, right?" I asked as if I already didn't know the answer.

She was in mid-conversation with her skating partner but sighed and turned toward me, her nose turned up, and eyes narrowed like she thought I was the most annoying person in the world. "Yes. Do you want an autograph?"

I laughed, the girl had spunk and this was either going to end up in some very angry sex, or she was going to turn around and leave my ass. I was hoping for the former. "No, I'm Blake Tremblay, Canadian snowboarder."

She looked down at my hand that I stuck out to offer a handshake. She barely held onto mine before pulling away as if I had a disease she might catch. "Pleasure to meet you," she muttered.

"Hey, Blake, I'm Logan, Kelly's partner." Logan stuck his hand out and shook my hand like he was trying to get the last of the maple syrup out of the jug. If Blondie wasn't giving into my charm, maybe her curly haired sidekick could help.

"Hey, Logan, at least you're friendlier than your counterpart here. Maybe you can convince her to go out with me and some of my other buddies into town for a few drinks. Those two guys behind me are Canadian skiers, Liam and Erik. They look goofy, but they're all right guys." I added an extra smile and looked right at Kelly with a wink.

Kelly opened her mouth to speak, but Logan got his words out first. "That sounds great. We could use a night out before the craziness begins."

She turned, her blonde ponytail practically whipping me in the face as she glared at Logan. "Are you serious?"

Logan just smiled and shrugged. "Why not? We don't have practice until later in the morning tomorrow, so let's have some fun. Maybe see the city."

"Well for one, we're all world class athletes with a reputation to protect. We can't just go around and get drunk and then end up on the news with some stupid alibi about being robbed that no one will believe," Kelly said, the crinkles in her forehead becoming even more pronounced. I hated to admit it, but she was kind of cute when she was mad.

"I think we can all handle our liquor, and this is the winter Olympics, we have better stamina," I replied, even though it wasn't directed at me.

Kelly turned in my direction, putting her hands on those oh so curvy hips that I wanted to put many parts of my body on. "And second, we don't know you. You're some dreadlocked guy in a Canadian track suit. I'm not going to throw out everything we've worked for just for a night of fun."

"When was the last time you ever had fun," Logan grumbled.

If I was going to ever win the bet, I couldn't give up on this. Win or lose, this girl needed to get the stick out of her ass, and I had just the one she could replace it with. "Look, Kel, can I call you that?"

"No." She shook her head.

I smirked. "Kel. I'm just another athlete like you that has a lot riding on these Games. I promise we won't do anything stupid. If at any time you want to leave, just tell us or I'm sure Logan here would be happy to take you home if we get too rough."

She chewed on her bottom lip, and I wanted to run my tongue along her perfectly pouty mouth. I knew this girl was going to be a challenge, but I didn't realize how much her being a challenge was turning me on. I'd have to adjust my pants before too long if she kept looking at me like that.

When she looked back at Logan, I thought she was going to tell him they needed to get the hell out of there, but instead, she raised an eyebrow. "Are you really thinking about this?"

Logan shrugged. "We could use a break, and The Games haven't even started yet."

Kelly rolled her eyes. "This is ridiculous."

"Is that a yes, then?" I asked.

Logan put his arm around Kelly. "We'll see you in the lobby of our dorms at nine."

"What did you just agree to?" Kelly snapped.

Logan smiled, pulling her toward the door with a wave. "See you guys later."

Kelly hiss-whispered at him, and they continued to argue back and forth as they disappeared inside the looming building.

Either this girl was going to show up in the lobby tonight with her skating partner, or I was going to have to figure out another way. Because even if this was a bet, there was something about the girl that I couldn't help but want to know more about. And that's what scared the hell out of me.

CHAPTER 2

Kelly

I stared at my reflection in the dirty mirror above the sink in my dorm. Was I really going to go through with this? Roam the streets of Pyeongchang with a bunch of Canadian snowboarders like some horny tourist who wants to pet their medals?

The only reason Logan convinced me to go was because he said he would refuse to practice until I agreed to get out of my dorm room. I had a feeling he wouldn't honor that promise, but I reluctantly agreed. Maybe while he was distracted, I could sneak back to the village and get in another practice of my own. Yes, that is exactly what I would do. Logan thought our final double axels were on point, but I knew we were half a second off and that half a second could cost us a medal and there was no way in hell I was going to get silver under that haughty Canadian, Alexis Roy.

Before I could think any more about half turns or sneaking away to the ice arena, the door to the dorm opened to my left with a giant hockey bag pushing its way in, followed by the wild curly blonde hair of my little sister and roommate for The Games.

She didn't even notice I was standing in the tiny bathroom until she was stripped of her sweaty hockey gear and standing in just her sports bra and underwear, then she opened the small fridge where we put our daily delivered meals and pulled out a bag of cheese curds, courtesy of our parents' dairy farm in Wisconsin. While we were both petite, with thin muscular frames, Becca built with quite the pair of toned thighs from playing goalie and adorned each of them with long vine tattoos that wrapped around her calves and up her thighs.

"Hey, Kel, going to a funeral?" Becca asked, holding out the golden ball of cheese.

"What? Why would you ask that? That's terrible!" I put my hand on my chest that was covered with the soft material of my black turtleneck.

"The long skirt and that throat-strangling sweater make it look like you're either going to teach Sunday school or Grandma died. But that you weren't going to tell me Gram died until after my first game," Becca said, pushing her way into the bathroom and sitting down on the toilet. She didn't seem to care that I was still standing there while she emptied her bladder and she placed her handful of cheese curds on the tiny white sink next to the toilet. Like the was the most normal thing in the world.

I looked over my outfit. Sure it was probably a bit matronly, but better that than to give the snowboarder any thoughts that I was out to do anything other than meet some of the athletes, maybe have a glass of wine, and get to the rink. Scratch that, no wine. That could get me tipsy, and no one wants to try skating while tipsy. "This is a very nice ensemble."

Becca wiped and flushed before pushing her way to the sink. "The fact that you called it an ensemble, tells me you need my help. Unless your plan is to dress up like those men who stood outside of UW with bibles to spread the good news, we need to scour your closet for something else."

"I think those are called Gideons," I mumbled.

"Didn't you have a skating partner with that name, too? That guy who you skated with when we were in that little rink in Milwaukee? Remember? I think he came out of the closet in like second grade and you made him cry so hard he quit skating and the coach suggested you go to singles skating instead of pairs?" Becca asked, pushing past me to my closet, throwing it open then thumbing through my clothes, which were mainly warm ups and performance costumes.

"You have a better memory than I do, what was that like thirteen years ago? And I didn't make him cry. It wasn't my fault he couldn't do a simple Double Axel. How did he think he'd get anywhere if he couldn't land that?" I asked, following her the few steps to our tiny closet.

"I don't know, when did you leave for New York? I was in fifth grade, maybe? You were still in middle school or just starting high school. Sorry, a few concussions fried my brain." Becca looked over her shoulder, blowing a wisp of curly blonde hair out of her face. "Seriously? We come across the world for The Games, and this is what you have to wear? Warm ups, costumes, and whatever the hell funeral outfit you're wearing."

I gawked. "What? This is nice. Presentable. I know this is your first Games, but we do news interviews and lots of press. I planned on wearing this for Good Morning America, so I guess I'll need to get it laundered, but still, what's wrong with it?" I asked, fanning out the silk skirt.

Something soft hit my head, and a black sheath covered my face. I looked up and pulled it off, holding out the very low cut black shirt. "What is this?" I asked.

"That's one of my shirts. Put it on with one of those push-up bras you wear for competition, some skinny jeans, heels, and you'll be good to go," Becca said, taking my blonde braid and pulling it forward until she had the ponytail holder out.

"And speaking of letting it go. This hair. You're not the ice queen, Kelly. Let it be free!" Becca held her hands up and my hair unraveled out of its ever present braid.

Turning to look at the small mirror across from us, I looked at the reflection of myself with my long blonde hair framing my face. I never wore it down. It was always easier for competition and practice, and the braid had become my trademark since my first Games.

Growing up on a dairy farm in Wisconsin, we always had to get up early for chores. Mom would braid both Becca and me's hair, and if we finished our chores early enough, we'd get to head to the pond to skate before school. Even now as I ran my fingers through my now curly hair and looked at my smiling sister, it brought me back to those cold winter mornings where I'd practice my Double Axels, and she would try and break the ice with a nearby stick.

I shook my head, knocking myself out of my memories and stared at my reflection. I looked like a different person that than the girl from Viel, Wisconsin. A girl with cleavage and wavy blonde hair. A girl who couldn't admit she found something incredibly sexy about the guy with the mesmerizing blue eyes and dreadlocks. Something that made me think about what could happen if I let go of my inhibitions and stayed around.

But I couldn't think like that. I was here for The Games, not for romance or anything else.

"Where are we going anyway?" Becca asked, knocking me out of my trance.

I turned away from the mirror to see her pulling on a pair of jeans. "Um, well, I'm not sure exactly. And you're coming?"

Becca laughed, tossing on a slinky red top. "Well, yeah, I'm not going to let my sister go on the streets of Korea without me."

I crossed my arms over my chest. "I won't be gone long, and Logan's coming too."

With my sister there, there was no way I could sneak off. She'd be watching me like a hawk. She gave me more shit than anyone about not having fun. Just because when she came to New York after making the Olympic team, I went to bed early to get up at dawn for practice while she stayed out all night. She didn't have the rigorous schedule that I did. Part of me envied that. But another part of me, would always choose gold over fun.

Becca smirked. "I think I could probably protect you more than Logan."

I smiled despite her statement. "Touche, Bex. Touche."

Becca put her arm around me. "Besides, how long has it been since we've really gotten to hang out? Sure we had trials and a few weeks in the summers when you went to visit, but if I get time with you before Mom comes in later this week, then I'm going to take it. I've never gotten to party with my sister."

"I wouldn't exactly call this partying," I muttered, my face paling as I thought of the drunk athletes and who would be breaking something and have us all end up in a bad light on the news. The judges did always have their favorites, and no one likes a hot mess on the ice.

"Whatever it is, don't tell Mom and Dad if they Facetime us," Becca said, raising her eyebrows.

I laughed. "Think Dad will make us talk to the cows too?"

"I wouldn't put it past him."

Waiting in the lobby of our dorm, I felt exposed. Vulnerable even. More so than when I was in a sparkly leotard on the ice with hundreds of people watching me in the stands and millions on TV.

"Stop tugging at your shirt," Becca muttered, turning away from her conversation with Logan who was still talking.

"I'm not," I grumbled, tugging on the ridiculously low top. I may not have had a very big chest, but the push-up bra and low cut top were making it look like I was about to bust out and hit someone in the chin with my breasts.

"You definitely are and someone else definitely noticed," Logan whispered and pointed his dimpled chin toward the elevators were out emerged Blake along with some other guys, two I remembered from when I first met him. I believe they were Canadian skiers or something. The other guys were talking amongst themselves, shoving, and laughing, but Blake's blue eyes were focused directly on me with a smirk that had parts of my body on fire that definitely weren't okay to be on fire in the middle of a dorm lobby during The Games.

"Hey, you showed up. I thought I'd have to come up to your room and drag you down," Blake said, his smirk broadening to a smile that was whiter than winter snow.

I always thought of snowboarders as being a bunch of hooligans who were missing some teeth or other random bloody body parts. I guess it was just what I was used to with the American snowboarders who were always up at all hours of the night during The Games. Even when they came to Lake Placid to train, they all had crazy hair and liked to drink a lot of energy drinks and yell while barreling down the mountains shirtless.

Before I could think of something snappy to say back to Blake, another guy with short black hair, put his arm around

Blake's shoulder. "Why are ya giving shit to the Ice Princess? Let's get out of here and get downtown."

The other skier, with long red hair, whose name I forgot, came to the other side of Blake and put his lanky arm on his other shoulder. "Be nice, Erik, Blake invited Kelly here to join us."

Erik's eyes practically bugged out of his head as he looked between Blake and I. "No, shit, really? You're banging Elsa?"

"What did you just call my sister?" Becca asked, strong-arming her way next to me.

Even though I didn't get to see my sister much, it was nice of her to always have my back. She may have been a few years younger, but the girl was strong and a firecracker. There was a reason she ended up with the boys traveling hockey team in grade school instead of figure skating with me. The reason being, she gave her first figure skating partner a bloody nose, and our coach suggested she try hockey instead. She never looked back.

Erik stepped back, holding his hands up. I couldn't see his arms under his long-sleeve thermal, but I doubted they were bigger than what my sister had crossed over her chest.

"Come on, Ana, let's be civil," Logan said, putting a soft hand on Becca's shoulder.

"A frozen reference? And me as Ana? I think I'm more of a Sven," Becca said with a laugh, looking over her shoulder at Logan and smiling.

"Hmmm, I was going to go with Olaf, but if you'd prefer the ice guy, we can go with that." Logan grinned, looking at her like she was the only girl in the room.

Logan had always looked out for my little sister like she was his own. When I was busy with extra practices or yoga, he would make sure she wasn't sitting alone in my apartment. My parents couldn't get away from the farm much, hence why it was just Mom coming in for The Games and not until the finals and later on in Becca's games. But Becca did try to visit when she could on school breaks. She liked skating in Lake Placid, and I thinks she too thought of Logan as the brother we never had. Assuming he thought of Becca and me as sisters too. But I'm pretty sure brothers didn't look at their sisters like that. This was the first time I'd noticed any sort of chemistry with them, and now I was starting to wonder what really went on with all of those alone time lunches and nights out they had together.

I let out a deep breath and turned to say something to my sister. But then I felt something warm on my lower back and looked up to see Blake smiling as his arm slid around my waist. "I think that's our cue to leave."

I wanted to respond and say something, but all I could concentrate was his warm fingers against the thin material of my shirt, so I just slowly backed away and tugged on Becca's arm. "Come on, Becca. Let's get a cab. The boys are ready to go."

"What, you aren't going to ride with me?" Blake said, holding out his arms.

I smirked. "We'll meet you downtown."

"Ouch," Liam said behind him with a laugh.

If we drove separately, I wouldn't have to think about the heat that still felt like he left on my body. A feeling I hadn't had in a long time and pushed away to focus on the sport. But now that I was feeling it, I wasn't sure I wanted it to stop. Maybe it would have been better off if I just stayed home or headed to the arena. Maybe.

I wasn't much of a bar goer, but I didn't expect everywhere to look like the street markets I saw on the Travel channel or for all of us to pile on some outdoor picnic tables with waitresses placing giant green bottles and small glasses in front of each of us.

Blake sat across from me and immediately grabbed a bottle and filled my glass.

"Oh, I'm okay. I was just going to order a glass of wine or something," I protested, waving my hands.

Blake laughed slightly and put the bottle down. "It's a Korean custom that you have to pour the other person's drink, and when your glass is filled, you must imbibe. It's considered impolite if you don't follow customs. You don't want to be looked at as another dumb American athlete, do you?"

I raised an eyebrow and scowled. "Is this some weird Canadian thing to get a girl drunk?"

He shook his head. "No, this is a dumb Canadian snowboarder doing some research on Korean customs. Go ahead, Google it, then pour my drink."

I looked around the table where the guys were pouring each other's drinks. I would have asked Becca, but she was already at another table, talking to a group in American warm-ups with Logan on her tail. It was now just Blake and me. This would be my chance to escape. To get back to the rink and perfect my double axel. But instead, my heart, or more like my libido, did the thinking.

I sighed and grabbed the bottle, pouring his glass before I sat the bottle down then lifted my own glass. "Here's to The Games, I guess."

He smiled and clinked his glass with mine. "To The Games."

I wasn't a big drinker. Ever. And I had no idea how many bottles of alcohol Blake, and I had gone through. Or when he got so funny.

Maybe it was the accent. It was a mixture of sort-of-kind-of-french and northern Minnesotan, which I guess was basically Canada. But when he spoke he rolled his Rs like a French man, and I couldn't help but stare at his mouth. And I should have stopped staring or stopped talking after the first glass. Then he just kept filling mine up, and I kept staring, and there we were, me laughing and staring at his beautiful mouth.

"You really had a Mohawk for Sochi trials?" I asked, almost spitting out my Soju that was a sugary vodka and supposed to be a very popular drink in Korea.

Blake laughed and filled my cup again. "Yeah. I wanted to stand out. You Americans can't have all the flair with your blue-haired swimmers."

I pointed at him and leaned on my elbow. "Hey! Those summer guys aren't the same, and you know it!"

He grabbed my hand, and a smirk crossed his face that brought out one small dimple on his cheek. I don't know if it was the large amounts of alcohol we consumed or that dimpled smile, but all of my body felt flushed, and I was sure my face had to be redder than the Canadian flag. "It's not nice to point, Miss Johnson. Even an American knows that."

I tried not to focus on how warm and rough his hands were on mine. His whole palm covered my fists, and I briefly wondered how big other things were before quickly shooting that thought out of my head, and pulling my hand away. I didn't need to think about sex, no matter how long it had been. This was The Games. Not a time for romance or lust. "I wanna see a Mohawk picture. Come on; I know you've got one on your phone."

"Only if you show me one of yours pictures. I'm sure you have some from your early days of skating. The American costumes in the nineties weren't exactly some of your proudest moments. Or at least that's what your movies showed me." He raised an eyebrow before taking a sip of his drink, which was more like a giant gulp.

Gathering some courage, I poured the rest of the bottle in his glass. "I don't even know what I have on my phone. Nothing exciting. No 1980s scrunchies or poofy sleeved leotards."

He laughed. "I'm sure you've got something. Now show me yours, and I'll show you mine."

I took a big gulp of my drink which was sweet like candy at first then burned all the way down my throat, even though I was about to choke on it from his statement. "Okay, I'll see what I can find," I managed to cough out.

He laughed, shaking his head and pulled his phone out of his pocket, swiping the screen a few times before he faced it to me. My eyes widened as I looked not only at Blake a few years younger with a bright, blonde Mohawk but the striking brunette with the evil smirk next to him.

"You know Alexis Roy?" I asked, trying to keep my cool, but it was hard to when I was pretty tipsy and staring at a picture of my skating rival and the guy I was currently fantasizing about in my head had his arm around her.

Blake pulled the phone back and looked at the picture, blinking a few times before sliding his phone into his pocket. "Oh, yeah, guess I didn't see her there. It's a small community; I guess you can say. Well, a big, small community. Her family likes to go to my family's ski resort, and we run in the same circles," he said, his eyes darting everywhere but my direction as if he was afraid she'd hop out from behind one of the wooden pillars.

I had a feeling that there was more to the story with her and maybe I'd get it out of him after a few drinks. Or if I found an embarrassing picture to share. I pulled out my phone and opened my photos app. Before I could even scroll through, Blake's rough hands were on the screen, yanking my phone.

"Hey!" I said, reaching for the phone, but he pulled back, swiping his fingers on the screen.

He laughed. "I knew you'd probably find the best picture you could, so I had to look for myself, and I think we have a winner."

The grin broadened on his face, making that dimple stand out as he ran his tongue along his bottom lip and I felt my cheeks grow even hotter from the sudden movement of his mouth. "I didn't take you for a cowgirl."

I grabbed my phone, to keep my attention and thoughts elsewhere than his tongue. I stared at the picture he was looking at. It was a black and white screenshot of a photo from the local newspaper. One of Becca and I as kids on the farm in our matching overalls and braids next to the cows and pictured next to that was a more recent photo of both of us in Team USA sweaters on the ice.

"My parents are dairy farmers in Wisconsin," I quipped, sliding my phone into my pocket.

"No shit? What's that like?" he asked, taking a gulp of his drink.

I shrugged. "Normal? I guess. We grew up with a lot of chores and snow, so, of course, we got into winter sports, and eventually, my folks saved up the money to send me to train in Lake Placid and the rest is history."

There was more to it than that. Like the fact that my parents had to save forever just to get Becca and I both into elite skating clubs and when I got to good for those, I begged to be sent to Lake Placid and be homeschooled from there when I turned fourteen. It took a lot for my conservative parents, who'd never left the state, to send their oldest daughter away, but I never forgot that generosity. After my first Games, and sponsorships came along, I did everything to make sure they and Becca were comfortable, including paying for Becca's college, and new milking equipment for the farm. I just wished I could always do more.

"What about your family? Becca and I checked out your Wikipedia page. Skiing parents and a reality TV show," I blurted out, before even thinking what I was saying.

He rolled his eyes. "More like a couple of guest spots on a Youtube channel. Don't compare me to your American socialites."

"None of them have dreadlocks. At least that I'm aware of. Are those even real or are they made of like nylon or something?" I asked, everything coming out like word vomit, which was better than actual vomit that was threatening to curdle in my stomach.

"You wanna feel them and see?" he asked, that smirk spreading into a grin, baring a set of teeth that were whiter than the snow on the mountains of Pyeongchang.

"Oh I don't think I could do that," I said, taking the tiniest sip of my drink to have something to focus on other than his smile.

I gasped as his hand snapped across the table and was on mine, pulling it to his hair. "Go on, feel it."

My eyes widened at his brashness before I sat my drink down, a few drops spilling over the edges and concentrated on the feel of his hair between my fingers. It was a giant tangle, rough yet somehow intricate and well worn like the ice before the Zamboni got to it.

"Now lemme feel your hair," he slurred, his rough hand reaching for my head. I thought he was going to yank the blonde out of my hair, but instead, he pushed a tiny fallen strand behind my ear, his fingers grazing on my lobe before trailing down my jawline.

A tingling sensation started from my toes and went all the way up my stomach until a flush went to my cheeks, making me crinkle my nose.

It had been a long time since I'd been touched by a man, aside from Logan in the rink or Coach Donahue when he was trying to teach us a new move. There wasn't time for romance. The only thing I ever had close to it was my former partner who I lost my virginity to in the locker room then found out he was actually in a serious relationship. Not just in a serious relationship, but practically engaged to a girl back in Britain. I found that out via social media. I told Coach I didn't want him as a partner and didn't give a reason. Since I was his golden goose, as he said, he found Logan without question and together we went to the Sochi Games in 2014, of course getting gold.

But none of that, the gold, men, none of that compared to that moment, staring into Blake's blue eyes and dimpled smile, wondering if maybe a one night fling at the Olympics wouldn't be a bad thing.

"Hey, Tremblay, we're gonna head back to the village. You coming?" A Canadian accent knocked me out of my stare with Blake, and I pulled back, his hand dropping from my face before I pulled the drink to my lips, downing the rest. I was in a trance just from his looks. I never got distracted. I was always on point, but there was something about him that had me captivated.

Blake looked at the guy, whose name escaped me then glanced back to me, raising an eyebrow. "I think Kelly and I are going to get another bottle of Soju, but I'll see you back there in a bit. Cool?"

The guys with him gave each other huge smiles then laughed, fist bumping Blake. "All right, man. We'll see you later."

As soon as they left, Blake turned back to me, and the smile fell from his face as he nodded at me. "I think your party's ready to leave too."

I whirled around to see Becca and Logan standing there with a few of Becca's teammates. "Hey, thank God we finally found you. Thought you might have gotten lost or snuck away to get a few more hours in of skating and already be passed out in the room."

I forced a smile. I wasn't exactly thankful for the interruption or for her assuming I'd be asleep, though I was pretty sure it was past my usual nine pm bedtime. "Thanks, but Blake and I were just about to order another drink. So I'll see you guys back at the village later?"

Logan raised an eyebrow and looked at Becca then back to me. "Are you sure about that?"

"What? Like he's some Canadian serial killer who is going to lure me away and string me up in the market? I don't think he would do that just because Canadian's pairs team is subpar. Unless you would?" I asked, turning toward Blake, realizing I was still a little dizzy and still very tipsy, but had to give myself an inner pat on the back for getting another dig in at Alexis.

He laughed and signaled to the waitress for another bottle. "I promise she'll make it back home. No need to worry about stringing her in the meat market or jeopardizing The Games."

I looked back at my sister and Logan who frowned at each other. Becca sighed. "Okay, fine, but if I find out he did anything you didn't want him too, I know a guy back home who said the hogs will eat anything." Becca looked past me at Blake and enunciated her words, "A-N-Y-T-H-I-N-G."

The cork of the bottle opened and I turned to see Blake smiling as he poured my drink. "Don't worry, Bex. I got her."

Oh, he sure did.

"I think it's about time we head back," I said, nodding my head behind Blake at the woman who had been serving us drinks all night. Instead of waiting on tables, she was sweeping. I guess that would have had to be the case since we were the only table left in the place.

Blake had polished off another bottle of Soju, and I was still sipping on the same glass since my sister and Logan left.

"Head back to your place?" Blake asked, wiggling his eyebrows.

When I was still tipsy an hour ago, I found him charming, now with his slurring words, it was a bit annoying, and I just wanted to go home.

"I'll go to my place, and you go to your own. Come on. I'll call us a cab or an Uber," I said, pulling my phone out of the pocket of my jeans.

Blake put his hand on my on top of the phone, and I looked up, meeting his smile. Even tipsy he was still sexy as hell, and I couldn't help but give him my full attention. "Why don't we walk back? It's a beautiful night. Look at all of the stars. I've never seen the stars on this side of the world. It's like everyone here is looking at a completely different set than we are. Isn't that crazy? There are millions of stars out there, and we only see a few of them," Blake said, staring up at the sky.

"Come on, drunky, let's get you back to the village," I said, pulling my phone back and pulling up the Uber app. "The guy should be here in a few minutes. His name is Hyun-Gi, and he's driving a silver Hyundai," I said, squinting at the name and car. At least I had sobered up enough to read clearly and think. If I had finished that bottle of Soju with Blake, I might not have been.

Blake put his arm around my shoulders. Even through all of the alcohol I could still smell the cedar scent of his hair oils as his dreadlocks fell over my shoulder. "Haaa Annnn Jeeee better not steal my girl," Blake said with a laugh, butchering the driver's name.

"Your girl? I don't think a few drinks qualifies me as your girl. And who even says that anymore? That sounds like something out of a bad movie, or a boy band song." I wrinkled my nose.

Blake laughed even harder. "Fine. Wanna be my Games girlfriend? It's like a regular girlfriend, but I get to fuck you while wearing my medals."

I gasped as soon as the words exited his lips. I'd never had a guy use words like that around me or so brash. I didn't have the typical college experience like most girls, and there weren't a lot of rowdy guys around, except when they came to train. Even then they didn't talk to me like Blake did. No man ever did.

The silver Hyundai pulled up just in time. I was afraid if Blake looked at me, or leaned into me any further I might have let him kiss me or do whatever else he wanted with his medals. Instead, I approached the car and opened the back door.

Blake put his free hand out. "After you, Games girlfriend."

I rolled my eyes. "That's still a horrible name."

When we got in the car and buckled in, Blake leaned in close, his breath hot on my ear lobe. "You won't be saying that when I have that tight little body unwound, and you'll be screaming my name," he whispered before his tongue slightly nibbled my earlobe.

A fire lit within me. Not just from the alcohol or from The

Games, but Blake Tremblay was turning me on like I never thought before. But I couldn't let him become a distraction. It was just one night of drinking. One night away from practice and that was it.

"So, your place or mine?" he whispered, his hand moving in small circles on my lower back.

"Both. I go to my place, and you go to yours," I said, staring straight ahead instead of into his blue eyes.

He squeezed my side. "We'll see about that."

CHAPTER 3

Blake

The harsh itch of carpet burn scraped my cheeks, waking me out of my sleep. Or, sort of woke me up at least. The sun streaming in through the curtains was too bright for me to open my eyes.

"Shiiiiitttt," I drew out, my throat dry as I slowly sat up. My head was pounding, and all I could think about was how bad I needed a drink of water and a shitton of Tylenol.

I was still in my clothes from the night before and almost forgot where I was until I saw the beige carpet of the Olympic village dorms. The same carpet they had in the lobby and boasted about on the tour my parents made me take when they tried to convince me I needed to stay there.

How the hell did I end up in the dorms? And on the floor? Did I win the bet? If so, why the hell was I still in my clothes? Shit that Soju was strong and the last thing I remembered was getting in a cab with Kelly. I wanted to kiss her so damn bad, but she turned her cheek to me. And that was all I could remember. There had to be something, though, or else why was I here. Unless I ended up in someone else's room…

"You're awake!" A soft voice gasped.

Slowly I turned in the direction of two twin beds. In the one closest to the wall sat Kelly Johnson with her perfect blonde hair tucked into a bun and a clean blue tracksuit on. Even though the beds were small as hell, she looked even tinier, sitting there with her knees to her chest and her eyes wide.

"Damn, that sugary stuff knocked me out. I don't even remember coming back here…" I slowly went to a standing position, cracking my back muscles in the process. I was getting too old for this all night drinking shit. Come to think of it, since I started training harder for The Games a year ago I couldn't remember the last time I drank. Explains why I was knocked out so hard.

"Did we…?" I asked, looking for any sign that I was still wearing a condom and would need to flush that ASAP.

She shook her head fiercely. "Oh no. By the time we finished that last bottle and left the bar, you passed out in the Uber. I didn't know where your room was so I brought you here, and you seemed pretty comfortable on the floor. You snore, though."

I laughed slightly then stopped, rolling out my shoulders. Damn that hurt even to laugh. I was going to surely get my ass kicked on the slopes today with practice. I guess this supposed luxury carpet wasn't as great as the tour guide boasted. "You just let me sleep it off? What about your roommate? Shit, I have to look like an ass."

Kelly pursed her lips. "My sister is my roommate, and she was up early to get to the rink. She didn't ask what you were doing on the floor, but I'm sure I'll get an earful after the opening ceremonies tonight."

"Fuuuu," I stopped and shook my head, trying to stop the pounding. "I forgot about those."

Kelly raised an eyebrow. "You forgot about the opening ceremonies? The entire reason we're here?"

I laughed slightly. How could I forget? My first opening ceremonies and my parents wouldn't stop talking about it. Or how different it was in their day when no one had smart phones and could actually watch the ceremonies instead of tweeting it. I wouldn't be surprised if they found a way to sneak in and carry the Canadian flag themselves instead of the Refugee bobsledder who was elected. "Yeah. I think I just had a brain fart. Blame the soju. Speaking of that, I'm hungover as hell, want to get some McDonalds? My treat. We can call it a breakfast date."

"Um, McDonald's doesn't sound appetizing, and I need to get to practice. We only have so much time on the ice today that isn't shared with every other country," she said, her words trailing as she finally stood up but her eyes wouldn't meet mine, they just stayed on the floor, taking tiny steps toward the foot of the bed.

I grabbed her hand before she could walk past me and there was a jolt of electricity. Not static electricity but a warm tingle that I usually didn't get just from holding some girl's hand. I had the same surge last night when she let me tuck her hair behind her ear. It may have started as a bet to get in the skater's panties, but part of me was glad I hadn't gotten that far with her. It meant I got to spend more time with the girl who cared enough to take a drunken Canadian snowboarder home and let him pass out without alerting the media.

"Thanks for taking care of me last night, Kelly. It's been a while since anyone's done that for me. If it were one of the guys, he would have probably left me for dead." I laughed it off but stopped when she smiled softly.

"It was nothing, really," she whispered, catching her teeth in her bottom lip and damn if that little bite didn't cause that surge of electricity to go straight below my belt.

I leaned in, fully realizing that after a night of drinking I probably smelled like ass and my breath was like a swamp donkey. So instead of trying to do what I really wanted to do to this girl, I put my hand on her hip and let my lips graze her cheek. "No really, thanks," I whispered.

Before she could say anything back, I let go of her side and turned to the door, getting out as quickly as I could then let out a deep breath.

This was only a bet. That's what I had to keep telling myself, even though after spending just one night, not even sleeping with the chick, and I was starting to wonder if I wanted to win because it was a bet, or because I liked this girl.

Even though The Games didn't officially begin until after the opening ceremony, snowboarding and other sports had qualifying runs that morning.

After grabbing a quick shower, I called an Uber and headed out to the mountain with coffee and a burrito in hand. My head was still pounding and not just because of the hangover, but because I couldn't get my mind off the blonde figure skater. Which wasn't going to help my situation, since I was about to meet up with Tweedle Dee and Tweedle Dum who I was sure would bring up the bet right away.

"Hey, look who showed up, the man whose now twenty-five grand richer," Erik said, clapping Liam on the shoulder who turned around to look at me as I sauntered toward the rail the guys were leaning on. There was an area all along the slopes for spectators to watch the preliminaries for slopestyle and another area for the athletes. Though, us snowboarders and skiers kind of took over the athlete area since there were a ton of us and most spectators with tickets waited until the actual events.

"Not yet," I mumbled, before stuffing my mouth full of burrito. I wasn't even sure why I said it. I could have lied. I mean I did technically sleep in the same room with her, just not screw her.

Liam raised an eyebrow and crossed his arms over his chest, his puffy coat crinkling with each movement. "Then what were you doing last night? Playing chess?"

I blew out a breath and shrugged. "I don't know, man. I guess I was too drunk and passed out. But we still have two more weeks, and a lot can happen in that time."

"For your sake, I hope you're right," Erik said, clasping his hand on my shoulder.

I could have said something smart back, but instead, I watched the American guy take his turn down the slope. I'd been immersed in snowboarding culture for so long I couldn't remember a life that wasn't surrounded by freshly fallen snow and a bunch of guys drinking energy drinks and trying to outdo each other.

I may have been pretty laid back with most things in life, but when it came to the sport, I was competitive as hell. I was always pushing myself to outscore the previous guy and anyone else at the top. I could blame my Olympic parents on that one, I guess.

But now that the score was a person, it was a different kind of competitiveness.

I couldn't deny that I wanted Kelly, the ice princess. The girl may have been tightly wound up. I thought she was nothing more than a snob when she turned her nose up at me. Then after a few drinks, I got to see the real girl. The shy and innocent one. The girl who took a drunk snowboarder home and didn't think twice about it. These douchebags didn't deserve her time, and I probably didn't either. But that didn't stop me from wanting a few more stolen moments with her. Bet or not, Kelly Johnson had me captivated.

"So you seeing her tonight?" Erik bumped my shoulder and wiggled his eyebrows.

"Probably. It is the opening ceremonies," I replied.

Erik laughed and put his arm around my shoulder and the other around Liam's. "And The Games are just beginning!"

I didn't even have time to shower after a run down the slopes before my parents were messaging me to see when I'd be at the village for Opening Ceremonies. It wasn't even close to time, and I was planning on downing a few energy drinks and napping before I even thought about heading over.

I swiped my messenger app open, seeing a bunch of missed messages. I guess they must have been trying to get in touch with me when I was out the night before and that morning when my phone died, so I left it to charge while watching slopestyle then heading for practice.

I typed in a quick message and agreed to meet them at the village for dinner before the opening ceremonies, briefly wondering what Kelly would be doing for dinner and how soon I would see her again.

Stepping into the shower, my thoughts flew to Kelly with her long blonde hair and that tiny hint of cleavage as she leaned over, giggling and sipping her drink. The girl could get me hard just thinking about her, which wasn't uncommon. She was gorgeous, sexy as all get out, and I was a man, so, of course, those thoughts brought my hands to my dick to release the pressure the thoughts of her bringing.

When I'd cleaned up and put on my opening ceremonies outfit and stepped out of the bathroom, Erik and Liam were already dressed and waiting in the living room, flipping through random shows on the TV.

"Dude, how long were you jacking it in there? Your parents have been blowing up your phone," Liam said, tossing me the device.

I caught it and saw their messages, questioning where I was. I didn't even think of the time passing. Their messages got more urgent saying they had someone "important for me to meet." Which probably meant one of their old colleagues or something that they wanted to use to brag about their glory days.

"You guys ready to go," I grumbled, putting my phone in my pocket.

"Yeah, man, let's do this shit," Erik said with a laugh.

The village was even more crowded than when we first got there, but like I had a GPS tracker on me, my mom found me within a few minutes of stepping onto the soil.

"Blake! Where have you been?" Mom's eyes widened, standing on the sidewalk with her hands on her hips. Even in her giant puffy coat and white knit cap, she still looked tiny.

"Sorry, Mom. I got caught up," I muttered.

"Well, hurry up, your father and I have someone important for you to meet," she said, looping her arm through mine and guiding me toward a small café.

"You aren't trying to set me up with someone again, are you? Alexis Cote was one thing, but if you're trying to find another athlete or even some socialite here for The Games, I'm not interested." Unless of course the athlete or socialite was Kelly Johnson, but I had a feeling my parents wouldn't be searching out American girls when they were our number one rivalry at The Games.

"Speaking of Alexis…" Mom's words trailed.

I stopped and looked down at my mother who wouldn't look in my direction. "Seriously? You blew up my phone, so you could set up a meeting with Alexis and me?"

Mom huffed as if I just said the most ridiculous thing. "Your father and I ended up sitting next to Alexis' parents on the plane ride, and they told us about this shampoo sponsor Alexis has. Paid for most of her trip and then some. They were able to set up a meeting with one of the company's PR people for you. It wouldn't hurt for you to have some additional sponsors, Blake."

I sighed. I wanted to object to that, but she was right. All the big sponsors had their guys. I had one energy drink company that only took a chance on me because of some

YouTube spots I did. I even had to buy my own board, and my parents fronted the money for the trip. As much as I hated to admit it, it couldn't hurt to meet with a sponsor, even if I had to deal with Alexis Cote.

And it couldn't hurt if the bitchy brunette did make Kelly a little jealous. I saw the way she looked at the picture of two of us that I even forgot I had on my phone. She and Alexis had some skating rivalry I guess and what better motivation to have a girl spark some jealousy and want payback on another girl than seeing me with the ex?

I stepped into the warm air of the café, and like an icy cold beacon, Alexis turned in her seat, giving me a tight-lipped smile. Shit, this was probably a bad idea. Even if it would make Kelly jealous or I'd have a chance at a sponsor, I forgot about the fact I'd have to stare at Alexis' bitchy face for however long this lasted.

While Kelly was petite and looked like a porcelain doll, Alexis was the hard to Kelly's soft with her dark brown hair pulled into a tight bun and extenuating those cheek bones I was pretty sure could cut glass.

Dad stood up from across the table and so did a gentleman with slicked back hair and a five-o'clock shadow. "Blake. I'd like you to meet Ben Broderick," Dad said, putting his hand on the guy's back like they were old friends.

Ben put his hand out, and I shook it, even though Ben slightly sneered his upper lip as if he just caught the smell of something nasty. "Nice to meet you, Blake, your father didn't tell me you kept the dreadlocks. I saw those on one of your

YouTube videos from X-Games and thought those were just a fun little thing. Not something you actually kept for The Games."

I looked down at the blonde dreads that fell just below my shoulder blades. "Yeah, kind of a trademark and they work better under my helmet than the Mohawk."

"At least the mohawk was clean," Alexis muttered.

"Cleaner than your pussy," I muttered under my breath so only she could hear as I took a seat at the table across from Ben.

She rolled her eyes. "Real mature."

"I guess we'll make this quick since you two have somewhere to be," Ben said with a nervous laugh, opening a leather folder.

"Okay," I said, not sure exactly what we were going to make quick or what the details would be.

"We'll have to get some contracts sorted out, and there is something that the guys in legal will want to add, and it'll have to deal with those dreadlocks," Ben said, glancing up at me.

"What about the dreads?"

"You're going to have to cut them. Can't exactly sell hair products when you aren't using them, and we don't have any kind of product hair style," Ben said, folding his hands on the open folder.

"You want me to cut my hair?" I asked, even though I heard him perfectly fine. Absently I ran my fingers through my hair thinking about how Kelly had done the same thing the other night. She didn't think of it as disgusting like Alexis or my parents. In fact, the way she bit her plump bottom lip when she looked at them made me think quite the opposite was true.

Mom let out a shrill laugh and put her hand on my back. "I think that's what Ben is saying is that after The Games, you know, it could be a new look for you.

You're almost twenty-nine, dear, don't you think it's time to give up the crazy hair?" Mom blinked slowly giving me a look that said; "Don't' fuck this up, this is your chance to do something."

I licked my lips, thinking about my options. On the one hand, I loved my dreads. But they were just hair. Hair that Kelly was attracted to. Wait? When did my decisions become about a girl? Dammit, maybe all the time in the snow was getting to my head. I had to think about my future and my career.

"Yeah. I can think about that," I finally said.

Ben smiled. "Good. We'll get it all set up for you and Alexis to get some photos done during The Games and then a before and after with the dreads. You two are going to make one hell of a campaign."

Mom and Dad beamed, and Alexis did her usual tight-lipped smile and I...well, I was just hoping I didn't throw up on someone. It wasn't going to be easy to win a bet, or to have any chance with Kelly if Alexis was involved during The Games. Getting her jealous was one thing, but if I had to spend time with Alexis for a campaign, between that, practice, and my events that left no time for Kelly. Time I wanted to make for her. Not just for a stupid bet. Now I just had to try and keep Alexis and Kelly as far away from each other as possible, which would be a problem since they were competing. I guess I would just have to make a bigger show of my feelings for Kelly, to get Alexis off my back, even though I had no idea what they were for sure. I guess I had two weeks to figure that out.

CHAPTER 4

Kelly

"AGAIN," Coach Donahue spat after I landed another perfect throw jump executed by Logan. Most of the other countries had left the rink to get ready for the opening ceremony, so it was just the three of us in the big arena that would soon be filled with hundreds of flashing lights watching us from the stands.

Logan wiped the sweat from his brow. "Coach. Really? We both need to shower before the opening ceremony, and we have this routine down. We had it down at nationals, and we're going to execute the short program flawlessly. There's no doubt about that."

I didn't want to bring up the half a second we were off on our first set of side-by-side Double Axels because that was my fault. My head wasn't in practice today and more on thinking about a blond, dreadlocked snowboarder. But I wasn't going to admit that out loud. Or ever. I was going to focus on The Games, which was what I came here for. At least that's what I kept telling myself.

Coach smirked, crossing his arms over his barrel of a chest. He looked like every single coach I'd seen in a movie with his round shape, balding head, and a thick mustache. I think it was the reason I wanted to train with him so bad. That, and he'd trained three other gold medalist pair skaters.

Coach held up one pudgy finger. "One more and if it's perfect, then you can shower."

Logan sighed. "All right."

After getting back to the room and showering, I emerged in just my towel to find Becca perched on the bed, sliding on her pants that I thought were cute yet not really practical for anything other than walking in an arena and I hoped I wouldn't have to cut them off myself and Becca after the ceremonies.

"Hey," I said, grabbing my brush and running it through my wet hair.

"Hey yourself Miss-brings-a-drunk-guy-home," Becca said, standing and pulling her pants over her hips with a loud grunt.

When we were younger, no one believed we were sisters. We both had the athletic figures, but while my features were petite, hers was extra muscular. I swore she could kill a man with her thighs. It had gotten even more prominent as we grew up and when she would visit me in Lake Placid, our personalities clashed even more than our looks. It was our mother's suggestion that we room together for the Olympics and get some sisterly bonding. I guess a few visits with me in New York where she used my ID to get into clubs wasn't enough.

Not that I didn't adore my sister, we were just completely different. Fire and ice as my dad used to say. I may have been in the spotlight as a skater, but I never tried to stand out amongst the crowd and avoided all conflict while Becca was the one you could pick out of a crowd, usually starting a fight.

I smirked, combing out a tangle. "He didn't know where his room was and I didn't want to just leave him outside."

"That and you kind of like the bad boy," Becca said with a wink before sliding her coat on.

I scoffed. "I do not. Why would you even think that? And he isn't a 'bad boy.' That sounds like a stupid cliché from a romance novel."

"Because of the way you just smiled before trying to act offended. Admit that you like the rowdy snowboarder. Or bad boy. Or whatever you want to call him."

My eyes widened. Did I just act offended? What was my face showing? I had the best competition face in the game. I could miss a turn and still smile like I was on top of the world. I guess that's why Blake's friends had no so eloquently called me the "ice queen." I knew how to freeze my face and usually my feelings for anyone.

Becca laughed. "And your reaction to that, tells me you do. Come on; you haven't talked about a guy, in well, ever.

Your life has just been training, and it's nice to see you even talking to someone that isn't your coach or Logan."

"I'll have you know that I have tons of friends and gentlemen callers that I talk to in New York," I said, adjusting my towel.

She raised an eyebrow. "Really? Name one."

"I, uh." Dangit. I had to have some friends. But now that I thought about it, there wasn't anyone I hung out with other than Logan, and that was just during practice. If I wasn't practicing, I was eating, sleeping, or watching reality TV.

Becca smiled. "It's totally okay, dude. I get it. It's hard when you're so passionate about something to find time for anything else. I don't remember the last time I had a date, let alone hung out with someone that wasn't in hockey gear. And have you seen the hockey dudes? Sorry, but I can't get down with a guy who has less teeth than me. Granted, a lot of them get falsies, and there was that hottie from Norway…but…" She shook her head then put her hand on my shoulder. "If you want to have fun with the snowboarder, I'm not going to judge you for it, just don't bring his drunk ass to the room. Find an open family restroom or something."

I wrinkled my nose. "Ew. That's disgusting. Do you know how many germs are in there?"

"Not if you don't let your naked bodies touch anything."

I thought for a moment how that would work then my thoughts lingered to how Blake would look naked with his lean body. He probably had a ton of tattoos. All bad boys did, didn't they? I wondered if he had the Olympic rings on him like all of those swimmers did, or maybe even a mountain that spread across his long back.

Then I started to think about what dipped below his V and my face heated up, so I had to stop thinking. "Okay. Enough talk about Blake. I need to get ready."

"AKA you need alone time in the bathroom," Becca laughed as I grabbed my clothes.

I glared at her. "No!"

That would have to be done when I knew she was good and asleep.

This was my third Olympics, and the opening ceremonies never got old.

All of the athletes from around the world together in one stadium, and even better was walking along with all of the athletes from the United States, and for that moment we are all together as one team. There weren't any politics or grievances; it was just all of us working for the common goal of the gold. Though, I assume there was more competition against people who had others from their country competing for the same medal. No one dared to try and compete against Logan and I. We were a powerhouse, and everyone knew it.

The only real competition we ever had was that bitch Alexis Cote and her haughty blond partner, Jacob Roy. The guy looked like a Disney prince, and with that stupid French accent, he had a way of making the judges swoon. I hated both of them. I never actually had a real conversation with either of them, but still hated the idea of the pair. We were always battling for gold at every competition, and I swore that neither of them ever smiled. They were the king and queen of resting bitch face. I wondered what Blake saw in her if it was really as a friend or something more. As soon as Blake entered my brain, I started to search the crowd. Canada was a ways away, but maybe in the sea of their athletes, I could spot his dreadlocked head.

"Looking for someone?" Logan asked, nudging my side as we walked to our seats to watch the performances.

"What? No, I was just admiring the beautiful atmosphere," I said, half-lying. So I may or may not have been looking. He didn't need to know all of my secrets.

When I glanced in Logan's direction his eyes weren't even on me but glued to his phone. "Oh, he just liked the selfie you posted of us on Instagram. I mean the atmosphere liked it, that is, if it's what you were really looking at," Logan said, peeking up at me.

"What? Really?" I couldn't pull my phone out of my jacket fast enough to open up my Instagram app.

There it was, staring right back at me. Blake Tremblay's name on top of thousands of other hearts on the picture of Logan and I, smiling with a sea of red, white, and blue behind us.

"Oh my God, are you blushing right now?" Logan asked, nudging my shoulder.

"I'm not," I said, quickly finding Blake's Instagram account and following it before Logan saw what I was doing, then shoved my phone back in my pocket.

"It's cute, and it's good to see you actually interested in something other than skating. Now we can have an actual conversation that isn't about a triple axel or what you didn't eat so I could lift you," Logan said, shaking his head as if he just had a thought but wasn't going to say it out loud.

Now was not the time to tell him that instead of eating one of the meals our sponsors had prepped and sent, I binged on cheese curds and root beer that Becca brought from home.

"Am I that boring of a conversationalist?" I asked, turning to face him fully.

He shrugged. "I wouldn't say that, but I will say that I've never seen you laugh or talk to someone as much as the dreadlocked snowboarder last night."

I rolled my eyes. "You sound like my sister. Like I have absolutely no life and that somehow this guy is just going to change all that. We only have two weeks here. It's not like a lot can happen in that time."

"Maybe it can," Logan mused.

Maybe it could. Maybe it really could.

CHAPTER 5

Blake

The great thing about my sport was that I concentrated on the giant and parallel slalom. I didn't have to spend the entire games worrying about qualifying for every little thing or practicing every minute. Though it might have been less intense if I focused on one thing, like my buddies that did halfpipe or slopestyle, according to my parents, "A Tremblay should be more than one event." Reluctantly I agreed with them like a scared little boy that was afraid his parents were going to make him get back on the bunny slopes with the too big of skies, so I agreed to train for giant and parallel slalom and never stopped.

Though I loved the mountains. I loved the smell of freshly fallen snow and the chill on my face I got when a cold burst grazed it. There was something completely freeing about just being alone with the board and the snow. It was always my solace. No matter what shit was getting me down, I always had the fresh powder beneath my feet.

But there were also very nice things about not being alone and somewhere warm with a girl underneath me. Probably why I spent just as much time in bed with the ski bunnies as I did on the slopes. Something else my parents never let me forget in my entire life. Maybe a medal in The Games would get them to shut up about the skiing part at least. Not the girls.

After the opening ceremonies, Liam and Erik hooked up with some skiers from Norway and headed over to our cabin near the mountains. There was a particularly sweet looking brunette who was giving me huge 'fuck me' eyes, but there was something holding me back.

No, someone.

I posted a selfie of Liam and me on Instagram while we were coming in for the opening ceremonies and briefly scrolled through the app. I didn't even think what I was doing when I looked up her name and saw the selfie of her in the same arena, but what felt like a million miles away.

I never thought much about a girl's delicate features unless I was thinking how small they looked when I was pounding into her. But Kelly was tiny, yet fierce with a smile that said she knew she was the shit and there was no one stopping her from getting what she wanted.

If the girl only knew how bad I wanted to and would have made use of the hundreds of condoms the Olympic committee had provided and had her on every single surface of her way too clean of room, I didn't think she'd have that same smile.

But there was also an aching guilt that came with looking at her smile. I wanted to feel her lips on mine. But not with the looming thought of a bet in my head. I could probably win it with her. The rumors may have been true that she was focused on her sport, but I'd gotten a glimpse of the girl that wanted to let loose. I knew I could be that guy, but under the pretense of a bet, something felt dirty about it. My mind briefly drifted to thoughts of just calling the whole thing off and letting Liam call me a pussy or whatever. But then what if he decided to take revenge and tell her about the whole thing? Or even worse…what if I did get that gold and he just took the medal money? That was going to be my down payment on a house. My future with sponsorships that weren't shampoo people who wanted me to cut my hair. No. I couldn't pussy out.

"Excuse me," a voice with a hint of an American twang said.

I was in the middle of the coffee shop, not paying attention to anything but how bad my coffee was. Seriously they needed Tim Hortons around The Games. I was pretending to look at my social media, but even that wasn't cutting my dreams of good coffee and Kelly. But the voice knocked me out of my thoughts, and I looked up to see Logan, Kelly's skating partner, standing in front of my table.

"Hey, what's up, Logan?" I asked, sliding my phone in my jacket pocket.

He pushed his long black bangs out of his face and gripped the chair in front of him. The guy wasn't much taller than me, but lean like a swimmer. The dude probably had to have some biceps if he could throw around girls on the ice, but in his big puffy coat and floppy hair, he looked like any other guy at the coffee shop. "Okay, probably not my place to ask, but I know Kelly definitely is too scared to. We're going to watch her sister Becca play hockey against Italy tonight if you'd like to join us in the stands."

I tried not to focus on my heart beating faster just hearing Kelly's name. What the hell kind of guy was I turning into? I didn't get worked up over a girl. Especially not a girl who was supposed to be just a bet. "I can think about it. I don't think I've got much going on, but need to check with the guys," I said, trying to play it cool.

Logan smiled, shaking his head. "You use whatever excuse you want to pretend like you aren't into her, but I'll save you a seat."

Before I could respond, Logan nodded and pushed off the chair, heading out of the coffee house and leaving me thinking about the blonde ice princess that was turning into way more than just a bet.

"Hey, Blake, we're gonna head to watch some jumpers. Wanna come?" Liam asked, coming out of his room and into the small living room of the cabin we shared with Erik.

"Naw. I was going to head over to the arena to watch some hockey," I said, sliding a thermal over my head.

"Hockey? I didn't think Canada was playing tonight?" Liam asked, raising an eyebrow.

"They're not, but his girlfriend's sister is playing Italy tonight," Erik said, coming out of nowhere, or the bathroom that he liked to stink up.

"You're seriously going to watch a bunch of chicks play hockey just to get into the ice queen's pants? Damn, man. No wonder you agreed to this bet. You like Elsa! Maybe you'll be the one to melt her frozen heart," Liam added the last part in a high pitched tone, clutching his hand to his chest and looking off into the distance like he was some sort of wannabe Disney princess.

"Shut up, okay? It's all just another game, and I'm the best at playing," I said, wishing those words didn't just leave my mouth. But what else was I supposed to say? Tell the guys that I actually liked the girl and have them razz me even harder?

No. If they were going to act like this just from me hanging out with Kelly, there was no way in hell I was going to tell them anything else. I'd never live to hear the end of it.

"Whatever you say, Man. Just don't let her get too close and freeze your fjord," Liam said, laughing at his own joke and threw his hand forward. I cupped my hand over my balls before he could get anywhere near him and turned in the other direction, his hand falling somewhere near my waist.

I tried not to let his words get to me as I shook my head and put on my coat. "Yeah, you do the same. I saw some of the teeth on those skiers last night. Better put a mouth guard on them."

Liam gave me a nasty look, but Erik laughed like a hyena and just like that the attention was off of Kelly and me. For that moment at least.

All I had to do was flash my credentials, and I was able to walk into the stands. It was kind of pathetic how many people didn't show up for women's hockey, especially when it wasn't the finals. But the Americans made sure their athletes were well represented with what seemed like half the Olympic village in their athlete's section.

It took me a minute to find Kelly's blonde head. Damn even from the back and in a jogging suit, she was beautiful. Her blonde hair fell in waves over her shoulders, practically sparkling in the fluorescent lights. The girl was a damn Disney queen if I ever saw one.

Jogging my way down the stairs, I slunk into the seat next to her with my phone out. I tapped on her shoulder, causing her to whip her head in my direction. I leaned in close to her and snapped a photo of the two of us before she could say anything.

"What was that?" Kelly quipped her eyes wide as she tried to grab my phone.

I laughed, looking down at the picture with me grinning and her staring with her eyes wide and nostrils flared. It wasn't the most flattering picture of her, but it was funny as hell. "That one's going on Instagram."

"I don't think so!" she shrieked, reaching for my phone again, but I pulled it away. She fell into my lap, her tiny hands landing right smack on my groin. If she wasn't so little, it might have hurt, but instead, it actually felt good. Really damn good and I was already straining against my boxers.

She sat up quickly and pouted. "Not fair. If you post that I'm going to post the pictures I took of you sleeping and drooling on my floor."

I shook my head. "You have no such pictures."

She raised an eyebrow. "Wanna bet?"

Pulling my phone back to my lap so she couldn't see my growing boner, I deleted the picture and pulled the app back up. The word 'bet' already had me calming down anyway. It was starting to feel like a dirty word that I didn't want to hear. "Fine. We'll get a new picture, but if you give me that fake smile then I'm going to recover that one and post it everyyyywhereeeee."

She rolled her eyes but then smiled as I pulled the phone up and leaned my head against hers. She smelled amazing. Like vanilla and mint, the perfect winter dessert that had my mouth watering and my smile even wider.

"Is this your real smile?" I asked, glancing at her.

"Yes!" she said, forcing her teeth to bare, her lips straining.

I slid my free arm around her waist and ran my fingers along her side. She squirmed as a light giggle escaped her lips, giving a genuine smile that lit up her whole face. I was lucky enough to snap the picture before she swatted my chest.

"Now that's a smile," I said, squeezing her side then let my hand stay there as she looked over my shoulder at our photo.

"You're lucky that turned out cute or I'd have to expose those pictures." She sniffed like she was making a point, but even beneath her words, I could tell she was smiling. I couldn't explain it, but I was already getting used to her voice. The way she spoke when she was happy. When she was upset. Everything about her was engrained into my memory like the slopes back home. I could glide them with my eyes closed, but there was no way I wanted to do anything with my eyes closed with Kelly. And just thinking about that had my cock already raring to go.

"Now to put this on IG, a good filter," I said, opening the app and adding a black and white hue to the photo before going to the next screen, all with one hand while I tapped my fingers on her hip.

"What are you going to say in the comments?" she asked, her chin resting on my shoulder and her blonde hair cascading down my jacket. If I turned even slightly my lips would be on her cheek, or that silky blonde hair would press against my ear. I was practically poking out of my boxers just thinking where else that hair could be, specifically splayed across my pillow.

"I'm thinking of something good," I replied, trying not to focus on that silky hair and her intoxicating scent.

"Like what? The Games hashtag and that we're at a hockey game?" she asked.

"If The Games have a hashtag, we should too. Something like Blakely," I said with a laugh.

"A hashtag? For us?"

"Yeah. The ultimate Olympic power couple."

"Um, we're not a couple," she said, slowly leaning back.

"What else would you call us?" I asked, not wanting her to leave my grasp. There was something not only alluring but almost necessary about having her touch. I didn't want to let go of her, so I ran my fingers up and down her side, hoping she didn't stop me.

"Friends? I think?"

"Friends don't think about their friend's naked," I said and turned to see her face flush.

All right, now we were getting somewhere.

"Fine, you can give us a stupid hashtag, but not Blakely," she grumbled.

"Okay, how about Klake? Then it sounds like the name of some Hollywood starlet's baby," I said, laughing at my own joke.

She shrugged. "I guess it's better than Blakely."

I typed in the hashtag then closed out of the app, sliding my phone in my pocket. I didn't even notice who was around us and finally realized that her skating partner wasn't next to her. "Where's Logan?" I asked, not that I cared too much because this meant I got a little more one-on-one time with her, but the guy did invite me.

"He's down there. He gets really into my sister's games," she pointed toward the glass separating the ice where his black hair was flying as he pounded on the glass and yelled obscenities.

"Holy shit, and I thought that he was a mild mannered gay guy. Guess he proved me wrong," I mumbled.

Kelly turned toward me and raised an eyebrow. "Logan isn't gay."

"Seriously?"

She nodded. "Seriously. He wanted to play hockey but didn't have the coordination with a stick, so his skating coach suggested figure skating. He didn't want to do it at first because of the stigma, so his coach set him up in pairs skating, and, after many failed attempts at partners, he found his way to me. Along with his old girlfriend that thought they were so in love she had to be in New York with him."

"Take it you weren't fond of the girlfriend?" I asked.

Kelly wrinkled her button nose, which was seriously adorable. "She was nice enough but clingy and jealous. She was always at the rink and got mad when we'd practice. After that, he didn't have any more romantic relationships and we both kind of stayed away from all of that. Easier to just have each other and the ice."

I raised my eyebrows looking between Logan and her. "You mean? You two?"

She laughed a melodic sound that was like church bells. "Oh, definitely not. We've just always had a mutual understanding. We chose this life of skating and going for the gold, and that's how it's always going to be."

"That's really all you do then? You two just skate? What about besides skating? What do you do for fun?" I asked.

She shrugged. "Watch reality TV I guess."

I laughed. "That's not doing something. Don't you have any other hobbies?"

"Who has time for hobbies?" she asked, her face serious.

I couldn't help but laugh even harder at this way-too-stuck up chick that still had me captivated no matter the fact that she carried herself higher than other people and didn't do much other than skate.

"How about I make a bet with you?" the words escaped my mouth before I thought about what I was saying. But this time the word didn't sound dirty as I said it. This way it was more exciting. It was something I would have with Kelly that wasn't a challenge. Something that I would enjoy a hell of a lot and hoped she would too.

"A bet?" she asked, raising her eyebrows.

"Yeah. You have to find one new hobby while we're here at The Games."

"One new hobby?"

I could think of a few hobbies I'd like to try with her, but I'd stick with at least getting her out of her rut. "Yeah. It could be anything. Hell, I even think they have a chess set at one of the coffee houses."

"I don't think I'm much of a chess girl," she quipped.

"Okay, just an idea."

"What about snowboarding?" she asked, a small, real smile crossing her lips.

"You really want to try snowboarding?"

She shrugged. "It's better than chess."

"Yeah, you got me on that one."

She blinked slowly. "So are you going to give me a lesson or what?"

"Right now?" I asked.

She laughed slightly. "Not right now, but I don't know, maybe some time."

"Tomorrow I have giant slalom, so it would have to be after that unless you're going to come be my good luck charm." I grinned.

She pursed her lips. "I'm not sure I'm much for luck, but I can see about coming out there. If it doesn't interrupt practice and isn't too cold."

"For someone who wants to learn to snowboard, you're making more excuses than my grandma when she doesn't want to go outside to get the mail."

She sighed, putting her hands out. "Okay, fine, fine! I'll be there."

I splayed my hand on along her side, feeling the warmth of her body radiating through me. "Good. I'll be looking for you in the crowd."

"Kelly! There you are! And, oh a, a fella?" A woman's voice said from behind us.

Kelly jumped practically across the seat then stood up, turning toward the voice. I looked as well to see an older woman with short, curly blonde hair and an older man with a USA trucker cap and plaid shirt stretched across his wide belly standing next to her.

"Oh, hey, Mom. Hey, Dad. Blake was just saying 'hi' before he met up with his friends. I. uh, didn't know you two were coming this early. Or that you were coming at all, Dad! What about the cows?" Kelly said, her voice wavering.

Did Kelly seriously just saw cows? I thought she was giving me shit about the dairy farmers. But there they were: real life Wisconsin dairy farmers at The Games in Korea.

"Well, we couldn't miss your sister's first game. Would have been here earlier if your father would have just agreed to use Uber. He seems to think it's going to get us murdered, so we had to wait forever for someone to pick us up that spoke English from the hotel. But we're here! And hopefully, Becca will be surprised too that dad's here!" The small woman took a few steps down and embraced Kelly in a tight hug.

I smirked, standing up. I couldn't resist meeting the family, so I put my hand out Kelly's mom. "Blake Tremblay, Canadian snowboarder," I said.

The woman's eyes widened, and she smiled brightly looking between Kelly and her husband who walked down to her side. "Oh! Good to meet a friend of Kelly's! I'm Diane, and this is my husband, Dwayne."

The woman shook my hand then I put my palm out to Dwayne, who took it in his sausage-like fingers, giving me a death grip that was either a friendly handshake or he wanted to strangle me for putting my arm around his daughter.

"Nice to meet you both," I said.

"As I said, Blake was just leaving," Kelly said with a nervous laugh.

"Why would I leave? This game is just getting interesting and I think there are enough seats for all of us." I shot a wink in Kelly's direction, and she glared.

"Oh, that would be lovely!" Diane said, and I stepped out of the seat, ushering her and Dwayne to take the inner seats next to Kelly with me on the outside.

"What's your game here, Blake?" Kelly asked through gritted teeth as she took the seat next to me with her mom on the other side.

"What? Me? Games. The only game I've got going on is the Olympics, babe," I lied, putting my arm around her shoulder.

I thought she would hit me or glare again, but instead, she sighed and left it there. "You know my parents are going to have a lot of questions about this."

"I'm sure they will," I said.

"Oh, I'm glad we didn't miss too much of the game! Only the first quarter!" Diane said, patting her daughter's leg.

"How's Becca doing? Get in any fights yet?" Dwayne asked.

Kelly opened her mouth then shook her head. "No. Um. I don't believe so."

"Sorry, sir, I think I've been distracting Kelly from watching the game, but you could probably ask Logan, if he'd ever stop yelling at the ref," I nodded my chin toward the glass where Logan was screaming so loud I couldn't understand what he was saying.

Dwayne laughed. "Logan's always been my girls' biggest fan. You know for a figure skater, he has one hell of a set of balls on him."

Diane swatted his chest. "Dwayne!"

"What? Did I say something wrong?" Dwayne asked, blinking his brown button eyes.

"I don't think the male figure skaters appreciate you talking about their balls," I offered, leaning forward.

"Is it okay for me to talk about anyone's balls?" Dwayne asked with a hearty laugh.

Kelly groaned. "Can you guys stop talking about balls? It's really weird."

"I'm just making conversation with your new friend, here, Kelly. Where did you say you were from again, Blake? Minnesota? That sounds like a Minnesota accent. Maybe even a little Upper Peninsula," Dwayne asked, leaning forward and putting his big bear-paw like hands on his knees.

"Canada, actually, sir."

Dwayne laughed. "Pretty damn close to the UP."

"Yeah, but with better coffee and manners," I said, pointing a finger at him.

That got Dwayne to laugh even harder. I couldn't remember the last time I was able to joke with my own father or get him to laugh. There was something that felt warm and inviting about being with Kelly's family and enjoying their company. But there was also a sick pain of guilt buried deep within me. All of this was happening because of a bet I agreed to. I bet I really didn't want to be involved with. But now I was in the middle of it, and there was no way I was getting out. Now if I could just keep this girl and her wonderful family from finding out.

"I think I like you, son," Dwayne said.

"I think I like you, too. Wanna switch seats with your daughter? I'm sure we could get the Olympic committee talking." I wiggled my eyebrows which caused another round of laughter to erupt from Dwayne's lips.

Kelly squirmed against me and opened her mouth to say something else but a buzzer went off, and the crowd stood, clapping.

"What just happened?" Kelly asked as we both stood and looked on the ice where the US skaters were all huddled together.

"That girl from Illinois. You know the one with the gap tooth? She just scored the winning goal!" Kelly's mom squeed. "I'm glad we were here for this!"

Kelly's mom embraced her husband then turned to Kelly and hugged her before she looked at me. "Come here, Blake. You're getting in on this family hug too."

"Okay, I can get with that," I said and let her embrace me. I couldn't remember the last time my mom had really hugged me for a celebration, and there was something warm about the woman who slightly smelled like mozzarella.

"We should celebrate with dinner. I'm starving. After that long ass plane ride with those little microwave fish meals that smelled worse than Grandma's basement," Dwayne said, rubbing his stomach before looking at me and raising a bushy eyebrow. "You wanna join us, Canada?"

"Oh, I don't think—" Kelly started.

"I'd love to," I finished.

I didn't look to see the glare Kelly was probably giving me. I hadn't eaten much that day, and I could use a bite to eat.

Plus it would give me a little more time with the girl. And if her family ended up liking me, well, the next step was getting her to like me. Then more.

CHAPTER 6

Kelly

I didn't know why Blake was at the game in the first place, but I had a feeling it had something to do with my floppy haired skating partner. The one who smiled like a Cheshire cat as we waited near the locker room for Becca to get out and head to dinner.

"It seems your new boyfriend and Dad are bonding. What do you think they're talking about?" Logan asked, nudging my elbow then pointing his chin toward where Blake and Dad were laughing.

I rolled my eyes. "I don't want to think about it."

Logan shook his head. "Come on. You know you wanted him here."

I scoffed. "Did not."

"Well, at least you wanted him here before you knew your parents were going to get in earlier than expected. I thought your dad wasn't coming anyway. Who is watching the cows?"

"I guess his new manager is watching them and he wanted to surprise Becca. Which was an even bigger surprise to me since dreadlocked wonder boy showed up," I muttered the last part.

"Do you like him, Kel?"

Raising an eyebrow, I didn't even look in Logan's direction. "What?"

"I mean do you really like him? I haven't seen you this fixed on a guy since that old partner of yours left. What was his name? British dude."

"I don't want to talk about Joe," I muttered. "And why does it matter? He's just here for The Games. We both are. Not like I'm going to fall in love or marry the guy."

"Well, at least I don't have to worry about going to Canada for a wedding." Logan laughed at his own joke, and I rolled my eyes.

"Just making sure if a guy is wasting this much time on you and you on him that it's a good time wasted."

I turned to face Logan. "What is that supposed to mean?"

Logan just grinned and looked past me at the girls coming out of the locker room. "I guess we'll find out."

Mom and Dad weren't adventurous eaters, and Becca said she was so hungry she could eat an entire cow, so we all ended up crammed in a corner booth at McDonald's.

"Do they have McDonald's in Canada, Blake?" Mom asked, unwrapping her cheeseburger.

"Mom!" I hissed, looking at her across the table where she sat against the wall with Dad at her side. Becca was on the other side of Dad and Logan in between me and Becca with Blake on the end. Probably should have found a way not to have him so close to my mom.

Blake laughed. "Yeah. We do. I think they're a little bit different than your American versions, but we do have them."

"Tremblay. That last name sounds familiar," Dad said in a gruff voice.

Blake hesitated with his burger in his hands. "It's a popular Canadian name."

Dad slapped his big bear paw of a hand on the table, causing all of us to jump and stare at him. "That's why that name sounds familiar. You wouldn't happen to be the son of them Canadian skiers? The ones who won more gold's than any other winter Olympians and were in that gum commercial for years?"

For the first time, I saw Blake shrink in his seat. The guy always carried himself highly with a smile on his face and a laid back attitude, but at the mention of his parents he was reserved and didn't even try to hide it. "Yeah. Those are my parents."

"Hot damn, they must be mighty proud of you for coming out to The Games, continuing their legacy like that. Hell, I think they were still skiing during Kelly's first games.

Breaking more world records before they retired," Dwayne continued.

"Yeah. I think they might have been," Blake muttered.

I wanted to ask him more about his parents and why he never brought them up. But then again it's not like we had many conversations that involved them after we talked about my dairy farming parents. I also hated to see Blake so reserved and not being the guy that was poking fun at me. Even though I acted like I hated it, there was something I liked about his little jabs. Something that made me feel normal.

"So, Blake, you ready for your event?" Becca asked, breaking the tension.

Blake smiled slightly. "Ready as I ever can be I guess. I'm not a star like Kelly, here."

And just like that Blake turned the conversation off of him and back to me. Something I was usually comfortable with, but tonight I wanted to know more about Blake Tremblay. And I just had to figure out how I'd get to do that.

My parents headed back to their hotel after dinner to beat jet lag. Logan, Becca, Blake, and I all stood awkwardly in the parking lot.

"Hey, some of the girls from the team are drinking at the condo they rented just outside the village and asked if I wanted to join. I think I may stop in if that's cool. Wanna come with?" Becca asked, looking between all of us.

"Sure. Couldn't hurt," Logan said.

"I think I'm going to call it a night," Blake said, which took me by surprise. Surely I thought after all of his talk at the hockey game he'd want to get me out of my element. But the look of defeat from dinner after talking about his parents was still there. Something I shouldn't have pried on, but I couldn't have helped being captivated by the guy.

"You know I think I'm going to call it a night too, Blake, would you mind walking me to my dorm?" I asked, blinking slowly.

Blake licked his bottom lip and nodded. "Yeah, I can do that."

Becca and Logan looked at each other before looking back to us. "Okay, behave you two," Becca said over her shoulder before she and Logan started down the path in the opposite direction of our dorm.

"I'm this way," I said quietly, pointing toward my dorm.

"Okay," Blake said, nodding and walking in step with me.

We were quiet for a few beats before I let out a deep breath, letting it hang in the air as a cloud of smoke. "So, not a big fan of your parents?"

Blake laughed slightly, shaking his head. "What makes you say that?"

"The way you went from carefree guy to ice cold in a matter of seconds." I smiled and nudged his shoulder. "The ice queen knows when a guy can turn to ice as well."

That got a genuine smile out of him. "I guess it takes one to know one, huh?"

Without thinking, I looped my arm through his, my fingertips grazing against his jacket. "So are you going to tell me why you're bothered by them or am I going to have to take unflattering Instagram photos of you until I get it out?"

He laughed, his body tensing. "Not much to say. They're Olympic royals, and I'm their kid who took way too long to get into The Games and a sport that wasn't skiing."

"Take it they're hard on you?" I asked.

He let out a breath through his nose. "Yeah. You could say that. It sounds really stupid. I'm twenty-fucking-six-years-old and I let what my parents think get to me."

I shook my head. "I don't think that sounds stupid."

"Yeah. To you. You have really great parents."

"I didn't always think that," I muttered.

Blake raised an eyebrow. "Really?"

I sighed. "Your parents may have always pushed you, but mine have been the opposite. They support me, yeah. But they've never really got it."

"What do you mean?" Blake asked, his free hand finding its way to mine, stroking it while I curled my fingers around his bicep.

I shrugged. "I mean you had the parents that probably spent money and time on all of this training and mine didn't even want to drive me to the rink. I had to beg my grandparents to drive me for the first few years of skating then finally my parents noticed I was really into it, so they signed Becca and me up together. But it was just local rink stuff. I had to beg for them to let me train in Lake Placid. I even saved up my own money to pay for part of my trip."

"They do care, Kel. I can see that the way they looked so proudly at you and Becca."

I blew a raspberry. "Yeah, now that I'm a multi-gold medalist and millionaire."

"Better than being the Olympic legacy who didn't get in until he was an old man."

I bumped his shoulder. "You're not an old man. If you are, then I'm practically geriatric."

"I think I did see a gray hair tonight at dinner."

I stopped and put my hand on my hair. "What? Where?"

Blake let go of me and turned with the smile finally returning to his face. "I'm kidding. Your hair is fine. Perfect," he murmured, his hand going to my hair and running his gloved fingers through it.

"Um. This is my dorm," I said, changing the subject and looking away, so I didn't kiss him. I wanted to, so badly. But what if he didn't kiss me back? What if all of this talk was just him being a nice guy?

He had to make the first move if he wanted this to be something more and I hoped he did.

Blake looked up. "Okay, I guess this is good night then. Maybe I'll see you tomorrow?"

I nodded. "Tomorrow."

He leaned in, and I parted my lips, waiting. Then he smiled, and his mouth went to my cheek, giving me the softest kiss before whispering in my ear. "Night. Good luck charm."

I always tried to catch at least some of the Olympic highlights on TV during the day. It was the easiest way to catch up on my competition, but I wasn't expecting to see a beautiful set of blue eyes on the screen when I turned on the TV. The eyes that I looked into last night, wishing I would have given him a real kiss goodnight.

Not only was Blake on the screen, but his parents sitting next to him. It was the first time I'd actually seen parents appearing with their athlete this early in The Games, or at all, but I guess it was different when his were Olympic royalty.

They also weren't what I was expecting. While Blake was wild with his dreadlocks, the tattoos poking out of his dress shirt, and a wicked smile, his parents were even more prim and proper than I was. His mother in her turtleneck and face that I swore didn't move even when she smiled and his dad in a perfectly trimmed graying beard and matching sweater to his wife's.

"So, Blake, what's the scoop with you and Kelly Johnson and that Klake hashtag that's been used over one million times?" A female, very smiley blonde reporter asked.

I widened my eyes, staring at the screen. Not just because Blake was looking especially good in his plaid button down shirts and jeans, and I thought about how my sweater still smelled like his manly and woodsy scent. But because his face genuinely flushed when my name was brought up and our hashtag. One-million times?

I grabbed my phone off the dresser and turned it on, notification after notification from social media popping up. I didn't even have this much on my feed when I made gold in Sochi.

Then I stared at the picture of us. Of his smile. And I thought of his arm around my waist; it seemed like those vibrant colored tattoos that went up, and down his arms radiated their own heat. He may have just been being playful, but I kept wondering how far those tattoos went up his arms. I may or may not have stalked his social media to get a better view of those tattoos. I was never one to care about ink on someone's skin. It usually repulsed me. But on Blake, the swirling blues and whites creating a mountain landscape down each arm were a thing of beauty. One that I wanted to see in person.

"We're both athletes, you know, here having a good time in the village," Blake's voice knocked me out of my phone trance.

"And? What else, Blake? That we're the power couple like you said?" I found myself raising my voice as I stepped closer to the TV. What the hell? I didn't care what we were. I was here for the gold, not to have a romance. My own words surprised me, yet I still found myself leaning toward the screen.

"Is that your way of avoiding the question?" the blonde reporter asked with a laugh.

"I think what Blake is trying to say is that he's here to focus on The Games. Not romance," his mother quipped with a haughty laugh.

"What do you know Canadian skier lady?" I found myself yelling at the TV like it was going to answer me back.

Blake smirked, visibly shrinking as his mother patted his knee. "I don't know how the Canadians would feel if I were to say anything more about an American figure skater."

"Okay, okay, we won't force a war between Canada and the US, but know that this is one hashtag I think we'll all be watching during The Games," the blonde reporter said.

"I'll make sure we keep posting then," Blake added, a smile finally crossing his face.

"Now, Robert, Debra. How do you feel that your oldest and only son has finally made it to The Games?" The blonde reporter asked, turning her attention toward Blake's parents.

Blake's mom, who I assumed was Debra, laughed slightly, squeezing Blake's knee. "Well, we're just happy he's here. And we hope he keeps his focus on the slopes."

"Ugh!" I groaned, not wanting to see what else his parents had to say. They didn't even know me, and they already seemed to hate me. Thinking I was some sort of a distraction. Or maybe I was reading into all of it.

"Ugh!" I groaned again. What does that all mean? Last night he was all talk about making bets and snowboarding together and now... what we were friends? That's what I said I wanted, so it should have been what I wanted. But I didn't. He met my parents. I thought we had a moment, even with the peck on the cheek. But now what?

Now I had to get ready for the qualifications tonight. I did what I always did best and focused on the ice.

Or so I thought.

"Since we aren't going to talk about American figure skaters, what about Alexis Cote? You two were rumored to be cozying up at your parent's resort in Canada during nationals," the reporter asked, turning her attention back to Blake, raising her eyebrows. Now my attention was back on him too.

I folded my arms across my chest. "Cozying up at nationals? I thought you two were just friends, Blake!" I spat his name as if he could hear me.

What the hell kind of jealous girl had I become that yells at the TV. I only did this when I was alone in my apartment watching The Bachelor, not at someone I knew on the screen.

Blake laughed, pushing up the sleeves of his plaid shirt. I found myself uncrossing my arms and staring at the way his muscles moved. "Well, you know, I think people are always looking for the fairytale romance. And what's more romantic than two athletes, some fresh snow, and a little games action?"

"Are you trying to hint at something to us?" The reporter prodded.

Blake smiled, shaking his head. "Nothing to hint at. I'm a single man if that's what you're asking. But don't tell too many people. My mom might try to hook me up with someone." He hitched his thumb in his mom's direction.

"Well, your secret is safe with us and our millions of viewers. I'm sure she didn't hear you either," the reporter said, and they laughed together.

"They'll be plenty of times for girls after The Games. And if Blake does as well as he's supposed to, I'm sure they'll be figure skaters, skiers, hey maybe even a few reporters after him," Blake's dad finally spoke, shooting a wink at the reporter who laughed even harder and I swore blushed.

"What does that mean?" I found myself yelling at the TV before I turned it off.

I sighed, shaking my head. This wasn't me. I didn't go crazy for boys.

But Blake was different than the other boys I was used to, and I wasn't sure if that was a good or bad thing.

"Again!" Coach yelled, even more frustration ringing in his voice as I missed another jump.

My head was always in the game, always on the ice and my movements. But Blake had me so twisted mentally; he gave me so much hope to dwell on, that it caused my focus to be on everything but what I was supposed to be concentrating on. This was why I didn't do relationships, hell, even friendships. They were all just distractions from my ultimate goal: the gold.

Yet I had two golds that hung in cases in my apartment in New York. I dusted them once a week and then looked at them when I needed motivation. I planned for possibly one more Olympics after this, but then I'd be almost thirty. There would be new blood, young blood who were thirstier for this moment than I was. Then what? After skating, I had nothing else planned for my life.

I was homeschooled due to my vigorous training schedule and never even thought about college. The problem with going to school was that I couldn't compete at a professional level and get paid according to the NCAA. I wasn't going to give up the sponsorship money I started getting at fifteen, so I didn't take a second glance at college. I didn't have experience in anything but skating which could get me a job in one of those traveling skater tours or maybe even as an Olympic correspondent. But that was it. All I had to show for years of dedication.

"Kelly! Where is your head?" Coach Donahue yelled his hot breath right on my face. He was so close I could see his nose hairs dangling from his flared nostrils.

I shrugged. "Sorry, Coach."

He shook his head. "I've been with you ten years. Ten years of dedication and one little distraction from some Canadian and you're all over the ice. Get your head in the game, Kelly. I know Alexis's head is there!"

I nodded, swallowing hard, my blood boiling just hearing her name. How did Coach know about all of this? I guess the whole world knew thanks to a little hashtag and the morning shows. This was something I was never going to live down unless I showed where my head was supposed to be and brought home a gold. "Yes, sir."

"Again!" Coach yelled, stepping back and clapping his hands.

Logan took my hand, guiding me toward our positions. He leaned in close. "It's okay to have a little distraction. It keeps us sane," he whispered.

"And what's your distraction? Hockey?" I asked, raising an eyebrow.

He grinned. "Something like that."

For qualifications, we settled on a waltz, the one that got us gold in Nationals. I'd had every turn and jump, and spin so memorized that I could do it with my eyes closed.

Logan and I stood on the side of the rink with Coach Donahue waiting for the Russians to finish their program, which lacked the depth and difficulty that ours did. At best they would make third after tonight and by tomorrow be out of the podium position.

I picked at the shimmering crystals on my shoulder blades. The long sleeve silky blue dress with its shimmering skirt made me look an ice princess from a fairy tale, and I was pretty sure that was the look our costume designer was going for when she put me in that with my blonde hair in a long braid.

Logan looked equally royal in his black trousers, puffy white top, and black vest. I smiled to myself thinking about how in our first competition together the judges and announcers talked about our chemistry. Like they believed we were a couple in love on the ice, moving together without knowing the world was watching.

That seemed like a lifetime ago, and I remembered thinking I would never be the girl that focused on a guy so much she forgot the world was going on around her.

But that was before. Before Blake had pushed my hair behind my ear and sent a jolt of electricity through me. Now he was all I could think about. Even as I straightened the jewels on my shoulder, I swore I saw his dreadlocked head in the crowd.

I did a double take. It really was him in the stands, and as soon as our eyes met, he waved slightly. Not only was he there, but he was sitting in the stands next to my parents and Becca. Like it was where he belonged.

I blinked once then twice, quickly turning away toward Logan, a small gasp escaping my lips.

"What? Did a jewel fall off? Is it going to knock that pompous Sergei on his ass when he attempts another Triple Axel?" Logan leaned in and whispered.

I shook my head, swallowing to gain some saliva in my throat. "It's Blake. He's here."

"Really? How the hell did you find him in this crowd? I think every single person who came to The Games is packed in this stadium, standing room only," Logan said, staring over my head into the crowd.

I didn't want to tell him that I had this almost psychic connection. Like I felt Blake's presence, and he was a beacon calling to me. That sounded crazier than a double five-rotation axel.

"From The United States, Logan Smith and Kelly Johnson," the announcer boomed which caused an eruption of applause from the audience.

I sucked in a deep breath and took one last look into the audience and swore I saw Blake wink, even though that couldn't have been possible to see since he was way up in the stands.

Maybe he was here for Alexis, who was skating after us. The thought of that made a lump form in my throat. Why did I care who he was with?

Maybe because deep down I really did like him and didn't know what the hell to do. Every time I wanted something, I went for it in full force. Like skating. I found Coach Donahue and begged my parents to send me to train with him. I kept training until I had the gold.

But a guy? A guy was something I didn't even know how to go about wanting and keeping. Logan said distractions were what kept us sane, but at this point, I was going crazy with my head everywhere else than the ice.

"Good luck," Coach said, squeezing both of our shoulders before Logan and I skated to the center of the ice.

I stood with my back to Logan, pressing against his stomach as he wrapped an arm around my waist and I put my hand on his face, my head down. I'd thought nothing of this pose and the thousands of times we'd done it, but now I was acutely aware of his hand on me and how it felt when Blake had touched my sides and how bad I'd wanted him to touch so many other parts of me. Blake's hand. Blake's lips.

Everything about him sent shivers through my body just thinking about him.

I was so lost in those thoughts that I was a beat off from our starting position. I quickly recovered, but my mind wouldn't get back on the ice. Luckily, I knew the routine by heart and could just go through the motions, like riding a bike to most people. I glided into each spin and jump then it was time for the toss.

Logan held me by the waist, lifting me into the air as we spun together. Usually, I focused on his face, mainly the tiny little freckle that was right below his left eye. But this time it just reminded me of Blake's dimpled smile, and I found myself looking up into the crowd for the snowboarder. And that was the fatal move that had me a beat off, my left skate hitting the ice before my right and my body going into a tailspin, hands on the ice to steady myself.

A collective gasp came from the crowd as I scrambled to get back to a standing position and forced a huge smile though all I wanted to do was cry. I messed up the move we'd done so many times, and that was going to put us off a point. I couldn't mess up the next Triple Axel, or we'd be off the podium.

Logan skated to my side, our fingertips barely touching. He glanced over at me with a nervous smile on his face and his eyebrows raised. I kept my wide smile, trying to assure him that I wouldn't mess up this time. But the downward spiral had already started, and I missed the landing, again my hands touching the ice followed by me scrambling back to a standing position as we skated back to the center ice and the final spin.

When Logan grabbed my waist, dipping me low as he crouched over me, I put my hand on his face as we did with every ending pose. But instead of beaming pride in his eyes, I could see the concern. The fighting back of tears.

But he shook them off as soon as the crowd erupted in applause and threw the flowers and bears that we grabbed a few of as we waved to the crowd and skated toward Coach to hear our scores that there was no way in hell I actually wanted to hear.

We breezed past Alexis and her partner, the smirks on their face evident like they pitied us. They knew that all they had to do was nail their performance and the gold was theirs. The gold and possibly Blake.

Before I could even dwell on that thought, Logan and I got to the bench. Coach sat between us on and leaned over as I put my skate guards on. "Where the hell was your head, KellyAnne?" he hiss-whispered.

I couldn't remember the last time he'd used my full name, and not just called me 'Kelly.'

"I guess just nerves," I whispered, before looking up at the scoreboard, waiting with bated breath for our standings.

I wanted to look out into the crowd and see Blake, but I knew if I did, it would just hurt more. I couldn't worry about the snowboarder anymore. If I did, this would happen with every competition, and I wouldn't even be considered for stars on ice.

When our numbers lit up on the board, we were sitting just outside of a medal position, which was pretty impressive for my screw ups, but not good enough. We'd have to pull out all of the stops to get gold in the finals, and that would require extra practices, which made me tired just thinking about it.

Coach walked ahead of us, mumbling to himself as we made our way toward the locker rooms.

"Since Blake came to see you tonight, do you want to go watch his qualifications after practice tomorrow night?" Logan asked, bumping my shoulder.

I raised an eyebrow. "Are you nuts? Didn't you see how much I messed up tonight? We're going to need quadruple the practice tomorrow."

Logan shook his head. "We can't spend our entire lives practicing, and I'm pretty sure Coach will work us like dogs tomorrow morning and well into the afternoon, so why not take a break? And if you can't stop thinking or staring at this guy, what better way to do that then watch how he moves in the snow?"

My face flushed just thinking about how his body would move in other places than the snow, and I had to shake the thoughts of his naked body out of my head. Letting out a deep breath, I nodded. "Shouldn't you be pissed at me right now? I'm taking you out of a medal position."

"Well, you did miss a jump that we've been practicing for almost a decade."

I sighed, putting my head in my hands.

"And that's why I'm not going to give you any more shit about it. I figure if you're messing up it's because of this guy, so you either need to go full force for him or forget about him. That way we can come back in the short program," Logan said.

"Okay…we'll see how I feel tomorrow."

CHAPTER 7

Blake

Number Unavailable: Hey, what are you doing tonight?

I glanced at my phone and the new iMessage. I tried not to make my phone number public, but it didn't take much more than a quick internet search to find it. I'd had more than my fair share of disgruntled ski bunnies texting me the morning after I left their apartment wearing nothing but my snow pants.

Me: Stuff. Who is this?

Number Unavailable: Your favorite American hockey player, Becca. Now stop being a dick and come to Kelly's qualifications tonight.

Me: And why would I do that?

Becca: Because you want in my sister's pants and the best way to do that is to sit through her boring skating routine with her little sister and parents. They're already asking me twenty questions about you.

Me: I might show up.

I didn't plan on going to watch Kelly in qualifications, but when her sister messaged me, I couldn't exactly say no. For one, I'd look like a huge dick if I blew her off and she'd probably tell her sister the same thing. As an only child, I didn't know much about sibling relationships, but I had a feeling earning her sister's trust was a big thing. For two, I also couldn't deny that I liked hanging out with her family. It was better than the scrutiny of mine any day.

"Just-friends-Canadian-snowboarder-Blake!" Diane said way too enthusiastically as I made my way to the stands.

I should have probably said "no" to this whole ordeal. This girl was supposed to be just a bet, and I thought dinner with her parents would be something to bide my time, but I didn't expect them to bring up my parents. Or get so excited to see me. It was a nice relief instead of the look of disappointment I felt like my parents always had when I was around.

"Hey, guys," I said, taking my seat next to Becca, but before I could fully sit, Diane already enveloped me in a big hug then handed me a plastic bag of some orange crummy-looking things.

"Uh, what is this?" I asked as Diane let go and took her seat opposite Becca and next to Dwayne.

"Those are cheese curds, all the way from Johnson Farms in Viel, Wisconsin. Ain't you ever had em?" Dwayne asked, adjusting the toothpick that was dangling out of his puffy lips.

"Uh, I'm not exactly sure I know what they are," I said, holding up the bag.

"If you're not going to eat them, pass em this way," Becca said, holding her hand out and squeezing her fingers over her palm.

"If you want em that bad, then I guess I have to try them." I opened the bag and reached in, my hand grazing over the bumpy, cold little balls of cheese. I pulled one out and stared at it. It looked like something I'd find after a cat puked, so I smelled it.

"Are you smelling the cheese right now?" Becca scoffed.

"Yeah. It looks weird," I muttered, rolling it between my fingers.

Dwayne laughed. "It's supposed to. It's just cheese crumbles, Blake. Stop playing with your food and eat the damn thing."

I nodded. "Okay…"

Slowly I put the curd in my mouth and let it roll over my tongue, the burst of cheddar hitting my taste buds before I could even chew.

"Holy shit, this is good!" My eyes widened as I bit down and another shock of spicy flavor hit my teeth then flowed down my throat.

"I told you," Becca sang as she stole a curd from my bag.

"Glad you like them," Diane said with a huge grin on her face, looking at me like a proud mama bear. I couldn't remember the last time my mom ever gave me that look, even when I made it to The Games.

The announcer called over the speakers that the first pair of skaters were up and the crowd rang in applause as a couple in very sparkly outfits went to the center of the ice.

"How long does this usually take?" I asked Becca between cheese curd munches.

"Hours. I usually bring a book to listen to," she whispered, stealing another cheese curd.

"Seriously?" I asked.

"Just enjoy your curds, and we can take bets on who's gonna fall."

I winced at the word 'bet' and how casually Becca said it. Sure the girl had no idea about my bet for her sister, but it still sat funny in the pit of my stomach.

This may have all started as a bet, but now I was getting in deep. I was sitting for hours with this girl's family. Eating their farm-made cheese and having them smile and act like I was a part of their happy little gathering. This could all blow up in my face very easily if I wasn't careful.

"What the hell was that?" Becca asked, leaning back and staring at me with her eyebrows furrowed.

"What was what?" I muttered.

"That look."

"What look?" I feigned innocence.

Becca rolled her eyes. "You acted like you ate a rotten piece of cheese when I talked about a bet. Afraid I'm going to make fun of one of your old girlfriends? Maybe that Canadian chick with the huge forehead?"

I laughed, letting go a deep breath I had been holding in. "I've never heard Alexis referred to that way and she's not my old girlfriend. We just used to hang out."

"Hanging out meaning fucking?"

Diane's hand reached across the seat, swatting Becca in the leg. "Becca! Language! And keep your voice down, some people want to watch the Swedes!"

"Fine," Becca whispered and turned toward me, leaning in. She smelled like cheese, sweat, and a hint of hair products in her wildly crazy hair. "So what's the story with you and Alexis? When Kelly and I googled you, she may have stopped at the basics, but I looked a little deeper. She was in a lot of stories with you. Good and bad."

I rolled my eyes, really not wanting to go into anything Alexis especially since things had a way of getting back to her. If I wanted a chance at a sponsorship with the shampoo company, I had to play nice. At least for now. "We've grown up together on the slopes. Yeah, we had a thing going on but not anymore. Okay? I like your sister," I blurted the last part without even thinking.

Becca leaned back and smiled. "Good. I hope it stays that way."

I hoped it did too. For this Wisconsin family's sake and my own.

When Kelly and Logan finally took the ice, it seemed like hours later, even though it was probably only about an hour since I got there and ate a bag of cheese curds.

Kelly and Logan skated to the center ice, both shimmering in their glitzy outfits. In the pictures, I'd seen of her online she always looked so poised and confident. But now that I knew her, I saw that hard exterior was a front. That the girl underneath was insecure but hid it with her icy bravado. She put her head up and smiled a fake smile, looking out into the crowd. I swore she saw me in the stands. It couldn't be right because there were thousands of people. But I met her gaze anyways and winked. That was probably my first mistake. Or my fiftieth if I was counting.

I didn't expect her to miss two jumps or to look right at me when she missed them. She probably didn't actually see me in the crowd, but I felt that jolt of electricity as soon as I saw those clear blue eyes and bright smile. This girl was going to be the death of me, and she didn't even know it.

This was supposed to be just a bet. A bet I didn't even want to go through with. But even with only a few times hanging out with the girl, I was starting to fall and fall hard. I'd never laughed as much or went out of my way to spend time with someone like her. I'd never gotten to know a girl's family like I had with hers. I knew nothing about Alexis or her parents other than they were filthy rich and worked in the oil industry. I wasn't exactly the kind of guy that a girl brought home to meet her parents. Especially not dairy farmer parents who brought me cheese curds.

After Kelly's performance, I looked down at my phone that had a bunch of messages from the guys and social media notifications. "Hey, guys, sorry to cut this short but I gotta jet," I muttered.

I stood up without looking back and heard Becca fumbling behind me. "What? You're not going to stay? Maybe get dinner at a real restaurant with us or something?"

I shook my head. I wanted to stay and talk with the family. Dinner that wasn't microwaved also sounded awesome. But I couldn't keep leading them on like this. Them or myself.

"Naw. I have to get ready for giant slalom tomorrow," I said.

"Maybe we'll see you there!" Becca yelled after me.

"Yeah, Maybe."

Trying not to think about Kelly or her family, I got my board ready and suited up for giant slalom that next night. Slalom was my only event, so I had to make sure I didn't mess up and got in my practice, landing every spin, ollie, and grab. And my parents also made sure I didn't mess up.

"He looks tight, doesn't he, Rob? Too tight. I think he needs to loosen up on that last turn," Mom said, not so quietly to Dad.

Usually, they stayed out of my way and didn't bother coming to practice, but I guess since this was The Games, they wanted to but in every step. That also included showing up at my morning talk show interview. I felt like a little kid being reprimanded the entire time and wished the news reporter would have just wanted me. But the only reason I was a story was because of my pseudo-relationship with Kelly and my Olympic parents. A medal would change that. I just had to keep my head in The Games today and not think about the blonde skater, who I thought about way too long in the shower thing morning.

"I'll see you guys at the finish line," I muttered to my parents, grabbing my board and heading where the other boarders were gathered. Some people were still doing interviews, but we were about to start up with the first run, so everyone was getting their game faces on.

Mom and Dad barely nodded at me and continued their conversation, staring at me and whispering as they headed to the crowd of spectators.

I let out a deep breath and got out my headphones as I approached the other athletes. I had a playlist for each run, and this first one had more Katy Perry than I wanted to admit to, so I wasn't letting anyone see my phone.

"Hey, Canada didn't know you invited your girlfriend to watch you biff," The Italian boarder whose name escaped me said, laughing as he looked down at the crowd. I put my phone up and followed his gaze.

There were hundreds of people against the fence watching us, but Kelly stood out amongst them all in her dark blue coat with her light blonde hair, spilling out of a white beanie. She wasn't alone, though, Logan and Becca were right beside her. I expected her parents to show up and breathed a sigh of relief when I didn't see the happy Americans in the crowd. I didn't think I could keep up this lie, this bet, and have to see their smiling faces. And my parents weren't anywhere near Kelly, so that was a plus. Another thing I didn't have to deal with.

"Hold this a second," I said to my coach, Ricky.

"What the hell do you think you're doing?" Ricky asked.

"I'll be right back, I promise!" I yelled but had already started making my way out toward the crowd.

The announcers were still doing some pre-performance interviews, so I knew I had the time to at least get in a little chat.

"Come to make sure I miss my jumps too?" I yelled, jogging toward Kelly.

Her eyes widened, and a slew of people aimed their camera phones at us.

I stopped, leaning on the fence and smiled. "How am I supposed to get in my jumps when I'm going to have to look at that smile? Unless of course you aren't smiling and just booing me."

"Blake, what are you doing?" Kelly whispered.

"Well, I was coming down here to say something, and then I got distracted by this head of blonde hair," I said, taking off my glove and running my fingers through the silky strands.

Her face turned bright pink as she nibbled on her bottom lip. I had to stop staring at her mouth, or I was going to be sporting some major wood.

"Don't you have to go and get ready or something?" she asked, her eyes darting everywhere but in my direction.

"That depends if my favorite skater gives me a good luck kiss and agrees to a date tomorrow," I said, wiggling my eyebrows. The quicker I got her alone, and on a date, the quicker this bet would be over. Then I could move on with my life. I didn't know if it was what I wanted to do. I was falling hard for this girl, and I couldn't admit that to anyone, even myself. And if I kept spending more time with her family, the harder it would be to leave. And, truth be told, I wasn't sure if I wanted to. This was way more than a bet now. This was me really falling for this girl and her American family. This was real.

Kelly shook her head, but she smiled slightly. "You're crazy! Go! Everyone's going to be waiting on you."

"Nuh Uh, not until I get my good luck charm. You don't want me to miss getting on the podium, do you? If I don't get that good luck kiss, it could be bad for all of us," I said, leaning closer and tapping my bottom lip.

"Blake," she whispered, her face turning an even brighter shade of red as she glanced behind her.

I looked in the direction of her stare and saw a few national TV cameras on us then the crowd started erupting in a chant. It took me a minute before I realized they were yelling "Klake," that hashtag I made up.

"Come on, Kelly, we can't leave the crowd waiting," I said, leaning in, my lips so close to hers I could practically taste her cherry chap stick.

She sighed and whispered, "Fine," before she closed her eyes and pressed her lips to mine.

It was just a peck, but it was warm. Inviting. A kiss that heated up my entire body and made me aware that she tasted and smelled better than anything I'd remembered. Her sweet scent of marshmallow and mint surrounding me as I went in for another kiss, putting my hand on the back of her head and opening my mouth slightly just to get another taste.

That was when the crowd erupted into applause and whoops, and she pulled away, putting her head down and her face redder than the flag on my jacket.

"I'll pick you up tomorrow after our morning practices," I said, squeezing her arm before I headed back to Ricky.

"Way to get all eyes on you, Blake," Ricky said, smacking my back and handing me my board.

"Hey, gotta make an entrance," I said.

He laughed. "Yeah, let's hope you don't mess it up now that you've got your blonde distraction in the crowd."

"Don't worry. I always get the girl and land the jump," I said, giving him a wink before looking at the red-faced girl in the crowd.

This was definitely turning into something more than just a bet. I just didn't know how much.

Landing a silver medal in giant slalom wasn't hard, figuring out where to take a girl on a date in the Olympic village was like trying to land a triple cork and not look like an idiot.

Usually, the only place I needed to take a girl was back to my cabin, and she was pretty happy with some whiskey and a backrub. That could work for Kelly or she would probably slap me.

Either way, I didn't want to just get this girl in the bedroom. She may have started out as a bet, but the more time I spent with her, the more time I was starting to really like the stuck up skater.

No, that wasn't right. She appeared stuck up, and that was the first thing I thought about the girl with the nose in the air. But I learned she was driven. All she'd known her entire life was skating and had never lived a life outside of that. Maybe sheltered wasn't the right word, but the girl had to get out, and if I didn't have to approach her for the bet, she might never have. But I couldn't tell her about the bet. As soon as I did, she would go right back to the girl who hated everyone that wasn't her skating partner, who I wasn't even sure she liked that much. I wanted to see this girl keep smiling and to be the one to make her smile. So I couldn't mess up our date.

Our date that was all I could think about while I had to have an awkward obligatory "family celebration" breakfast with my parents that morning after my run. I think the place was supposed to be Americanized Korean food but everything tasted the same, and I wasn't hungry. I just wanted to get this over with, so I could get out with Kelly. I didn't know if I wanted to get over my time with her or prolong it. My head was going in a million different directions and by the time the day was over I was pretty sure I'd need multiple stiff drinks.

"So, Blake, we've heard there have been some rumors about you and an American figure skater. The one who we saw you kiss on the big screen at giant slalom," Mom said not so subtly raising her eyebrows as she put down her wine glass.

I smirked, swirling my fork in the sauce covered noodles. "Yeah. I've been hanging out with Kelly Johnson."

"Any chance she's shared contacts to her sponsors?" Mom asked.

I groaned. "Really? That's the first thing you ask? Not 'Oh is she just a fling or are you serious?' But about sponsors? You have to be kidding me right now."

Mom blinked hard. "What? It was merely a question. Do you want me to ask about your love life? If you'll be moving out of the house now that you have a medal and maybe a shot at some sponsors? That is if you continue to board or what else you had in mind."

I blew out a deep breath. "Kelly and I are friends. I haven't asked about sponsors and, yeah, with the medal money I plan on putting a down payment on a house somewhere. Maybe New York."

Mom's eyes widened at the last part. "New York? As in America? Is it really that serious with you and the girl?"

I didn't even know where the idea of New York came from. I'd toyed with the idea of moving to America for years. I always thought it would be southern California so I could be near the mountains or the beach. But with Kelly in the back of my mind, New York just came out. And the more I thought about it, the more it didn't sound half bad living near her. Maybe starting something. That is if anything happened after The Games. If this really was more than a bet.

I shrugged. "Maybe. I guess I'll see what happens after my next event."

Without really thinking where I was going after breakfast, I found myself at the rink just as Logan was leaving. Kelly was already back at her room; I guessed getting ready for the date I was supposed to take her on in an hour.

"Hey, shouldn't you be somewhere else?" Logan asked, raising an eyebrow as he stepped out of the men's locker room.

I pushed off the wall I was leaning on, realizing that I looked like a creeper hanging outside of the men's door, especially since I was still dressed up in a button down and dark jeans from breakfast instead of the warm ups everyone else was in. "Um, yeah, which is why I'm here to talk to you."

Logan glared. "If you're about to tell me that you're going to ditch Kelly today, I don't want to hear it. I don't want to freaking hear it. She fucked up at qualifying, but if because of you, we're off the podium, I don't even fucking want to know until I'm beating your ass because of it," he said, pushing his backpack up on his shoulder and starting toward the doors.

I walked in step with him and shook my head. "No, man, not at all. The opposite actually."

Logan stopped and turned toward me, his brow still furrowed. "And what's the opposite of that?"

I blew out a breath and ran my fingers through my dreads. "Look, you're like the only friend Kelly has besides her sister. To be honest, she's too damn good for me, and I can't just take her to some bar in South Korea again and expect that to impress her."

It was true. I could probably take her to a bar again, pound some drinks, and get back to my cabin. But if this was the last shot I had with her, then I had to take it. I knew how easy it would be to avoid her after this. If I finally had all of her, then I'd admit how this started. I'd just have to figure out how to say it without sounding like a dick.

Or I could never tell her. We could go on this date, be happy, and then once The Games were over I'd go back to Canada, and she'd go back to New York. If I was lucky maybe I'd have a house by the spring and we'd reconnect. No bet around us. At least that sounded good in my head, but I knew it would be hard to stay away from her, no matter what.

"I don't know what you want me to tell you, Blake. It's not like there's a lot of fancy restaurants around the Olympic village," Logan said, shaking his head.

Realization dawned on me, and I nodded, forming an O with my lips. "Oh, I get it. This explains everything now..."

"I beg your pardon?" Logan crossed his arms over his chest.

"You've been going along with everything because you secretly like Kelly and you're hoping I fail at this so she can fall into your arms and you can be the good guy to save her. I get it, man, and I don't want to..."

Logan raised his hand and cut me off before I could say anything else. "I don't have feelings for Kelly that way. I love her as a sister and teammate, but that's it."

"Okay..." I said, drawing the words out. Figuring this guy had to have some other ulterior motive than just winning gold medals with this girl. I guess maybe that was all it could be. That's how I thought Kelly was. Just in it for the gold. Then again, people can surprise you.

Logan sighed, running his hand over his face. "It's her sister, okay?"

"What?" I couldn't have heard him right.

"Her sister, Becca. I have a thing for Becca, and if you screw up things with Kelly it's going to turn them both into man-haters together, and I'll never get my shot," Logan said, crossing his arms over his chest.

I couldn't help but laugh. "You...You like Becca?"

I looked over the long and lanky dude in a leotard, thinking that the hockey goalie chick could probably bench him.

"Yeah, I do. And if you tell her or Kelly that, I have no problem kicking your ass."

I raised an eyebrow, the words sounding forward coming out of the prim and proper guy's mouth. "You? Kick my ass?"

He nodded. "Yeah. You may underestimate me but years of skating, gymnastics, and a black belt can make a guy like me pretty lethal."

I put my hands up. "Okay, okay. I surrender, man. I won't screw things up, but that means you gotta help me impress Kelly."

"Only if I know what your end game is on all of this." Logan fixed his stare on mine.

I stuffed my hands in my pockets, looking at my shoes instead of the guy's eyes. "Nothing, man. I just want to take her out, okay? Just have a good time while we're here."

The words sounded foreign coming out of my ears. It was all I'd been saying to the guys since we came to The Games, but that was before. Before I met Kelly's family. Before I spent time with her. Before I tried not to admit even to myself that I was falling for her.

"This isn't some sort of game you and your other snowboarding or skiing buddies or whatever have cooked up? First one to nail the ice princess gets a prize?" Logan asked, standing straighter.

I snorted and shook my head. "That sounds like something out of one of those romance novels. That's not real life, dude."

So it definitely was real life and a real bet, but he didn't need to know it, and I figured using that excuse made it seem like everything was legit. Though, was everything legit if I was going this far out of my way to plan a date with her? This was just for a bet in the beginning, and after spending the first night with her, I knew I could get her to let her guard down with a little prying and then it would be easy to make a move.

But the more she let her guard down, the more I had to admit to myself that I was falling for her. I just couldn't let the guys know that one. Then what if they told her? Then I'd lose any chance I had with her, romantic, sexual, or otherwise.

No, she couldn't know the truth, though I was wrestling with the idea of telling her myself. I couldn't lose the girl or the bet that would earn me another twenty-five grand. That would get me a good down payment on a house in New York. I could have the girl, the medals, the house. I'd be all set.

"Okay, if you're really into her, then I'll help you, but if this turns out to be some sort of game, I swear to God—"

I lifted my hand, stopping his words. "No game, man. No need to swear. No need to bust out a triple axel."

He smirked and put his hand out. "Okay, man, let's get you up to speed on all things Kelly."

I shook his hand and forced a smile. Maybe this was a little bit of a game, but we were at the biggest arena to play. Logan nor Kelly would ever know about the bet and that was if I even talked to either of them after The Games were over.

At least that's what I had to tell myself, so I wouldn't feel so damn guilty.

CHAPTER 8

Kelly

"So where is Canada taking you on this date?" Becca asked, zipping up her tracksuit. She had another game today, but I didn't have the free skate until later that night which left my entire day free, aside from the grueling morning practice that still had my bones sore even after a massage and an ice bath.

I shrugged, checking myself out in the mirror one last time. I may have been fully clothed in a long white sweater, I purchased in one of the ski shops after practice, leggings, and riding boots, but I'd never felt more exposed. The shirt hugged what little curves I had, barely covering my behind. This was as tight as the clothing I was used to wearing on the ice, and that was with a million people watching me. But no one looked at me or made my entire body feel as if it were weightless like Blake did.

"And you're keeping your hair down?" Becca stood next to me in the full-length mirror, her fingers barely touching my hair that fell in loose waves down my shoulders and framed the slight dip in my sweater. I didn't have much for cleavage, but what I did have was on full display. I planned to cover it up with a scarf, and then possibly take the scarf off. If the moment called for it.

I wasn't a sex on the first date kind of a girl, but all the rumors about the Olympic village were true. I'd been sheltered from the crazy sex fests when I was a teen, but now it was like a full-blown orgy with condoms being handed out left and right. Even Becca had admitted to catching the looks of one or more of the guys on the Norwegian hockey team. I didn't know if that meant she'd done anything with them and I didn't exactly want to know those personal details of my sister's sex life.

And with the hormones and all of the competitive energy, sex was at the forefront of my mind. Parts of it, even more so than getting another gold medal. Don't get me wrong, I wanted another gold around my neck more than anything, but if I could have the gold and maybe an orgasm that wasn't by a battery operated boyfriend, I'd be okay with it. The thought of that made me blush. I didn't pack the toy on the trip, but it sat in my apartment back in New York in my night stand. I came into womanhood while being away at a training camp, losing my virginity to a man that was almost ten years older than me and being the last time I was ever touched.

I shook all of those way too hormonal thoughts out of my head. I was being silly. This was just hanging out with a man. Albeit, an incredibly sexy man. But nothing more. We would go out, probably for lunch or coffee; maybe there would be kissing then I'd go home and compete.

The worst that could happen would be that I'd end up in his bedroom. But maybe that wasn't the worst case scenario.

"How long has it been since you've had sex?" Becca blurted.

I gasped and whirled around. "Becca!"

"What? It's just a question. And, you know, our coach gave us a bunch of condoms, so I could loan you some," she said walking toward her hockey bag where she pulled out a handful of condoms in every color of the rainbow.

I wrinkled my nose. "Um. No thanks. I won't be needing those."

"Are you on the pill? You know the pill doesn't protect you from diseases. What if Blake has some Canadian STD that they can't treat it here? Something like moose warts on his dick. Then you'd miss your program tonight because we'd have to fly you back to the states or, hell, to Canada to have a doctor treat your junk," Becca asked, her face completely serious.

"I don't think that's a thing. I don't think countries each have their own STDs."

"Well then he could have a regular STD, and you're going to feel really shitty out on the ice with American genital warts."

I put my hands up and sighed, closing my eyes slowly before I opened them. "It's been a long time for me, okay?"

I said changing the subject. I never told my sister about my old partner. I figured it wasn't something you discussed with your sister. I also didn't think one talked about Canadian STDS, but here we were.

"Like long as in a couple of weeks? Months?" Becca asked cautiously.

I sighed and opened my eyes. "Years," I whispered.

"Years?" Becca's eyes practically bugged out of her head.

I rolled my eyes and sat on the bed. "I shouldn't have said anything and just let you keep talking about condoms and STDs."

"Has it been years because of your training? Is that why you're so angry all the time? Pent up sexual frustration?" Becca asked, slowly sitting down on the bed next to me.

I groaned. "You're not going to call me Elsa now too are you?"

Becca's arm slowly slid around my shoulder. "Kel, I'm your sister. I might not be interested in knowing all of the details of your sex life, but I do care about you. And if you're about to go out with a playboy snowboarder, you should probably be protected. Sexually or otherwise. I don't know the gun laws in South Korea, but I'm sure I could talk to one of the girls to see what kind of piece we could get you."

"It's not about protecting my body. It's about protecting my heart..." I sighed.

Becca leaned back. "Your heart? Don't tell me that after a week you think you're in love with this guy?"

Love wasn't the right word, but there was something about him that had my body fluttering. Maybe it was just hormones, and a roll in his sheets would get rid of that. But I knew that wasn't it. The way he looked so defeated when I talked about his parents. The way he smiled and made me genuinely smile. He was a good guy. A good guy that I wanted to be with not just at The Games, but after. If I could get over the feelings of my last relationship that made my heart freeze over.

Shaking my head slowly I looked up at Becca. "No…it's just…"

I sighed. "Did I ever tell you about Joe?"

She raised an eyebrow. "Your old partner with the mustache?"

I nodded. "The one. My first partner. The one I was supposed to go to my first games with."

"Was he..the…?" Becca's words trailed.

I swallowed hard. "Yes. He was my first and my last."

"Wasn't he like old?"

Laughing, I shook my head. "As old as I am now. I was a teen, yeah. I guess the whole partner chemistry and forbidden older guy thing had me going." I let out a deep breath before I continued. "I thought we had something; then I found one of his old social media profiles and photos of a girl. A fiancée."

Becca's eyes widened. "No shit? The guy was cheating?"

Nodding, I swallowed hard. "Yes. She was back home in Britain, waiting for him. Instead of confronting him, I told Coach Donahue that our skating partnership wasn't going to work. Since I'd been with Coach for two years and was a lot younger than Joe with a long career ahead of me, he sent him off, and Logan started skating with me. The rest I guess is history."

Becca shook her head. "I had no idea…I guess that explains a lot."

I snorted. "Why I'm such a bitch?"

"I didn't say that, but dude, it's totally understandable. If I found out a guy I was sleeping with, had a fiancée; I'd be pissed and swear off men too."

I laughed even though it wasn't funny. "I figured maybe I wasn't meant for relationships and was meant for gold medals. So it was all I focused on. That is, until now."

Becca put her hand on mine. "You deserve the gold and to find someone, even if it's just to get over your ten-year slump."

My parents had purchased Becca and me international plans for our cell phones before we left for The Games, but Blake only had Wi-Fi to message me whenever he was in his room, or wherever he was staying.

He sent me a message when he was leaving his place and said he would be at my dorm in about half an hour.

What dorm was he living in that it was taking him that long? Was he snowboarding over?

I pulled my coat tighter around me as the brisk air picked up outside of the dorm.

It had been exactly thirty minutes since Blake messaged me and I'd paced my room enough, staring at the array of rainbow condoms that Becca had left on the bed, before I picked up a few, shoving them in my purse and decided to step outside. I thought for a moment he'd be late, then a horn blared from halfway down the street, causing people on the sidewalks to turn and stare.

A black, narrow van pummeled down the street until it came to a screeching halt in front of my dorm.

I stared wide-eyed as the window rolled down and a smiling Blake stared at me. "Looking for someone?"

I shook my head. "You're nuts. You know that?"

He shrugged, adjusting the blue beanie on his head. "I've been called worse."

I went around the front of the car and got in the passenger side. I expected the van to smell like sweat and the locker room, but instead, I inhaled the scent of pine and chocolate.

"Do you have an air freshener in here to hide the boy smell?" I asked, buckling my seatbelt before Blake tore off down the street and I found myself reaching for the door handle, so I didn't fly forward and hit the dashboard.

"No. Does it stink in here?" he asked, looking at me out of the corner of his eye.

"No, the opposite actually. I was expecting more of a..." I put my hands in the air, twirling them in the circle as I searched for the right words. "A boy smell I guess."

"And what does a boy smell like?" He asked, raising an eyebrow with a ghost of a smile on his lips.

I felt a blush creep up my cheeks. I wanted to say 'you' as I thought about his woodsy scent, but instead, I chewed on my bottom lip for a moment before responding. "Sweat and ice?"

He laughed. "I didn't even know ice had a smell."

"It does." I nodded to myself. "It's that clean, fresh smell. The one that makes every bone in your body tingle. You take it all in, in one big breath and can't help but feel alive."

Just thinking of the smell of the ice took my mind to the arena. The cold rush that surrounded me as I spun in the air. The way I felt alive. Every time I stepped into an arena, I'd take in that scent, and I knew it was where I belonged.

I didn't even realize how lost I was in my own thoughts until I turned to see Blake grinning.

"What? Are you making fun of me?" I asked, gently shoving his shoulder.

He shook his head, a silent laugh escaping his nose. "No, just the opposite actually. I was taking in what you said. The smell of ice. You're right. That's how it smells to me when I'm on top of the mountain. It's the thing that makes me feel alive. I've just never heard anyone describe it that way."

"Maybe you and I aren't so different after all," I whispered, more to myself than anything as I sat my hand down on the console between us.

He glanced down then put his hand on mine, interlacing our fingers. "Nope. Maybe we're not."

I thought we would just end up somewhere in the village, at a nice restaurant, or even downtown Pyeongchang, but instead, Blake drove out toward the mountains where I could see skiers in their bright coats sliding down the slopes.

"Um, where are we going exactly?" I asked, looking around at the scenery.

"What a drive through the mountains isn't enough for you?" he asked with a smile.

"Oh, um, well it is a lovely drive," I mused, looking out the window, but couldn't help but be acutely aware that his hand was still on mine, sending an electric current throughout my body.

He laughed, a deep laugh that came from deep in his throat. "I'm joking, Kelly. We're almost there."

I looked around the mountain landscape expecting to see a lodge, or maybe we'd even come to a village, but instead, I only saw one little sign with some Korean lettering pointing to a pathway that didn't even look like the van would fit on it.

"Better hold on. It's kind of bumpy," Blake said with a laugh, dropping the gear on the shifter and turning toward the path.

The car vibrated underneath me, slowly making its way up the curvy path that followed the mountain. A little bumpy was an understatement as the car scooted up the mountain. Instead of just a little vibration, it was an all-out rollercoaster ride with me holding onto the dashboard with my free hand, wondering if the van had airbags.

"Is this safe?" I asked, my words shaky.

That made Blake laugh even harder. "Don't worry. I do this all the time."

"Somehow that's not much of a comfort."

He squeezed my hand but kept his eyes on the road ahead. "Don't worry, babe. I got you."

I would have objected or said something snarky, but when he smiled and held onto my hand, all I could focus on was the butterflies in my stomach.

This was my third Olympics, and another athlete had never approached me unless they wanted my autograph, let alone to want to hang out with me, and especially not go on a date. This was more than what I felt with Joe and what I ever imagined we had. That, I attributed to being a horny teen girl who was away from her parents for the first time and had an older guy touching her. This was something else entirely. This was not only lustful feelings but something else. Something more that had me connected to the dreadlocked snowboarder.

"And we're here," Blake said, pulling the car into a circle.

I was so enthralled in my own thoughts that I didn't look to see if we were in some mountain town.

When I looked around, I didn't notice much until I found the view in the side mirror and gasped at the beautiful sight.

It was as if we could see for miles with nothing but snow covered hills and electric blue sky, striped with fluffy white clouds. On the snow-covered bases, rows of trees covered in white dotted the landscape as if they were just the sprinkles on top of the beautiful sundae.

"Wow. This is something," I said breathlessly.

"And the view is only the beginning," Blake said with a grin, getting out of the van and opening the back door.

I raised an eyebrow and quickly followed him to the tailgate where he stood with two snowboards.

"You aren't serious, are you?" I asked.

"What? You said you wanted to learn to board, so who better to teach you than me?" He put down both boards and grabbed some boots out of the back as well.

"I thought you were just kidding about that hobby thing," I muttered.

It wasn't exactly disappointment that rang through my head, but curiosity. I expected dinner, drinks, and then back to his cabin. The fact that he wanted to spend time and teach me something made my heart beat even faster.

He laughed and sat on the tailgate, securing his boots. "Nope. I'm just hoping I got your right size. The board is one of mine, but I had to borrow the boots from Lorelei Lysacek, she's a slalom girl."

Something in me boiled thinking about the fact that he was talking to another girl. I didn't want this to be another situation like with Joe. I already had enough to worry about with his former fling with Alexis. I couldn't worry about yet another girl. The worry must have shown on my face because he laughed, patting the seat next to him. "Don't worry. I'm not Lorelei's type, but your sister might be."

I let out a deep breath that I didn't know I was holding in and took the seat next to him. "Oh. And my sister's not into other girls if that's what you were insinuating."

He laughed again. "Well, I didn't think she was. But now I don't know how I feel about the jelly Kelly. It's kind of cute," he said.

"Jelly Kelly?" I raised an eyebrow.

"Yeah. Jealous. You gave me the same look when I mentioned Lorelei as when you saw that picture of me with Alexis. It's this little crinkle in your forehead," he said, pointing between my eyebrows.

I swatted his hand away. "I am not jealous."

I tried to sound confident, but my voice wavered.

"Don't worry, Alexis may be my country's ice queen, but I think you skate better than her. Just don't tell any other Canadians," he said with a wink then nudged my elbow. "Now get those boots on. Your first lesson is about to begin."

With that he put on his own boots and hopped on his board, effortless as if he'd done it a million times before and could probably do it in his sleep.

"Okay, but if I got hurt, my coach will probably kill you, and he's from Texas and a hog farmer. He once told me that they'll eat anything, including teeth," I said, sliding off my riding boots and into the furry boarding boots, trying to put thoughts of Alexis and Lorelei out of my head.

"I love it when you talk dirty to me," he said with a laugh.

"Okay. The boots are on. What now," I said, dangling my legs off the tailgate and trying not to think too much about what he said about talking dirty, even though it definitely had me thinking how much of a dirty talker he would be in the bedroom.

"Okay, Imma help you down, and we're going to strap in your front foot first," he said, taking my hand and helping me hop out of the van.

I put my right foot up, and he held it before securing it in the binding along with the ankle strap. "Okay does this feel snug but not enough that it's going to hurt you?" he asked.

I wiggled my toes. The shoes were about a size too big but at least they weren't squashing my feet. "I think I'm good."

"Okay, now you're going to put your other foot in the other binding and stand straight, with your knees bent and your arms at your side," Blake instructed.

I put my foot in the other binding and then stood up, slightly bending my knees and looking at him. "Done."

"Don't get too cocky, it's now time to see if you can move," Blake smirked. "Now you're going to lean on your front foot to move forward, and if you want to slow down, you lean on the back foot."

"Easy," I said and sucked in a breath, leaning forward slightly, ready to coast down the hill.

But instead of the board moving, My body was the only thing that moved, face first into the snow with my legs and board in the air.

"Ack!" I yelled, spitting out a mouthful of powder.

Blake laughed like a hyena and offered me his hand. "Not bad for a first try, but you've got to make sure to stay straight, only bend those knees slightly."

"I think there's a step you're not teaching me just so you can watch me fall on my face," I muttered as he helped me to a standing position and I dusted off my coat.

"I'll hold your hand, and we can glide together. How's that sound?" he asked, raising his eyebrows and standing next to me before he held out his hand.

I let out a deep breath, letting it waft in the air as a cloud of white smoke. "Okay," I said and put my hand in his.

"Ready?"

"Ready." I nodded, putting my free hand to the side and bending my knees.

"And…Go!"

Blake started gliding forward, and instead of me following him, only my arm went forward before my face followed, right back into the snow.

I looked up, spitting out the snow and saw Blake had turned around and leaned over before putting his hand out. "I think maybe you moved a fraction of an inch that time."

I took his hand, but instead of letting him help me up, I yanked his hand forward, and he lost his footing, crashing down next to me.

I laughed, rolling over to a sitting position.

"That wasn't cool. I was trying to help you out," he said, sitting up and wiping snow off his face.

"Aw, I'm sorry," I said, giving him a sweet smile.

His look of disdain turned into a small grin. "It's okay… you can make it up to me…"

He leaned forward, his hand on my cheek. I thought he was going in for a kiss, but then I felt the shivering cold snow trail down my neck and back as he used his free hand to shove a snowball down my coat.

I screamed, shaking the snow out as he pulled back, laughing.

"Oh, you're going to get it, Blake!" I grabbed a handful of snow and shoved it at him, landing on his face.

He spat out the snow and wiped his gloved hands over his mouth before a large grin spread across his face. "Oh, it's on."

Unsnapping his boots, he then gathered a handful of snow, pawing it into a ball.

"You wouldn't want to hurt this sweet face now, would you?" I asked, batting my eyelashes.

He smirked, tossing the snowball from one hand to the other. "That depends. How fast do you think you can run with your board still on?

I looked down at my boots then back up to Blake's smirking face before I quickly made work of the bindings, which were nothing like the laces on skates and I fumbled, trying to get them loose.

By the time I got the bindings undone, Blake's toes were right at the edge of the board. I looked up, meeting his eyes. "I'll give you a ten-second head start," he murmured.

I couldn't help the giggle that escaped my lips as I slowly crawled forward until I was able to scramble to my feet. I looked behind me to see that Blake was already coming toward me in a slow march.

"You might be fast on a board, but I bet I can out run you," I said with a giggle, picking up a handful of snow and throwing it over my shoulder.

He ducked, the snow landing on his arm before he started moving faster, jogging toward me.

I squealed, trying to run, but the snow started to quake beneath me, and it was like moving through wet cement. I looked over my shoulder just in time to see Blake pouncing on me, wrapping his arms around my waist.

I giggled as he pulled me to the ground and we fumbled until we landed with him on his back in the cold snow and me lying on top of him.

"Who's the winner now?" I yelled, holding up a snowball.

He laughed, the sound vibrating in his stomach and straight to my core that was so close to his belly button and another very hard part.

Before I could drop the snowball on him, he'd tossed a ball of snow up, hitting me in the face.

I screamed. "Oh, you're going to get it for that one."

Leaning over, I grabbed a pile of snow and smashed it into his dreadlocks as he thrashed his head from side to side. Then he took both of my wrists, holding them above his head.

"Now what are you going to do?" he asked, raising his eyebrows.

I sucked in a deep breath, staring into those endless blue eyes. As if he knew what I was thinking, he leaned in, pressing his lips to mine.

Our first kiss was just a peck. A very explosive one. But this was different. This one caused a deep growl to emit from low in Blake's throat before he fisted my hair and I opened my mouth to his. He nipped at my bottom lip before licking it then his tongue met mine slowly in a delicious torture of kisses and lip nibbles.

I'd never been kissed like that. A kiss that lit my whole body on fire and gave me a rush more than skating ever could.

I moaned without even thinking what I was doing, which caused him to pull me closer to him, his lips trailing from my mouth down to my neck, pushing aside the thick fabric of my coat.

I pushed my core into his groin, grasping onto his coat sleeves as he continued to bite, suck, and kiss down my neck. The thin material of my leggings did nothing to hide the friction of his jeans against me, and I bit down on my bottom lip, already on the brink of orgasm from just some making out and grinding my body against his. I should have been embarrassed that I was dry humping this man in the snow, but he felt so damn good against me, and it had been so long. And he wasn't stopping me. At least not at that moment.

Blake slowly kissed up my neck and jawline then leaned back with a small smile on his face. "As much as I'd like to continue this, I'm getting snow in my ass."

"Oh, uh, right, sorry," I muttered and stopped moving, a flush crossing my cheeks. Maybe I should have calmed myself down before humping the man. Slowly I sat up before climbing off of him, hoping there wasn't a giant wet spot on the front of my leggings.

He stood up and took my hand. "This gives us a perfect opportunity to warm up."

I raised an eyebrow, wondering what he meant by that,

then he pulled me toward the van and opened the back door. I watched as he folded down the back seats and then took a few blankets and laid them on the flat surface.

"Um, what are you doing?" I asked, wondering if this was his idea of a date that included a snowball fight and sex in the back of his van. Not that I would have obliged at that point, but maybe preferred a bed if we were going to get that far.

He laughed and sat down on one of the blankets, patting the spot next to him before he grabbed a book bag with his other hand. "It's lunchtime."

"Lunch?" I asked, taking the spot next to him.

He scooted all the way back, so he was leaning against the seat and ushered me next to him so I slowly crawled back until I was sitting down and leaning against the seat. "Yeah, I talked to Logan today about what I should do for this date, and he suggested some fancy Korean restaurant and maybe a foreign film or something, and none of that sounded good to me."

"Oh. Well, I guess a snowball fight is better than reading subtitles," I muttered, not sure of what else to say.

He grabbed another blanket, putting out over our laps. Then he pulled two thermoses out of the bright orange backpack next to him. "I didn't agree with either of those, but he did tell me you really like this lemon thyme soup with pine nuts and peppermint hot cocoa."

He opened one of the thermoses and poured the soup into a metal cup. He handed me the filled cup, and I inhaled the scent of pine and lemon. I couldn't remember the last time I had that soup, probably before Olympic training. Before I had a sponsor that sent me a week's worth of prepared meals that were sitting in the fridge in my dorm currently. As much as I liked chicken and sweet potatoes, a year of those could wear on a person.

"Where on earth did you find this?" I asked before taking a sip and letting the warm liquid fill my mouth.

"It was a pain in the ass, and I had to call around to a few places, but eventually I talked to a luger who owed me a favor and brought his chef with him who had no problem whipping this up." Blake took another cup out of the backpack and poured himself some of the soup. "I also brought Baileys for the cocoa in case you hated all of this and we just needed to get drunk."

I laughed. "I don't think I could hate anything you did, especially when you put so much effort into it."

He smiled, his blue eyes shining as he looked at me over his cup. "A lot of effort doesn't always guarantee the best results."

I took my free hand and put it on his. "Well in this case it did."

CHAPTER 9

Blake

The girl had me hard as a rock just from watching her sip her cocoa and soup. I never thought much of the girl or any figure skater, not even Alexis, but holy shit the way Kelly kissed me, instantly got me hard and didn't stop as we sat in the back of the van.

She didn't just kiss me. The girl was practically fucking me with my clothes on. Her heat on my dick, her kisses savouring me. I wanted to take her right there in the snow. But I didn't think getting naked in the thirty degrees weather was the best idea, and though she looked and felt hot as hell rocking against me, the movement was causing snow to creep in my boxers. Nothing drops a boner like ice on the balls.

"I'll admit, I thought this soup would be weird, but it's not half bad," I said, looking at the mountains instead of her sexy legs in those thin pants. I don't think she even knew how beautiful she was. I wanted more of this girl. Not just today. Or for The Games. But I wanted that blonde hair splayed across my pillow every morning. I wanted to make love to this girl.

Love? I had to shake those thoughts out of my head. I couldn't love someone I hadn't even had sex with and only known a few days. Or at least that's what I told myself.

"It's an acquired taste, the same with the hot cocoa, which could be really good if you add that Baileys," she said, and I turned to see a mischievous grin on her face.

I laughed, shaking my head as I sat down my cup and grabbed the bottle of Baileys and the cocoa thermos from the bag. "If I didn't know any better, I'd say you were trying to get me drunk and take advantage of me. For not being much of a drinker, as you say, you're pretty good at pushing it."

"Me? Never," she said with mock sarcasm.

I opened the thermos and poured us each a cup then added a few shots of Baileys, give or take, on top of that.

Kelly sat her soup cup down and then scooted closer, her hand brushing against my thigh under the blanket as she picked up her cocoa. I twitched, sucking in a deep breath just thinking how close those hands were to my cock. She only pulled her hand away to take a big gulp of her drink.

"Are you still cold?" she asked, her voice low and almost sultry.

"Kinda, are you?" I asked.

"I wouldn't object to a little body heat," she said, scooting closer.

I grinned, putting my arm around her. "The Baileys get to you that quick?"

"Baileys…or the tent you're pitching in your pants," she said with a smile.

I laughed. "Didn't take you for the kind of girl who'd want to take advantage of me in a van."

She widened her eyes and held up her free hand. "I'm not saying that."

I leaned in and put down my cup then grabbed hers and set it down next to mine before putting my hands on either side of her hips. "Good, because I want you to want this as bad as I do. To feel your tight little body underneath me and scream loud enough, so they hear you down in the village when I make you come."

She shivered, her bottom lip quivering. I didn't know if my brash words would turn her on or have her running, but I got my answer when she leaned in and kissed me fiercely, her tongue dancing behind my lips as she wrapped her arms around my neck. She tasted like peppermint and Baileys, her blonde hair surrounding me. I couldn't get enough of this girl.

Deepening our kiss, I wrapped my arms around her waist, pulling her as close as we could get with our coats still on. Obviously, she saw the problem of too much clothing and didn't even break the kiss as she pulled off her jacket then made quick work of unzipping mine.

"Eager?" I whispered before nipping her earlobe.

She gasped, sliding her body on top of mine and straddling my hips to face me before her gaze focused on mine. "Very," she whispered and slid her sweater off. She had an athletic body with small curves and full breasts that were at least a handful, spilling out over the top of her lacy white bra.

"Oh my god, that's cold!" she said, shivering and covering up her chest and stomach with her hands.

I laughed, shucking off my coat then my sweater before I wrapped my arms around her waist and pulled her to me and slid the blanket over our bodies. "Don't worry, babe; I'll warm you up."

She kissed me again with even more passion, her hands on my cheeks then down my back, her core grinding into me as she kissed and nibbled my lips.

I grinned beneath her mouth then tip-toed my hands up her back before unhooking her bra. Leaning back slightly I kissed from her lips, down her neck, and to her chest. Her little pink nipples were already hard and aching for me, so I took each one in my mouth, swirling my tongue around each hardened bud before nibbling. This caused Kelly to buck harder against my hips, a little sweet moan escaping her mouth.

I looked up at her, kissing back up to her neck then to her ear. "Don't come yet, baby. I'm just getting started."

I moved my hand from her back to her waistband between us, sliding my fingers underneath her thin pants and silky panties. She was completely bare and already soaking wet by the time I got my thumb to her clit, circling it as I hooked a finger inside of her.

It didn't take long for her to ride my fingers and come hard, moaning into my neck.

"That's one down," I whispered, grabbing onto her hips and flipping her onto her back as I sat up and hovered over her beautiful body splayed on the van floor. "Let's see how many more times I can make you come."

"Multiple times?" she asked, her eyes widened.

I smirked, pulling off her boots, leggings, and panties, tossing them to the side. She was freaking beautiful with all her creamy white skin and just the right amount of pink on her nipples and now very swollen clit that was begging for me to taste it.

"Is that a problem?" I asked, bending over and swiping my tongue down her center.

She moaned. "Not at all."

I grinned and sucked on her clit, lapping her up before adding my thumb to the mix. It was only a minute before she was coming hard, her screams ringing in my ears.

I felt her body build to the brink again and she pulled my dreads, forcing me to look up at her. "I want you in me. Please do me, Blake. Don't make me beg," she panted.

I grinned, forcing my mouth and thumb from inside of her as she made a sweet little moan before I shucked my pants and boxers off then fished through my pockets for a condom.

Before I slid on the latex, I looked down at her wide eyes staring at my cock. "Did I hear you gulp?"

She shook her head. "No, I was just admiring your artwork," she murmured, moving her hands down my arms then to my hips. She traced each line of the mountain landscape tattoos on my arm then the Canadian flag on my hipbone with her fingernails. I swore I was going to blow all over her right there from her gentle touch.

"If you keep doing that, I'm never going to get inside of you," I hissed.

She held onto my hips, and her eyes met mine, pulling me closer until the head of my cock was at her wet entrance.

"Don't tease," she growled, her nails already pressed into my lower back.

I didn't expect the ice queen to melt this quickly, but once I slid inch by inch and filled her up to the hilt, I didn't know why I didn't do this sooner. She was so wet and tight, her body clenched around me as I rocked my hips against hers.

She moaned sweetly, her legs wrapped around my waist and her hands on my back as she kissed up my neck.

I circled my hips against her, her tiny body going to the same rhythm as mine as I felt her tighten and arch her back. I slid my hand down the center of us and massaged her clit as I continued to rock inside of her.

She moaned loudly, throwing her head back in passion and quivered underneath me, her orgasm taking hold, crying out so loud I swore it echoed on the mountains.

I knew I wasn't going to last long with her, so I grabbed onto her hips, rolling over, so she was on top. I pushed her up, so she was sitting and gripped onto her sides as she straddled my waist.

"I've never been on top," she whispered, her cheeks flushing.

"Seriously?" I asked.

She nodded, biting down on her bottom lip.

"We can take it slow, baby. I'll help you drive."

She put her hands on my chest and slowly rocked forward, her breasts bouncing lightly. Her tight pussy clenched around me as she continued to move. I moved my hands from her sides to her ass.

"You can go harder, baby. I'm not going to hurt you," I murmured, arching my back.

She moaned, rocking harder, her breasts bouncing as she tilted her head back, her mouth forming a perfect O. I moved one hand from her ass to her clit, circling the swollen bud.

It didn't take long for me to come after watching her sweet face as an orgasm took hold, her body quivering around me before she collapsed on my chest. Her head pressed against my neck as she breathed heavily against me. Our hearts beat to the same rhythm. My cold sweat mingling with hers and the scent of our sex.

We laid like that for a few moments, her running her fingers through my hair as I placed soft kisses on her neck.

"Warmed up now?" I asked, leaning on my elbows and meeting her beautiful blue eyes.

"Very, but I should probably get cleaned up before I head back to the village and my performance," she said, slowly moving until I was out of her then she crawled to grab her clothes.

I smiled, sitting up. I didn't want to pull out of her, hell I could have stayed there all day, but I was pretty sure all of America would kill me if I kept their beloved figure skater from the ice. "The house I'm staying at is just down the mountain. You can use the bathroom there then we'll get an Uber back to the village," I said, tossing her her sweater.

She laughed. "So that explains how you found this place, but why Uber? Don't feel like driving me back?" she asked, fastening her bra.

I leaned in and kissed her before grabbing my boxers. "Do you really think I'm not going to watch your short program tonight?"

She raised her eyebrows, putting on her sweater. "Are you sure you want to do that?"

I waited until her arms were in her sweater before I leaned in and put both of my hands on her face. "I want to be wherever you are. Just think of me as another guy in the crowd, another guy cheering you on, who will also give you multiple orgasms to celebrate you winning gold."

Her face flushed which was just about the cutest damn thing ever. "Well, I don't think we'll get that after my performance in qualifications, but maybe silver if we're lucky."

I laughed and kissed her again. "Either way, we're celebrating with my cock inside of you."

CHAPTER 10

Kelly

I'd never had a guy talk dirty to me, and I never knew how much it could turn me on.

The last time I had sex was, well, with Joe. It was awful the first time, and I remember wondering why people liked it so much. Every time after I kept going through the motions, thinking it would get better, but nothing. I did it because he wanted it. Now I knew he just used his pent up frustrations for sex instead of landing his jumps, or calling his fiancée. We had a mild connection on the ice and in the bedroom, but it was nothing like the passion or the multiple orgasms that came with Blake Tremblay.

After seeing Blake at qualifications, and falling twice, I was initially nervous at the thought of him watching me in preliminaries. Now instead of feeling fear, there was a new burst of excitement. Adrenaline.

I guess this explained why everyone screwed like rabbits during The Games. I definitely missed out on this with Joe. If only he would have told me he was engaged to someone else, instead of having to find out via MySpace, I could have moved on with my life and not waited this long to find someone again. Maybe I wouldn't have been so closed off for so long. Then again maybe I would have never been this good of a skater and had two golds around my neck. Or made it to these games to meet Blake and find out what I'd been missing.

Was this just the high of coming down from multiple orgasms or was I feeling something else with him? Not only did I enjoy his company inside me, but when we were hanging out, I couldn't stop smiling. He made me feel good. No matter if we were kissing or just laughing about a stupid hashtag. Being with him was the most relaxed I'd ever been at The Games. Maybe ever. When the cameras weren't around, and it was just us, I felt alive. I felt real. Something I didn't know I'd been craving for so long.

"So does that count as a snowboarding lesson or will I need some more practice?" I asked as we got into the car and I made sure my sweater wasn't on backward. I was pretty sure my hair was messed up and looked like I just walked out of 1980's music video, but I didn't care. I'd fix it again for competition. And right now I wanted to spend all of the time I could with Blake instead of worrying about my hair or makeup being perfect. I'd spent too long worrying about everything being just right instead of just being. It was nice to sit back for a change.

Blake laughed, shaking his head and starting the engine. "If by practice, you mean I get to take you out here and fuck your brains out in the back of this van again, then I'll take that."

I swatted his chest playfully. "Blake!"

"What? You know you were thinking the same thing."

"I'm not just going to become your sex doll all of a sudden, you know," I said, trying to straighten myself in the seat. Though I wasn't exactly sure what a sex doll was, but it sounded good.

"I wouldn't expect you too. We need breaks for other things, like snowboarding, skating, and of course eating. Or me eating you, whichever comes first."

I went to swat Blake again but he ducked out of the way with a laugh then grabbed my hand, bringing my knuckles to his lips as he intertwined our fingers before kissing the back of my palm. "You're easy to get a rise out of."

"I am not," I pouted, though it was true. It didn't take much for me to get riled up. I always wanted to stay calm, cool and collected like the ice, but one little mess up or something out of order and unfortunately I turned into the dragon lady.

"It's okay. It's cute. As long as you don't come after me," Blake said, squeezing my hand.

"How are you so calm all the time? Even when you're bothered you just smile and nod," I asked.

He shrugged. "I don't know. I guess years of being razzed for everything kind of made me push it to the side. If I keep getting worked up over every little thing, what does that accomplish? Not shit."

"That doesn't really help anything or answer the question," I replied.

"Sex. Also a lot of sex. Even if it's with myself. So we might have to work on that for you. The more sex, the less you'll worry." He smiled, looking at me out of the corner of his eye.

"You're too much. You know that?"

"And you love it," he said, kissing my hand again.

It was a short trip down the mountain, and a little off the main road before Blake pulled down a gravel drive and into a circular parking area in front of a small cabin. The structure had the traditional South Korean architecture with the peaked roof that looked like a children's fort, or any of the other small buildings I'd seen in my travels to this part of the world. I just didn't expect it to be somewhere Blake stayed, especially when it was so far from the other athletes. And from me.

"This is where you're staying? Why not the village?" I asked, staring at the cabin and noticing the large Canadian flag hanging over the doorway like a beacon letting everyone know this was where Blake stayed.

Blake grinned, parking and opening the door before jogging over and opening mine then helping me out of the van. "You've been where my event is, it's like an hour from the village. No reason to be in the village and drive an hour every day to the mountain, but I will if you're going to let me have you in your bed instead of the back of the van," he said, nuzzling my cheek.

I giggled, even though we just got done, I was already ready for another round. What kind of girl had I become? Maybe this was what a sex doll was. Though a sex doll would probably just lay there and after feeling what it was like to be on top of Blake and ride out my orgasm, there was no way I was going to just lay there. Now I wondered about all of those positions that I'd seen online when I was casually looking for skating positions and happened to come up on other positions. They all looked impossible at the time, but now I was thinking of how much fun it could be to try them out with Blake.

He kept his hand on mine, and we walked into the house, which was much smaller than I thought it would be with a living room that had floor-to-ceiling windows facing the mountains and a tiny galley kitchen to the right as soon as we entered.

"I just gotta change real quick," Blake said, not looking up from his phone. "I put in for an Uber, and he should be here in a few minutes. So if you see a guy named Yu in a white Hyundai don't let him leave without us!"

"Okay." I nodded, not sure what else to say and wondered if there were any roommates. I'd lived alone ever since I moved to New York and living with my sister the past week was a new experience. I didn't realize how messy another human being could be, or what it was like to have personal space invaded so much. Especially in the bathroom. The girl could stink anyone out with one of her post workout bathroom showers and whatever else she did in there.

Blake grinned, putting his phone in his pocket then looked at me before he leaned in, pressing his forehead to mine then kissed me slowly. I thought kissing a guy after his tongue had been in my private regions would be disgusting, but tasting my own arousal on him made it even hotter.

I licked his lips and pulled his dreadlocks, giving me better access to his mouth.

He grinned beneath our kiss and nipped at my bottom lip. "Already ready for round two? We have a few minutes before our ride gets here, enough for one of us to come at least. That one person being you."

I giggled as he wrapped his arms around my waist and lifted me up, carrying me toward the small gray couch that faced a flat screen TV mounted above a metal fireplace.

I sat down on the hard cushions, pulling him on top of me, kissing him fiercely and working the zipper on his jacket to get it off as soon as possible.

Before I could even get there, the door opened with a loud bang and I froze, Blake jumping off me and looking at the door with a glare.

Erik and Liam from the first night at Pyeongchang came through the door, laughing about who knows what, but stopped and stared at us. Liam crossed his arms over his chest and sauntered toward us. Dammit, he did have roommates. I guess I should have expected that. Maybe they'd leave once they saw he was busy.

Liam took a few steps closer until he was at the edge of the sofa. He was an attractive guy with his short chestnut hair and deep brown eyes that went along with the tall, dark, and handsome look, complete with chiseled cheek bones. But the look he was giving Blake and I made him look more like a cartoon villain than a Disney prince.

"Sup, Liam? We were just about to head out," Blake said, standing up and adjusting his jacket. His back straight as if he were a cat about to pounce.

"Hey, Blake didn't think you'd be here, or Miss Johnson. Take it by her messy hair and the fact your breath smells like pussy; you won the bet?" Liam asked with a cocky smirk.

"Bet?" I asked, sitting up and smoothing my hair down.

"Back off, Liam," Blake growled.

Liam looked down at me, cocking his head to the side and put his hand on his chest. "Oh, sweetheart, you didn't know? You thought this dreadlocked piece of man meat actually liked you?" he asked, hitching his thumb in Blake's direction.

"Drop it, Liam," Blake snarled, glaring at Liam before looking down at me. "Don't listen to a thing this idiot says, okay? He's just trying to be an ass."

I stared between Liam and Blake then whispered. "Blake, what is he talking about?"

I'd seen plenty of movies and read books where the guys in the story make a bet for the girl's virginity or who can sleep with a girl first. I didn't think that happened in real life. I had to be wrong in thinking that when he mentioned a bet. At least I had to hope I was.

"Don't worry about it, babe, come on, let's go wait outside for our Uber," Blake said, taking my hand and pulling me up.

Before we could even move, Liam was in front of us, putting his hands up. "Whoa, are you telling me that you really didn't know this was a bet for Blake to screw you? He freaking put his medal money on the line and I for sure thought he was going to lose."

Liam put his hand out in a handshake position. "Gratz, man, that twenty-five K is all yours, bro. Nice job de-icing the ice queen."

"Shut the fuck up, Liam, I mean it," Blake growled again, tugging my sleeve. "Come on, Kelly."

I pulled back, tears pricking my eyes as the realization of the situation hit me. The first night he approached me with Liam. The way they both grinned like idiots. How his friends laughed every time, he was with me. It's why he made a big spectacle on social media about us. Just to get me to think this was real. To give myself to him in the back of a van. All of it was a bet. All of it was a lie. But why? Why did he go so far just to hurt me? What the hell kind of guy would do that? If he went this far, was some of it real? No. I couldn't think about that. No matter what happened, it was all because of a stupid bet.

"Come on, Kel," Blake reached for my hand, and I yanked it back.

"No!" I screamed, louder than I intended.

"Uh oh, someone's pissed," Liam said with a laugh.

"Fucking drop it asshole," Blake snarled.

"A bet? Please tell me this isn't true," I whispered, trying to meet his eyes. You could always tell when someone was lying if they wouldn't look you in the eyes and Blake's eyes were on the ground as he ran his fingers through his hair.

"Blake?" My voice cracked.

He let out a big breath. "Yes? Okay, yes it started out as a bet. That's why I approached you." He finally looked up and took a step closer. "But then I got to know you, and I fell for the girl that everyone said was an ice queen, but ended up being the warmest, funniest, and sexiest girl I've ever met." His voice was low and sincere, but I couldn't trust his words. Not with a guy that made a bet to sleep with me. None of this was real. That's why he could be so laid back about everything. Because he didn't care. Not about me. Not about anything but winning a bet.

I shook my head, taking a step back and then turned toward the door. "A bet. A fucking bet," I said through gritted teeth, not carrying that Erik and Liam were laughing behind Blake.

"Babe, please, can we talk about this?" Blake put his hand out, and I threw my arm back, reaching for the door behind me and throwing it open, the cold wind hitting the side of my face. "I think you've said enough. Don't bother coming tonight. Or anytime, unless it's with your hand. Thanks for the Uber ride oh and for the sex, guess I should ask for my cut of your medal money, huh?" I asked, sarcasm oozing from my voice. This was why I didn't trust men. This was why I didn't get involved with anyone. My only focus should have always been the ice.

"Fuck the money and fuck the bet, okay? I want you. All of you. You have me, Kelly, you know you do. I may have just been the dreadlocked Canadian snowboarder to you in the beginning like you were nothing but the ice queen to me, but then we both unmasked each other. We got past our layers and found each other. I don't want a mistake to ruin that."

The crunching of tires on snow and gravel alerted me that someone was in the driveway. I glanced behind me to see a small white car, guessing it was the Uber.

"Well, Blake, it was a pretty big mistake. And we both know that in The Games, one mistake can cost you everything."

"Kelly…"

"Goodbye, Blake. Good luck in your competition," I said, before slamming the door and running to the car, not looking back as I got in and tears streamed down my face.

I would never trust anyone again. The Games weren't meant for fun. The Games were meant for winning, and I was losing pretty badly in The Games and in love.

CHAPTER 11

Blake

I felt Liam's hand cup my shoulder. "Tough break, man."

All I saw was red as I turned, swinging my arm back before my fist connected with his jaw.

Liam's head snapped back before he put his hand to the side of his face. "What the hell, man?" He snarled.

Erik stepped in between us, holding his hands out, stopping us from getting any closer. "Everybody calm down now!"

Liam spit out some blood on the hardwood floor. "Tell it to the fucker who just hit me. I have finals tomorrow. A black and blue face is gonna be great to explain to the press. What should I tell them? My asshole roommate decided to hit me?"

"Kind of like how I just had to try and explain why your assholish self decided to tell Kelly she was a bet?" I snarled, not holding back.

Liam put his hands up. "Hey, man, you're the one who agreed to the bet, don't get mad at me for calling you on it."

I blew out a big breath and raked my fingers through my hair, stepping back and shaking my head. "Fuck, man, fuck. I didn't even want to do this shit. I agreed to it for you guys to get off my back and now I'm fucked. Totally fucked," I muttered the last part.

"Don't tell me you actually like that stuck up chick, man?" Liam asked, but it was more of a statement.

I glared at him because I wasn't sure what else to say and Liam shook his head, a broad grin crossed his face. "Aw, man, never thought I'd see the day Blake Tremblay would get pussy whipped by a girl. Especially not some American bitch."

I lunged forward, ready to beat the shit out of him, or at least get in another good punch, but Erik stepped in between us. "Both of you, stop. This is fucking ridiculous on both your parts. I don't know why you guys are acting like a bunch of teen girls and fighting like we're in the cafeteria, but grow the fuck up. I don't know why either of you made the bet because it's not like we had enough shit going on at The Games. Why don't you too just drop this and move on?"

"Hey, I'm not the one who attacked his buddy here," Liam said, shrugging out of Erik's reach.

"Blame doesn't help either one of you. I know you both are give'rs and do everything one-hundred-and-ten percent, but does that mean you two need to get in a kerfuffle over a girl?" Erik asked, looking between the two of us.

"This isn't kerfuffle about a girl. This is about Liam making the stupid bet in the first place then instead of being a decent guy he goes and tells the sweet girl she was a bet," I muttered.

"Why the hell did you do the bet in the first place then? If you have such a hard on for this girl?" Erik asked.

"Because I didn't think? Okay? You guys just kept talking, and I wanted you to shut up, so I gave in. I didn't think anything would happen with Kelly and it did. Now instead of my head in the game, it's all twisted, and I sound like a pussy for even saying it out loud," I groaned, raking my hands over my face and stepping back.

"Why didn't you just tell us you wanted out of the bet? You would have just owed me a lot of money and been done. Though, technically you did win," Liam said with a smirk.

Instead of getting into another kerfuffle, I shook my head. "Whatever," I muttered and pulled my phone out of my pocket, walking toward the door.

"And where do you think you're going?" Liam asked, crossing his arms over his chest.

"I'm calling another Uber to take me to the village," I grumbled, looking at the app and seeing it would be almost an hour before anyone got to me.

"Then what? You try and make some grand romantic gesture and make yourself look like an ass?" Liam asked.

I'd tried to get Kelly's attention so many times. Using the media or her parents or whatever else I could so she wouldn't say no. The only time I'd gotten her to fully open up to me was when it was just the two of us. But there was a slim chance I'd ever get that to happen again. And I didn't have any ideas in how the hell I was going to make this all up to her. If I even could.

I shrugged. "I don't know. But I gotta try."

I ended up at the village almost two hours later; I had absolutely no idea what I was going to say or do as I stared up at her dorm. All of the looming buildings looked the same like the skyscrapers did to me in New York. But I still remembered standing in front of Kelly's dorm that night after dinner. I remembered the way she looked at me full of genuine concern. The way she held onto my arm and laughed as we walked in the freshly fallen snow. She really seemed to care about me and was interested in what I was saying. I wasn't a bet to her. I was real. Like she was to me.

While I could remember everything about that night meeting her parents, I couldn't even remember what room she was in. The one I drunkenly slept in that first night. I should have thought about that before I took the long trip to the village. I stared at my phone in my hand. I was within the range of Wi-Fi so I could message her, or maybe even Logan, or Becca, but then what? If she'd already gone back to her room and told them what happened then, they would just think I was an hoser. I'm sure they already did. I wouldn't have put it past Becca to hit me either.

Just as I was about to pull the door open of the dorm and try to figure out what to do and how the hell to find Kelly or her room, I came face-to-bitchy-face with Alexis.

"Blake! I didn't expect to see you here," Alexis practically purred, her eyebrows raised as she exited the dorm. Maybe she was supposed to be smiling, but her face always stayed in that same half-scowl.

She must have been on the way to the arena with her red track suit, hair in a high bun, and a book bag over her shoulder. She would be living at the same place that Kelly was and competing. Maybe even getting ready in the same locker rooms. I didn't think the two girls actually talked, but I wondered how their conversation would go. If Kelly would talk about herself being a bet and then Alexis would take it as her chance to get back in bed with me. Or maybe they'd both be smart and laugh about my stupidness and find someone else to occupy their time. But I couldn't think about that option. Not when Kelly's naked body and sweet smile were still in the forefront of my mind.

"Yeah. I was just in the neighborhood," I muttered. I didn't want to go into the details of was going on with Kelly, and it wasn't her business anyway. If she found out later then so be it, but I wasn't going to be the one to open up that wound.

"Walk me to the arena? My hair and make-up artist are waiting, but I can take some time to walk with an old friend, especially if you buy me a cocoa." Her lips pursed together.

I wanted to tell her 'no' and to get the fuck out, but I didn't have any other plans on what to do with Kelly, so I found myself nodding. And figured that it would give me some time to think and I'd be at the arena anyway. I'd figure out what to do once I got there. At least I hoped I did. "Yeah, okay."

"No double double?" I asked, referring to a coffee with two creams and two sugars, very popular in Canada but Americans acted like we were hosers when we ordered it at the coffee shops there or anywhere in the village.

She laughed. "No caffeine before a performance. Gets me antsy."

That was the exact opposite for me. I needed the energy drink or coffee to get me pumped up. Not that adrenaline wasn't already coursing through me, but there was something about downing a few energy drinks in freezing weather then powering down a mountain to make you feel alive.

Almost as alive as I felt on that mountain with Kelly. I shook the thoughts of her out of my head as I headed into the small coffee shop with Alexis and ordered her a cocoa and myself a double double, using the American wording.

"So were you at the dorm hoping to catch that American girl or me?" Alexis asked, taking a small sip of her cocoa as we exited the coffee shop into the cold air and walked side-by-side to the arena. It wasn't too far of a walk, but the way my head was buzzing, it felt like an eternity. There were too many athletes around. Too many smiling people with cameras. Too many people that had no idea I may have just made the biggest mistake of The Games by taking that bet, and it had nothing to do with winning a medal.

"I think you know her name, Alexis," I muttered before taking a big sip of my coffee.

Alexis nodded. "I do. I'm very familiar with Kelly Johnson. I think the media likes to call her my biggest rival, though I've hardly spoken to the girl, to be honest."

"We always hate the people we compete against, especially those damn Americans who always seem to get on top," I grumbled, thinking of the cocky redhead who took gold in giant slalom.

"Then why hang out with the blondie? I mean, I get it, she's gorgeous, but if we're all competing here, then why her? Was it to make me jealous?" Alexis asked, raising an eyebrow.

I laughed, shaking my head. That statement was one of the most ridiculous things I'd heard all day. I'd known Alexis for years. Romantically and otherwise. The girl didn't get jealous of anyone. She just took what she wanted, and if she didn't get it, she acted like she didn't and was going to get something better. "Wouldn't have a reason to make you jealous."

"So all of those nights at the ski lodge were nothing? I hardly believe that seeing as you kept coming back to my room at all hours of the night and morning," Alexis said with a smirk, taking a small sip of her cocoa.

I shrugged. "You know sometimes things just happen. Hookups are hookups."

"We were definitely more than a hookup."

I stopped, turning toward her. "Look, Alexis, I don't know what you're trying to get at here, but I'm sorry if you thought we were something more. I never thought that. And yeah this is going to sting, and it probably sounds dickish of me, but we're not gonna happen."

She narrowed her eyes. "So what? You think because after ten years you finally qualify for The Games and you can be a hoser? Chasing after stuck up American girls? You know when this is all over you'll be texting me, and you know what? After this, I'm not answering."

"That's fine, Alexis. I was trying to be the nice guy and kill some time before heading to the arena anyway."

"You can kiss that sponsorship goodbye without me you know?" She glared.

Those words were the one that slapped me harder than any other. Silver in giant slalom wasn't going to get sponsors crawling at my door, I'd have to get gold in parallel, which was a possibility, but what if this mess in my head had me screw up my moves? What if I didn't make the podium? Then where would the sponsors be.?

"Maybe they like me for my charm," I smiled, trying to add some light-heartedness to the conversation.

She rolled her eyes. "I think I can walk myself to the arena."

I put my arm on hers. I used to get some kind of jolt at least, or at least my dick did, from touching the tight little skater's body, but now it did nothing. Absolutely nothing for me. "I'm sorry. I'm having a rough day. I didn't mean to be an ass."

She raised an eyebrow. "What's with this Dr. Jekyll, Mr. Hyde thing?"

I shrugged. "Game pressure I guess."

"If you want this sponsorship or anything, we can't just be fighting on the streets like this. We're supposed to be a team, not that stupid little hashtag you came up with, with the American girl. What was that about anyway?" Alexis asked, putting her hands on her hips.

I couldn't think of a good answer, so I just shrugged.

Alexis rolled her eyes. "I think you've hit your head on the slopes one too many times. You're not even making sense. Maybe that's why you're saying so many crazy things."

I nodded. "Yeah, you're probably right."

I was at the end of my snowboarding career. I couldn't make enemies with anyone in Canada if I wanted to keep up some kind of presence in the winter sport world. As much as I wanted to tell Alexis to fuck off, I also knew that I needed her.

"Can I still walk you to the arena?" I asked.

She smiled and looped her arm through mine. "Of course."

CHAPTER 12

Kelly

I didn't look at anyone passing by as I got out of the Uber and ran into the dorms. I wiped all of my tears on the sleeve of my coat and sucked in a deep breath as I got off the elevator. I didn't want to think about what my makeup or hair looked like. I just hoped that a paparazzi didn't sneak in and make that the big story of The Games. The ice queen falls apart was all I needed to see as a stupid headline.

Becca's game was earlier in the day so she'd be back in our room if she wasn't with her teammates. For the first time ever I would have to tell my sister why I was crying and that it was over a boy. A boy who she probably knew would screw me over but pushed me toward him anyway even after I broke down and told her everything about Joe.

I unlocked the door of our room and turned the lights on. I thought for a brief second that maybe Becca was gone, but then I heard some whispered swearing in a male's voice.

I put my hand over my eyes and stepped further into the room. This definitely was not what I wanted to come home too. We needed to come up with a system if this was going to happen again and this was the last thing I wanted to come home to after what I'd just been through. I groaned. "Becca, if you have a man in bed with you, can you both please cover up? Or I'll go wait in the bathroom or something."

"Um, yeah, just a sec," Becca said, whispering and then I heard the guy muttering something back.

I kept my eyes on the ground with my hand shielding what was in front of me. That was when I spotted something very out of place on the ground. It was a Team USA warm-up jacket, but not just any warm-up jacket, this one had Logan's name embroidered on the front.

"Um, Becca? Is there a reason Logan's jacket is here?" I asked, hoping my first thought was wrong and he wasn't in her bed. Maybe she got cold at the arena, he happened to be there at the same time for some reason, and he let her borrow it. Even though my sister never got cold and I didn't know when they'd be at the arena together at the same time. That thought at least sounded better than the other option of my sister sleeping with my skating partner.

"We're just getting dressed then Lo-, uh, the guy is going to leave," Becca sheepishly said as I heard the fumbling of bodies and zippers.

I sighed and dropped my hand. "As if my day couldn't get any worse," I muttered and looked up to see Logan in nothing but his sweatpants with his hair tousled every which way and Becca in nothing but her bra and underwear.

I wanted to scream at both of them or be even more upset by the fact that my sister was sleeping with my skating partner, but instead, I just sat on my bed, defeated enough by the enormity of everything that happened with Blake.

"Well, that wasn't the reaction I was expecting," Becca said, the side of the bed creaking as she sat down next to me.

"Have you been crying?" Logan asked, walking toward me as he put on his t-shirt.

"This is a weird conversation to have right now, maybe a weird one to have ever," I muttered.

"Do I need to put on a shirt? Will that make it better? Maybe even pants?" Becca asked, putting her hand on my shoulder.

I shrugged. "That probably couldn't hurt."

Before Becca could even get off the bed, I sighed, mentally and physically exhausted. I'd done seventeen hour days training for most of my life but nothing tired and pained me more than the revelation with Blake. "I was a bet. Nothing more than a stupid bet," I said through gritted teeth.

"What did you just say?" Logan asked, kneeling down in front of me. I almost forgot he was in the room then the wave of nausea hit me that I just walked in on my sister and skating partner in bed together.

I covered my face with my hands. "This has been the most messed up day ever," I muttered and laid back on the bed, my head hitting the very scratchy comforter that reminded me of the flannel blanket in the back of Blake's van. The van I thought we had incredible sex in. Sex that was meaningless. Not just meaningless, but nothing more than a wager between a bunch of Canadian buddies. And the fact that it meant something to me. That it was more than just a fling or connecting of our bodies. That I was really falling for this guy and giving my all to him was the thing I thought would bring us closer together. Not tear us apart.

I found the tears streaming from my eyes again, and Becca was at my side, pushing my hair away from my face. "Kelly, shhh, it's okay. You don't have to talk about if you don't want to," Becca murmured.

"Like hell, she doesn't. That guy made a bet? Is that what you're trying to tell us? Like one of those bad romance novels or some frat boy move where they take a wager on who can sleep with a girl?" Logan growled from the end of the bed.

I raised my head to see Logan's hands clutched into tight fists at his side. People always gave male figure skaters a hard time about not being masculine enough, but they'd obviously never met a real male figure skater. Logan was tall, lean, and could lift me effortlessly and I was one-hundred and ten pounds. Then that made me think about how he was lifting my sister, and the bile rose in my throat again.

I nodded. "Yeah, that's basically what happened. I was a bet. *A bet to de-ice the ice queen*," I said, doing air quotes with my fingers."

"I'm going to go to the mountains now and sucker punch that dreadlocked, maple-syrup chugging little prick and his little buddies. Who the hell do they think they are?" Logan snarled, heading toward the door.

Becca was off the bed in a flash, her hand to his chest as she put her body between him and the door. I saw a flicker of something almost carnal in Logan's eyes as he looked down at her, licking his lips, but then looked back to me and he sighed.

"Logan, if you do that, you know it's just going to get you in more trouble, and you two have to get to practice before your program," Becca said, keeping her hand splayed on his chest.

I sat up and wiped my eyes. "You're right, Becca. No use worrying about some guy who doesn't care about us. We have a country to make proud."

"That isn't exactly what I said," Becca said tentatively.

I stood up and walked over to the closet, grabbing my outfit for the performance. "I'm going to shower quickly and then head over to hair and makeup. I'll meet you at the arena, Logan."

"Are you sure about this? Maybe you want to talk some more?" Becca asked, following me to the bathroom door.

"There's nothing more to say. I made a stupid mistake with a stupid boy, and now I need to go back to focusing on the reason we're here," I said, nodding to myself and shutting the door before Becca could say anything else.

Logan and she had a whispered conversation outside of the door, so I turned on the shower. That way they couldn't hear my tears that were going to be the last ones I ever cried for Blake Tremblay.

I sat in the chair, staring at the girl in the mirror while the man with bright blue hair and striking eyebrows secured my hair into an intricate updo.

I'd been getting my makeup airbrushed and my hair professionally done for competition since I was in the fourth grade. I'd gotten used to the poking and prodding, even found some of it therapeutic. The less I could feel physically when the blue haired man stuck pins in my head then the less I had to worry about feeling emotionally. This is why I was the ice queen, as Liam so eloquently called me.

I didn't need to worry about my emotions. Those were for silly girls who fell for boys and thought they liked them. Girls who weren't me. These games were about one thing and one thing only: bringing home the gold.

"All right, Ms. Johnson. Any other touch ups?" the blue haired man asked in a high-pitched tone.

I put on the plastic smile that I always did for competition and looked at the bright blue eye shadow that matched the sparkly blue leotard with the wispy skirt. Blake had said I had a fake smile for competition and the real smile I had was with him. He might have been right at the time, but that was before I knew our relationship was a lie. Now I wasn't sure if I'd ever be able to have a real smile again. "Yes, thank you."

"Yes, a vision of a loveliness," Coach said, his reflection coming into view as he stepped in the dressing room.

"Thank you." The blue haired man nodded then skittered out of the dressing room as Coach took long strides until he was at the back of my chair, his large hands gripping onto the faux leather.

"Thanks, Coach," I muttered, turning toward him as he stepped back and let go of the chair. I kept my head down as I grabbed my skates, sliding them on.

"So I've been told of some rumblings about a social media hashtag and that maybe a certain Canadian snowboarder has been breaking your concentration?" Coach asked, his voice gruff.

I froze, my hands still on the laces. Swallowing hard, I shook my head, pulling up the leather tongue. "You don't need to worry about that, Coach. It's a thing of the past."

"Is that past why I had to watch my two-time-Olympic gold medalist skater fall on her ass twice in qualifications?" he asked, his voice even firmer.

I tried to focus on lacing my skates and not the shaking of my hands. "It won't happen again, Coach. I can assure you. No boys. No friends. Only the ice. If you want to be a champion that's all you need," I said, trying to repeat the mantra I'd had since I was just a scared little girl coming to train with the great Coach Donahue.

Coach's hand was under my chin, forcing my eyes to meet his. "Do you need me to take care of him?"

I pulled my head back and raised an eyebrow. "What? Take care of him?"

Coach moved his hands to his pockets and shrugged. "You know, talk to his coaches or the committee and make sure he doesn't show up at the arena and break your concentration?"

I stood up, holding my head high. I was a damn multi-gold medalist. I wasn't going to let some Canadian boy stand in my way. "No, Coach. I'm a big girl. I can handle this."

Logan and I stood in waiting for our turn to be called to take the ice. Another waltz. Another program where I wore all blue and smiled for the crowd as their American ice princess.

It was all I had ever thought about all my life, and now that I'd experienced something more than just skating, I was starting to question it. Which was definitely not the time in the middle of the Olympic games.

I didn't have any lifelong friends that I could chat with for hours about nothing, and if I did, I'd have nothing to talk with them about except skating. No ex-boyfriends. No nothing. My life had always been the ice and training for The Games. Blake was right about one thing; I did need new hobbies. I just didn't think that one of my hobbies would turn into falling for him and then losing him just as quickly. But I guess you couldn't lose something you never really had.

Alexis and Jacob just got off the ice, and I tried not to glare at the put-together-brunette. I normally wouldn't have even spoken to her, but she stared right at me and did a small little wave as she walked to her seat to wait for the results. What the hell was that about?

"So are we going to talk about what happened?" Logan asked quietly, his head down and his overly gelled and slicked back hair gleaming against the bright lights.

"About Blake using me as a bet or you sleeping with my sister?" I hiss-whispered.

Logan sighed. "Both."

I shook my head. "Not now."

"Then when?"

"Possibly never. We just get out on the ice, we ace this performance and hopefully get in medal position then prepare for the free skate, get gold, and go home," I said all in one breath.

"And the ice queen is back," Logan muttered.

I snapped my head in his direction, glaring. "What was that? Did you really just use that name on me?"

Logan looked around. All eyes were on us since we were next to take the ice. He leaned in his lips practically on my ear. "Look, Kelly, you know I love you as a partner and a friend, but we both know that you push everyone away that you deem as a distraction. And maybe, just maybe this Blake guy became more than a distraction. He may have fucked up with starting to talk to you because of a bet, but when I talked to him, I could tell he really did like you and you'd be stupid to throw it away because he made one mistake. Would you want the judges to only focus on our mess ups in the qualification round and not let us compete in finals because of your mistakes?"

I glared at him, and before I could say anything, the announcer called our names to hit the ice.

"It's show time," I whispered, my voice cracking.

CHAPTER 13

Blake

I wanted to run onto the ice and stop Kelly. To make some big grand gesture to show her that she was more than a bet. Then I watched her on the sidelines with Logan as he whispered in her ear and rubbed her back. She visibly relaxed as soon as she was with him in the center of the rink.

This time I made sure to stay hidden and stand in the shadows instead of where she could see me and become a distraction. That, and I couldn't face her family. Her family that had welcomed me with open arms into their little circle. They'd shown me more compassion in the little time I had with them than my parents did my entire life. Now I'd lost Kelly and them. And I was more upset about the second part than I should have been.

Watching Kelly on the ice was a thing of wonder. She really was an ice queen and not for her cold demeanor, but the way she glided on the ice like it had always been a part of her was something of sheer beauty. This time she didn't falter. Every spin and jump were effortless, landing with ease and a smile. A smile that I wished I had put there. But I knew it wasn't her real one. It was the one for the crowds. The fake one she always put on. I didn't know if I'd ever see that real smile again.

The crowd cheered and threw her roses as she and Logan bowed then skated off the ice with huge grins. Even after their mess ups in the qualifying round, this would surely get them a medal position. If it weren't for me, there would be another gold around her neck. But obviously, she was already over me and not even thinking about us if she could skate like this. Just like that, I was out of the picture.

"Are you just going to stand on the side like a creeper or are you going to come sit with my parents and me in the stands?"

I looked over to see Becca standing there with her arms crossed over her chest. The only resemblance I ever saw between the two sisters was their short stature and bright blonde hair, but the glare in Becca's was just like the death stare Kelly had given me. I didn't want to see that same glare or look of disappointment on Kelly's parents' faces. I'm sure she hadn't given them all of the details, but they'd soon find out too. I couldn't bear any more people giving me that damn look.

"I was just leaving," I muttered, shoving my hands in my coat pockets.

"Are you really going to pull a pussy move like that?" Becca asked.

I raised an eyebrow, definitely not expecting that bravado, but I should have from the foul-mouthed Wisconsin-bred hockey player. "I have no idea what you're talking about. I know Kelly probably told you what happened and that I'm an asshole, but I wanted to see her perform. I didn't want her to get flustered seeing me up there, so I thought I'd hang back."

"Like I said, pussy move," Becca growled, her biceps bulging in her thin sweater. I never thought much about girl hockey players, but I was pretty sure Becca could break me. Which meant she was probably also a beast in the sack. No wonder Logan was into her.

"What do you want me to do? Want me to grovel? Want me to get on my fucking knees, crawl out on the ice and tell her I'm a fuck up?" I asked, putting my hands out and pointing toward the rink.

Becca shrugged. "Better than being the creeper in the stands. Or talking to that brunette Canadian bitch."

"What are you talking about?" I asked, raising an eyebrow.

"I saw you two walking here together. I glanced out the window when my sister was in the shower and saw you going into our dorm. I thought maybe you were coming to apologize and say it was a mistake, but then that bitch came out. And instead of coming in to do what you should have done, you walked with her to who knows where, but you ended up here. I don't know what you're trying to pull, but that's a dick move, even for someone who made a bet to get into my sister's panties," Becca said.

I winced as if her words had slapped me. "Who I hang out with or fuck is none of your business."

Becca's hand snapped forward, and before I knew it, a sharp pain hit my chest when her fist connected.

"Ow, what the hell was that for?" I asked, trying to catch my breath. I wouldn't hit a girl, but damn, she hit harder than any guy I'd ever sparred with.

"That was for saying something so dickish, and for hurting my sister. Why don't you apologize? Or sit with my parents and me, watch the program, then you go and tell her that you were an asshole."

I groaned. "Well, I'm not going to do that. It's better that she thinks I'm an ass than break her concentration."

"So what? You expect her just to think she was just a bet?" Becca asked, raising an eyebrow.

"She was."

"Keyword: was. Which by the way is the stupidest thing I've ever heard. What kind of grown ass man makes a bet with another guy about sleeping with someone? That's like something I read in those damn romantic comedies that fill up my e-reader," Becca said, shaking her head.

I blew out a breath. "It was stupid, okay? Liam and I were just having some fun, and I didn't think there was any harm in it."

"Then you fell for my sister? Or was she really just a bet that had you running back to your Canadian girl."

"Alexis and I are nothing. Okay? She's helping me out with getting some sponsors, and yeah, I'll admit I hooked up with her a few times. But who hasn't hooked up with another athlete?"

For a brief moment I thought I saw Becca's cheeks tinge red then she crossed her arms tighter across her chest. "Not my sister. She's always been about the ice. I've never seen her go so crazy about anything other than skating. I should thank you for at least getting her out of that rut, but now you've made it worse and possibly cost her a medal. For that, I should aim for your face instead of your chest."

I put my hands up. "Hey, now, there's no need to get into a kerfuffle."

She snorted. "That's a really Canadian word. It sounds too polite. Just call it a brawl or something."

I rolled my eyes. "Like your American slang is any better."

"I'm not about to get in a North American war with you here, but I'm here for my sister. The one you hurt."

"Nothing I'm going to tell you is going to make a difference, so why should I try?"

Becca blew out a big breath. "You know I love my sister. She's full of life and always smiling. She can also be a pain in the ass, determined, self-centered. But that's all elite athletes, which is probably why you two are perfect together," Becca mused.

"Like you and Logan?" I dared to say.

"Hey, this isn't about my relationship, Dreads."

I couldn't help but laugh at the impromptu nickname. "Fair enough." I squeezed and unsqueezed my hands in tight fists, unsure of what to do. What to say. Where to go.

"What do you want me to do then? Give up my sponsorship opportunities with Alexis? Go run and be some crazy guy from the movies and put her over my shoulder all caveman-like? Because I'm out of options and don't even know what to say or do at this point."

Becca shrugged. "I don't know. I didn't come here with a plan, that's your job. If you want to be with my sister, you'll figure it out."

I opened my mouth to say something else then closed it and nodded.

She offered a small smile. "I'm going back to the stands to watch my sister get to medal position. Probably will be silver or bronze, but she earned it. You coming with?"

I shook my head. "Naw, I think I'll stay shadow boy for a little bit longer."

Becca rolled her eyes. "Suit yourself."

Instead of going back to my cabin, I ended up wandering around the village. I had no idea how long I had been walking until my stomach started to growl. I'd have to get food and go back to the cabin to sleep at some point I figured, but I knew there was also another option. An option I didn't want to take, but now it seemed like the best one.

I sucked in a deep breath and knocked on the wooden door, staring into the peep hole. This may have been a mistake for coming here, and I was probably going to get shit for it, but it was either this or go back to face Liam and Erik, and I was too tired to get into another kerfuffle.

The door opened, and I stared back at my mom's bewildered expression. "Blake! What are you doing here? Is everything okay?"

I should have thought about what time it was and the fact that my parent's hotel room was pitch black with both of my parents standing there, their hair wild with bedhead and both in their flannel pajamas.

"Yeah. I. Um. Can I crash here tonight? Do you have a pullout couch or something?" I asked, raking my fingers through my hair. I couldn't look either of them in the eyes. This was one of my lowest moments.

The creaking of the door alerted me it was opening wider. "Of course, Blake. Come in. We'll make up the couch."

I followed my parents into the space that looked bigger than the cabin I was staying in. A large set of sliding doors faced the front door and looked onto the mountains. Next to the door was a large couch and flat screen TV mounted on the wall. There were two doors immediately to my left which I was guessing was the bedroom and bathroom, but I didn't go near either and went toward the couch, helping my dad to pull it out as Mom went into the other room and grabbed some pillows, sheets, and a blanket, making the bed as soon as it was pulled out.

"Is there anything else you need?" Mom asked once the bed was made.

I shook my head. "No. I'm good for now."

"Are you sure?" she asked again.

I nodded. "Yeah. Thanks, Mom. I appreciate it."

She smiled and leaned in, giving me a stiff hug. "You're welcome, honey. I'll set the alarm for you in the bedroom, and we can drive you back to your cabin. Or to the mountains. Wherever you want to go."

"Thanks." I nodded.

This was possibly the nicest my parents had ever been to me, and I had no idea what was up. I was also too emotionally and physically exhausted to care, so I sat down on the couch bed and let out a deep breath.

I didn't expect the creak of the bed or for my dad to sit next to me. "Is this about the pressure of the game or girl problems?"

"Does it matter?" I muttered.

Dad sighed, running his hands through his beard. "Well, if it's games problems, I'd give you some inspirational speech about how I overcame the pressure or I'd talk to Ricky about more practices. If it's girl problems, then I'd probably tell you that you may need to grovel a little, even if she is American."

I looked at my dad, raising an eyebrow. "I don't know if either of those are good options and I really can't remember you ever giving me advice on The Games or girls. Especially not an American girl."

Dad laughed. "Well, you've never come to me with problems about either."

"That's true."

Dad cupped his arm on my shoulder. "Listen, son; I know you think your mom and I have been hard on you. Hell at your age, we already had you and a few Olympic golds. But that was a different world. A different time. If I didn't meet your mother in junior nationals, I might have had your same story."

"I'm not sure what you mean?" I said, tilting my head to the side.

Dad smiled, shaking his head. "I'm not even going to pretend I understand a lot of what goes on in the snowboarding world, or your bravado with the ladies. But what I do understand is liking someone a lot and then messing that up. I don't know if that's the case with you and this American skater or what's going on, but I can say that, like in The Games, if you want something, you don't give up. One little mistake can't falter your whole run. You get back up, and you do something that's going to wow those watching. Something that'll get everyone's attention. Whether it's on the slopes or in this girl's heart."

"So you think an extra kick flip will do it for Kelly?" I asked, smiling slightly.

Dad smirked. "If by Ollie you mean maybe an apology? Then yes, go with that."

"I don't think she'll even accept that," I muttered.

"Well, maybe what she needs is time. Maybe you do too. You sleep here tonight, then you go and get that gold medal and tell her that you're Blake Tremblay, Olympic medalist. And if she doesn't take you back, hey at least you've got the gold, right?"

"Right," I mumbled.

Dad sighed. "I know it shouldn't always be about the gold, but you know, that's what you have to aim for. In life and The Games. Don't do something half-ass, Blake. You either give it everything you got and if you don't make it to the podium or win this girl back, at least you know you put it all out there."

For the first time one of my dad's gold medal speeches made sense and I smiled for what felt like the first time all day. "Thanks, Dad. I'll do that."

Dad patted my back before standing. "No problem, son. Now get some rest. Tomorrow you can worry about medals and girls."

CHAPTER 14

Kelly

Bronze position was better than I expected to be in after the short program. It wasn't gold, but with all of my distractions, it was a damn good thing to even get this close to that position. Of course, Alexis and Jacob were in the gold position. There was something about her smile and niceties that had me think she was planning something. Of course, that could have also just been everything else that was going on in my crazy head and making stuff up. Maybe my relationship with Blake was all just made up in my head. Maybe it wasn't real.

But even as I thought that thought, it quickly exited my head. What I felt with him was more real than anything I'd ever felt in my life. Having him admit that we were a bet broke that one little sense of realness I had in my life and pushed my anger to the forefront of my mind.

That anger helped to get the fire back in me to get ready for the free skate. There was no way I was going to walk away from The Games without a medal around my neck, and if we skated our asses off, it would be gold.

"Hey, wanna take a site-seeing trip today?" Becca asked, drying her hair as she got out of the shower.

I shook my head as I packed my skates in my duffle bag. We may have been in medal position going into freeskate, but we could just as easily lose it if I messed up again. "No, I'm going to head to the rink for another practice."

Becca stepped in front of me, putting her hand over my bag before I could zipper it. "You already practiced for umpteen hours this morning with Logan. It's time for a break."

I shook my head. "I had a break. We had lunch, and now it's time for more practice. The Games aren't about fun. It's about winning."

Before I could grab my zipper, Becca took the bag with one hand and threw it behind her, with a crash it went slamming against the wall.

I widened my eyes, staring between the wall and Becca. "What the hell was that?" I snapped.

"That was me, for the first time ever, standing up to my big sister and tell her to stop being such a diva," Becca snarled.

"You have some nerve," I muttered, trying to step past her to grab my bag.

Becca blocked my path; her arms crossed over her chest. "Look, you don't want to talk about what happened with you and Blake or with Logan and me and we don't have to. We've been sisters all of our lives, and this is the most time we've spent together since we were in grade school. We're going to take this opportunity to at least get a few hours together and do some sisterly bonding, dammit."

"What are you talking about? We spend all night together," I scoffed.

Becca laughed, but there was no humor in it. "Yeah, sleeping. That doesn't count for shit. And if you're not sleeping, you're practicing or eating. At least when you were with Blake you did a little bit more, but now you're back to hyper-skater, and you need a break."

"This is The Games, Becca. This might be your first one, but you should know being an athlete all your life that we need practice. I can't walk away with a bronze and end my skating career with that," I muttered the last part.

"Yeah, and it isn't going to kill you to take a couple of hours off. I promise, just a few hours then you can go and skate all night if you want. Please? For me? These two weeks at The Games is all we have for a while. After closing ceremonies, you go back to New York, and I go back to Wisconsin and who knows when I'll see you again," she said, her words softening.

I sighed, melting at my little sister's words. She was right. After The Games were over, I'd fly back to New York, and she'd go home for Wisconsin and go back to school. I didn't know where my career would go after these games. By 2022 I'd be almost thirty. Ancient in the sport of skating. Would I stay in New York? Go back to Wisconsin? I didn't know.

I guess I had to figure that out at some point and maybe spending some time with my sister could help that.

"Okay. Let's go on an adventure."

The Uber car drove out of the village and toward the mountains instead of downtown PyeongChang where I assumed we were going. The hairs on the back of my neck stood on end as I remembered this familiar road. The last time I was on this road was when tears were streaming down on my face, and I was in the back of an Uber, leaving Blake's cabin after finding out we were a lie.

"Where exactly are we exploring, Becca?" I whispered, staring out the window.

"You ask a lot of questions. Isn't exploring all about the unknown?" Becca asked in a huff.

"We're going to watch Blake's finals aren't we?" I asked, raising an eyebrow.

"Dammit, how are you so good at figuring shit out!" Becca hissed, pounding her hand on the seat between us.

"You know you could have lied then I wouldn't have figured it out until we got there," I offered.

"Yeah, but you know I'm a terrible liar."

"Not that bad, you kept you and Logan from me," I muttered.

"Lying and secrets are two totally different things," Becca said, crossing her arms over her chest, the puffy coat crinkling against the seat.

"How do you figure?"

Becca threw her arms in the air. "Seriously. Can you just be happy and not question things or be a killjoy?"

Becca's voice raised enough that the Uber driver looked at us from the rear view mirror. Pretty sure he couldn't speak English or knew for sure who we were, but he was at least sensing the tension in our conversation.

"Me? A killjoy?" I asked, pointing at myself and widening my eyes.

"Yes, you. What? Can't expect someone to give you criticism when you're America's, darling?"

"I didn't say that." I glared.

Becca groaned. "Look, Kel, I love you, and you know that even if we haven't seen each other much in the last ten years. You know why that is?"

"Because I've been living in New York and you stayed in Wisconsin?" I asked.

Becca rolled her eyes. "Because you've had a stick up your ass. Even Mom and Dad hated visiting because all you would do was complain that you needed to be at practice or go to bed early and leave us in the living room of your apartment twiddling our thumbs. It's always been about you and whatever it's taken you to get to the top."

I winced as if Becca's words slapped me. "That's not fair, Becca. You know I'm dedicated. I didn't move to New York or come to The Games for fun. That dedication has made me a millionaire, paid for your college, and equipment for the farm, so how's that for a kill joy?"

"It's not about the money or the fame, Kel. It never was. Mom and Dad just wanted to see you happy and to see me happy. You put on a nice fake smile for the judges but the only time I've seen a real smile on you lately has been when you're with Blake or talking about him."

"That was before I knew I was just a bet," I muttered.

"Do you think a guy would show up at your events, make a big show for social media, and, hell, talk to your little sister and skating partner if it was all just for a bet?"

I shook my head. "I don't know what I think."

"You wanna know what I think?" Becca asked.

"Not particularly."

"Imma tell you anyway."

I watched the woodsy area at the base of the mountains, filled with people. There were flags from all of the different countries, and I found my heart skipping faster as I realized that even though he might not see me again, I was going to watch Blake for the first time since everything went down. Since I found out, I was a bet. My heart shouldn't have been beating as wildly thinking about seeing him, but the truth was that I missed him. I missed his touch. His company. His everything.

Becca sighed. "I think that Blake may have started talking to you because he was dared or made a bet or whatever, but I could see it when you two were talking that first night and the other night at your short program finals. You probably didn't know it, but he was there watching you. If you were just a bet, I don't think there would be any way in hell that guy would stay around."

I shrugged. "Maybe and maybe not."

The Uber driver pulled to stop where a bunch of people were gathered at the gated entrance to an area where a huge course was set up in the mountains.

I never paid attention to the sport of snowboarding before Blake came along. I figured it was just another thing that boys did in the snow, but watching him spin and jump and the way he did everything so effortlessly made me rethink the sport. Made me rethink his passion for it. Someone with that much passion for a sport had to have it in everything in life. At least I thought he had that passion for me. Maybe he really did, like Becca suggested, but I couldn't get over the pretense that it was all because of a bet.

"So this is slalom huh?" Becca asked as we flashed our credentials and walked to an area at the base of the mountain where a few other athletes were milling around.

"Yeah, it kind of reminds me of that time I was home for the summer when you were in middle school, and you dragged me to that skate park because you liked a high school boy who hung out there," I replied, casually looking around for a familiar face in a red and white jacket with dreadlocks.

Becca tossed her arms out. "Avril Lavigne was big, and I wanted a skater boy, okay? You didn't have to come."

"What else was I supposed to do? Stay on the farm and do both of our chores?"

"Probably would have been more fun than watching a bunch of fourteen-year-old-boys fall on their asses over and over," she said with a laugh.

"Speaking of boys, are we going to talk about when this all happened with Logan?" I asked, raising an eyebrow.

Becca adjusted her scarf and lowered her beanie. "He's just a hook-up. Everyone has them at The Games."

"Oh, so you can have a hookup, but for me, it must be something more?" I asked, crossing my arms over my puffy coat.

Becca sighed. "What do you want me to say? That I've had a crush on my sister's skating partner forever? That he's a hot geek and kind of reminds me of that know-it-all guy from Criminal Minds that I know you binge watch too?"

"I wouldn't go that far. I don't think Logan's like him. Maybe the hair," I added.

"The point is, I've liked Logan for awhile, but it's always been weird because you know he's older and your partner. But the more time I spent with him in New York because you were too busy doing hot yoga or something and then at The Games, well one thing led to another..."

"And somehow hanging out turned into him hanging out in our bedroom? Maybe he just fell on you over and over and over?" I asked.

"Real mature, Kel," Becca said, pushing my shoulder, which I think was supposed to be a gentle shove but I was pretty sure I'd have a bruise.

"So what's going to happen with the two of you then? Are you going to try for something more?" I asked, genuinely curious. I'd never thought about Logan as anything other than a partner. Or my sister in a romantic relationship with him. Two of the most important people in my life together could either go good or turn out catastrophically bad.

Becca shrugged. "I don't know. We'll see what happens I guess. A lot can change over the next week we're here."

"That it can," I whispered, thinking of how much my own life had changed in the past week. I'd gone from being completely focused on The Games and another medal, to worrying about this dreadlocked boy who was talking to me, to falling hard for that same guy, then ultimately going back to being broken. To just focusing on The Games and nothing else. At least that's what I thought I could focus on, but I couldn't deny that part of me was still broken. Part of me that I thought Blake had fixed but ended up just smashing again.

When we got to the athlete's area, I expected to see some familiar faces, especially with all of the Americans who trained at Lake Placid. We had people from all over the world in summer and winter sports that trained in everything from swimming to bobsledding, so I met a lot of athletes from around the world. But what I didn't expect to see was Alexis Cote.

Every hair on the back of my neck stood on end, and I tried not to stare at the statuesque brunette, standing in the middle of a group of guys in ski caps. She had her gloved hand wrapped around a Styrofoam coffee cup and took slow sips in-between some haughty laughs.

I don't know why I hated her so much. I barely even knew the girl outside of competition. I just knew that we were always taking silver and gold on the podiums. Sometimes I got gold, and sometimes she did. It had been a toss up between the two of us the last four years since we took gold and silver in Sochi and now I didn't want to be on the lower end of the podium. Especially knowing she had a history with Blake. She was younger than me, this only being her second Olympics, so she would ultimately be the next leading lady of the ice. I should have been happy for someone else to come up and keep attention to the sport, but instead, I thought about the younger, brunette skater taking the hearts of fans and even Blake Tremblay.

He said she meant nothing to him when he showed me the picture. Was that what he would tell people about me too? It shouldn't have bothered me this much. I didn't have any romantic relationships with boys back home. I may have only been in middle school when I left for New York, but while I crushed on the pee wee football playing boys, they all looked at me like I was the weird girl who never went to after school activities because she was too busy skating. I never had time for anyone, and it made me an outcast. That's why it was so easy to always leave. If I was nothing, then nobody could miss me, and I couldn't miss anyone.

"Hey, American, are you going to stare at me the entire time or are you going to join us?" Alexis shouted, her French accent ringing through the crowd and I felt the heat of a few eyes on me.

I shook my head out of my reverie and saw Alexis staring at us with wide brown eyes.

"Do we have to go over there?" Becca asked. "She reminds me of a Kardashian and not the friendly one."

"She's still staring at us, I don't think we can get out of it," I whispered out of the corner of my mouth as Becca, and I slowly moved forward.

It wasn't until we were standing right in front of Alexis that I realized the guys with her in big puffy coats were none other than Liam and Erik, Blake's friends he made the bet with. As if she knew how awkward this would be for me, Alexis smiled like a Cheshire cat and looked at the boys then to me. Did Alexis know what happened? I was sure I was the laughing stock of Canada now if she did.

"Erik, Liam, I don't know if you've met her, but this is American pairs skater, Kelly Johnson, and, I'm sorry, but I don't know your name," Alexis said, holding her hand out to Becca.

"It's Becca. All-American hockey goalie or you can just call me a badass," Becca replied with a smirk, shaking her hand firmly before looking at the two men and hitching a thumb in both of their directions. "And I already know these assholes. I don't even mean that in a nice way."

Liam, Erik, and Alexis all stared at each other open-mouthed for what felt like at least a full minute. The joke was always that Canadians were super polite and obviously, they'd never met a foul-mouthed girl from Viel, Wisconsin like my little sister.

"Good to see you again, Becca, I think we're gonna head over there before this gets any more awkward," Erik said, putting his hand on Liam's shoulder before they both turned and headed in the opposite direction.

"Good move, Pussy," Becca muttered, and I nudged her side.

"What? He's an ass. I could have shouted it, but then I'm sure someone would get that on camera, and that would be my sound bite for the entire Games." Becca shrugged.

"Well, now this is super awkward," Alexis said, taking a long sip from her cup.

"I didn't expect it not to be," I muttered.

"So what is going on with you and Blake anyway, if you don't mind my asking? I'd seen you two all cozy together on social media, and since Liam and Erik are his roommates, I thought maybe something happened?" Alexis asked, raising her eyebrows.

I wasn't about to dish out all of my troubles to someone I considered competition, so I just shrugged. "You know how The Games are. All hormones and hookups. He's been fun to hang out with during The Games. Since he went to me perform in qualifications and short program, I figured I should watch him on slalom as well."

Alexis nodded, pursing her lips together in a tight smile. "I see."

I sucked in a breath as the first guy took his place on the ramp. But instead of watching him jump and flip and whatever else he did, I looked past him, hoping for a glimpse of a red coat and dreadlocks. Because the truth was, I may have said it was nothing and tried to get over the guy, but he was way more than nothing. He was the one person to have me focusing on something other than the ice in years. Even if it ended up being nothing, in the end, Blake Tremblay made me feel alive, and that was worth something. I just didn't know what, yet.

CHAPTER 15

Blake

There were a few other countries going before me, and I stood on the side with the other awaiting athletes, my Beats on, the loud music drowning out everything else. One of the things I loved about snowboarding was that I was allowed to have my music during competition. It helped reduce the crowd noise, and I could focus on the beat of the music and the board, nothing else. Nothing else except Kelly Johnson who wouldn't leave my mind.

I should have listened to Becca and done something, but like the hoser I was, I just left after her performance. I didn't even wait for the results. I took a photo outside of the arena and tagged it as #Klake with nothing else. That, of course, led to a lot of questions in the comments, but I couldn't even begin to explain it. I just hoped the one person I wanted to see it would, but every time I checked my phone, there weren't any notifications from Kelly.

With not much going on for sleep on my parents pull out couch, I left early that next morning and headed to the slopes to get some practice in. I was definitely ready for the slalom. I was doing pretty good after qualifying rounds to get myself in a medal position. It was just between the cocky American and me for gold. My first and last gold I'd ever get in The Games.

Sure, I could have tried again for 2022, but by then I'd be even older and practically a grandpa in the sport. I already felt like that running around with the kids I was at least ten years older than.

"You ready for this, man?" My coach, Ricky, asked. He was only a few years older than me and should have been an Olympic gold medalist himself but was injured the first time he tried out for The Games and never fully recovered, so he started coaching. I'd been with him for five years now and never looked back. The tall, balding guy with a facial tattoo and nose piercing was like my better half. Well, in the least sexual way possible. He made me a better and more focused boarder. My parents weren't sure about the guy at first when he showed up at their ski resort, but after they saw him on the board and what he taught me after one practice, they were settled on going with him instead of the other coaches that tried to get me to The Games. When I qualified, I swore my mom almost kissed Ricky, right in the big tribal tattoo on his cheek.

"Ready as ever, man," I said.

I was about to put my mask down and get into the zone, then I glanced at the big screen and had to do a double take. There were cameras and screens all over the mountain so spectators could watch us up close and see our little interviews and what not. But some American news reporter was interviewing people in the crowd, and the blue-eyed beauty lit up the big screen behind me. I was mesmerized and couldn't look away. There was no way in hell I thought Kelly would show up at my event. Maybe she did see the hashtag. Maybe there was a chance I could get her back after my monumental screw-up.

The American reporter pulled his red ski cap down and held the microphone up to his pale face. "And down here on the sidelines we have athletes supporting athletes. Sisters Becca and Kelly Johnson came out to cheer on, well is it Team USA or is Team Klake?" The reporter laughed at his own joke and shoved the microphone practically in Kelly's teeth.

I waited with baited breath, staring at the girl on the screen. I had no idea where she was in the crowd, but all that mattered was that she was there. Maybe there was hope for us after all.

"I'm just here supporting all of the athletes. Taking a little break before freeskate," she said with the smile I learned was her performance one. Not that smile that I was falling for that brought out the tiny lines around her eyes. No, this one was the fake smile she put on for an audience.

"Blake? You ready?" Ricky yelled, cupping his hand on my shoulder.

I finally turned away from the screen. I wasn't going to let Kelly be a distraction. That was never what I meant for her to be. She was going to be the one that pushed me to be greater. This wasn't about sponsorships or about how badly I wanted that gold around my neck. This was about how much I loved the sport. The smell of the powder and the rush I got from being in the air. The same rush I felt in my stomach when I was with Kelly.

This win wasn't going to be for a bet. This win was for her.

The announcer called out in a few different languages, and I put my mask down and adjusted my hat and scarf. I'd done this a million times in practice and for the first time in The Games the other day. But this would be me final Olympic event ever. If I messed up, that was it. I'd just be known as the guy who had a fling with a figure skater at The Games and fucked up. Hell, people probably wouldn't even remember I was the son of Olympians unless they looked at me as their failure son.

The start button dinged, and I sucked in a breath before making my way down the slalom. I hit every single jump, twist, and let the air take hold. I was on fire. Faster and hitting every point better than ever before. I was in my element on the board. I may have fucked up everywhere else in my life, but in this slalom, I was king. There was no way I was going to walk away without some kind of medal around my neck.

When my board hit the powder, and I came to a final stop, I whipped off my mask and hat, tossing my dreadlocks in the wind. I had to wait for my final score, and usually, I did a little dance for the cameras. But not today. The crowd cheered, and I looked out, spotting her almost instantly.

Instead of going to wait for my results, I unhooked my boots, grabbed my board and darted for the fence. There may have been hundreds of people there, but I spotted the top of her bright blue cap in the crowd of athletes who were all patting my back and cheering as I leaned against the fence.

"Hey, Kelly! You see that?" I yelled, pointing behind me at one of the giant screens.

Becca looked at me, her eyes somewhere between narrowed and raised with question. Then Kelly's eyes slowly went toward me but then darted at the girl on her other side. I followed her gaze and recognized the brunette standing next to her with a smug smirk.

Oh. Shit. What the hell was Alexis doing? I should have known not to trust that bitch as far as I could jump her. Did she know about the bet? Did Liam and Erik tell her everything? What the hell was she telling my girl?

I shook the thoughts out of my head about Alexis and turned to Kelly, waiting for her to say something. Anything. When she didn't respond, I blew her a kiss and put my fist in the air and yelled, "that one was for you, babe. Klake forever, whether you like it or not."

That caused the crowd to erupt in even more applause and chant "Klake." Like Dad said, I had to put it all out there.

I hoped it would be enough to at least get a real smile out of the girl or something that told me I still had a chance.

I thought I'd get a better reaction out of Kelly. If nothing else a blush of her cheeks and a smile and for Alexis to know we were over. I may have fucked up my chance at a sponsorship, but if this run was really something, I'd walk away with a good chunk of change and something for my future with a gold on my resume.

Instead of Kelly even smiling, what I got was her looking away and tugging on her sister's coat before she turned and walked away from the slopes. The cheers got louder, but she didn't turn around. She didn't walk back.

"Blake, how does it feel just hitting a world record score and having your girlfriend here to watch it?" A reporter asked, tapping my shoulder.

I turned around and looked at the screen, my eyes practically bugging out of their sockets. There was only one guy going after me, and he was barely in medal position. I was going to make gold for sure. I should have been thrilled. I should have been like King Kong and banging on my chest. But instead, I felt like the biggest fraud in The Games. The guy who made a bet to sit here in this very position. The guy who made the wrong bet with the wrong girl. A medal wasn't going to celebrate with me at night, and neither was Kelly.

I offered a small smile to the guy and let out a breath. "It feels, well it doesn't feel real, man."

"Will you be celebrating tonight with the other half of Klake? It looks like you might have embarrassed Kelly Johnson who one of my colleagues is trying to catch up with."

I shrugged. "Well, hopefully, the girl can forgive me. She's the better half of Klake, you know?"

The reporter laughed, patting my shoulder. "Well, that medal around your neck should help."

A sour feeling sat in my stomach. This bet all started out with a wager over medals. Now I'd have my gold. The American messing up on his first ollie solidified that one. Instead of being over the moon, I felt like the biggest hoser.

Standing on the podium, I watched as the Canadian flag waved in the breeze, our anthem playing. I had so many emotions running through me. The gold meant a lot of things could happen for me. I didn't need to worry about being nice to Alexis for some shampoo sponsorship. At this rate, someone else would want me. I'd move out of my parent's house, maybe even take up coaching. Who the hell knows.

When I got off the podium, I was greeted by Liam who was still wearing his gold he won earlier in the day. "I guess I should give this one to you, ey?" he said with a smirk, fingering the heavy metal piece.

"Keep it," I muttered, pushing past him.

"Hey, don't be like that, man. It was all in fun," Liam called after me.

"Blake! Congrats! A gold medalist and world record holder!" Mom crushed me in her arms before I could even step another foot outside of the arena.

"Thanks," I muttered half-heartedly.

When Mom let go, Dad embraced me, patting my back. I thought he was going to let go, but then he whispered,

"Remember what I said last night? Now's your chance to get the medal and the girl."

I sighed. "I don't think that's going to happen."

Dad pulled back and raised an eyebrow. "That doesn't sound like the mantra of an Olympic gold medalist."

"Yeah, but somehow I don't think that's going to impress her. I don't know if you saw Kelly on the big screen…"

"Oh I saw her," Mom cut me off, stepping forward. "We all did. Look, I'll admit that we've both pushed you. We've wanted you to go for sponsorships and everything we achieved in our lives. We thought if you got everything we did, you'd be happy. But the only time I've truly seen you happy in these games is when you were down in the crowd with her. So, I'm telling you, Blake, you're a Tremblay. You've got your gold; now it's time to go for it all. You put your heart and soul on that board tonight. Now put it out there for her."

I raised an eyebrow. "Not what I was expecting you to say."

Mom laughed. "Stop being a hoser and go get your girl."

I hugged Mom and Dad again. "Thanks, guys. I'll catch up with you later. Victory dinner or breakfast?"

Mom sucked in a deep breath and exhaled as she let go of me before patting my shoulders. "Our couch is open to you for as long as you like. And breakfast or dinner is always welcome for you."

I smiled and shook dad's hand before running toward the many cabs surrounding the arena to head to the village.

I had to make this right. I might have been a newly minted gold medalist, and as Dad said, I should go for the gold and the girl. But I was still an asshole. An asshole that had to make it up to his better half.

CHAPTER 16

Kelly

I don't know why I thought I'd be fine watching Blake. I should have just called another Uber and left Becca instead of watching him. At least my parents didn't come. Then there would have been more questions, though I was sure some reporter or blogger would be up my ass soon.

Of course, Blake had to come out and make a scene. And of course, I still kept staring at him. The guy wasn't just amazing when it came to the bedroom or the van as it be, but when he was on the board, it was like magic.

I'd done my fair share of jumps and spins in the air, so I knew the feeling of the wind whipping through my face and nothing holding me up but the air around me. I couldn't see Blake's face beneath his mask, but I could feel it. I could feel the rush as if it was me up there, gliding through the air alongside him.

When he came down and unmasked, it was as if I unmasked myself. I couldn't help staring at his smiling face. The face of someone who knew they were about to get on the podium. A rush I'd felt so many times and could never get enough of. But instead of basking in that glory, he searched the crowd to find me. Me. The girl who was just a bet. Or so I thought.

If that's all I was, why was he still trying?

I couldn't think about that. I had to work. My freeskate performance was tonight. This time I couldn't mess up, I couldn't be focused on a boy instead of getting in medal position. And that was what I was going to do.

Logan met me at the arena instead of coming to the room. Since neither he nor Becca were talking about what happened, that came with Logan avoiding our room or the general vicinity of my sister.

He was waiting for me by the locker rooms in his blue track suit and hair standing up all over the place like he just got out of bed or had been running his hands through it a million times. For a second I imagined instead of Logan waiting for me, it was Blake. That he would take me into his arms and not let me go until I spoke to him. That I would get wrapped up in his manly scent with a hint of cool mint and he'd kiss me. Telling me that it was all just a bad dream. That he approached me because he felt the electric connection I did the moment I saw him as well. But this wasn't a fairytale, and things like that didn't happen in reality.

Of course, none of my Blake dreams were real, and that was evident by the frown on Logan's face when I approached him. "Geez, don't look so happy to see me."

I rolled my eyes. "You're the one with bedhead. Don't tell me you were in bed with another hockey player, Becca will probably beat you. And I know you can lift me, but I've seen her workouts, and I think she could bench both of us together."

Logan smirked, shaking his head. "No other girl. Just took a little nap while you were busy being on the big screen watching snowboarding. Didn't happen to see a big bruise on him, did ya? I heard Becca socked him the other night."

I raised an eyebrow. When would that have happened? He probably deserved it, and a small part of me smiled thinking about my little sister giving the guy a hit for me, as petty as it was. He deserved it a tiny bit for making me hurt. "Where did you hear that?"

"You're not the only one who sleeps in a bed next to your sister. Well, I mean, we aren't sleeping..."

"Gross!" I wrinkled my nose, raising my hand to cut him off before he could finish that sentence. Though part of me was happy that even though he was avoiding my room and they were avoiding talking about each other, they were still seeing each other. If there was hope for the two of them to stay together, maybe there was hope for my love life.

"Anyway... She told me that during our short program she found Blake hanging out in the stands and had a few words and maybe a few jabs," Logan said, running his fingers through his already tousled hair which just messed it up even more.

"Why didn't Becca tell me?" I asked out loud, even though it was more to myself. I don't know if it would have made a difference if it were her or Logan who told me she hit him, but why didn't she tell me? Did they have an entire exchange about me? What did he say to her?

"I guess she probably tried to. She's better at just hitting things instead of actually talking about them. She's more of a doer, no pun intended," he muttered that last part.

"Gross!" I half-shrieked, trying to get the image of my half-naked partner and sister together out of my head, but that was going to be burned in my memory forever.

Before I could walk away toward my dressing room, Logan put his hands on my shoulders. "Look, Kel, I should have maybe pushed you harder instead of being so nonchalant after we did so bad in qualifying. I thought maybe if I went easy on you, you'd go easier on yourself. But you know what? Fuck all that. Instead of being upset or angry, let's put it all out on the ice. Let's skate our hearts out tonight. Let's get out all of our frustrations, our joys, just everything. Let's show it in this program. We may be out of the gold right now, but fuck it, if this is our last Games, let's give it all we got. No mistakes. No distractions. Just you and me, doing what we're the best at."

I wanted to ask what he had to be upset about, besides my performance. I didn't know if he and Becca were having problems, but I didn't want to think about that. We were there for The Games. We'd been together and training for almost ten years. This was our last chance to get on the medal stand in the Olympic Games, and we were going to do it. Sisters or boyfriends or bets or whatever be damned

I nodded and smiled. "All right, Logan, let's do this."

After getting my hair and makeup done, Coach and Logan met me outside the dressing room, ready for our final performance.

This was the last time I'd don a blue dress with thousands of Swarovski crystals that glimmered in the lights of the arena. The last time Logan would wear his puffy shirt and vest, grinning from ear to ear as we glided across the ice together. This had been our life for so long. Our look. Our moves. It was all we ever wanted in life, and we'd made it to these games so many times. But now that it was our last time out there skating for competition, I felt tears prick my eyes. If I didn't have the ice and I didn't have Blake, what did I have?

Coach put his hands together, looking between us. "You know, they call these the Olympic games and games have players. Some players are good, and some are bad. There are games that are pure luck and games of skill. Figure skating isn't like hockey with a definite back and forth of scoring points. It takes precision. One mess up and you can't always come back from it."

I put my head down, feeling like this conversation was pointed at my mess up in qualifying. I couldn't let that happen again. I'd let down Coach, Logan, and the country.

"But, you two have proven that you're some of the best players out there. You have heart. Something that other players like to keep frozen," Coach said.

That one had me looking up and trying not to roll my eyes. I was pretty sure I was the notorious ice queen. Even though it was a horrible nickname, I knew it. I was great at skating and keeping my feelings in check, that is until recently. Blake Tremblay unfroze my heart, but then all it took was one thing to freeze it again quickly.

"I've been hard on both of you. As a coach that's what I've always done is push you to go further. To be the best. But on this, your last night skating for competition in The Games, I want you not only to do your best, and to fight hard, but to skate with heart. I want the judges to feel this performance. Skate with heart, you two. Show them the real king and queen of the ice."

Logan grinned, putting his arm around me and Coach did the same, enveloping me in a hug. I'd put everything I had into the ice, but my heart wasn't put into anything. Never. That was the part that did stay frozen.

But not anymore.

If I was going to go out of the skating world, it wasn't going to be as the ice queen, but the queen of the ice.

I took the hugs from Coach and Logan then headed out to the ice, catching the end of Canada's performance. Alexis and Jacob landed their double axels then went into a final spin before their pose. The crowd, of course, erupted in applause, throwing stuffed animals and roses down on the ice. The two looked like an evil version of Ken and Barbie in their bright pink, sequined outfits. If they weren't right in front of me, I might have made gagging faces at Logan. Pink wasn't either of their colors, and I'm pretty sure Alexis might have pulled off the leisure suit Jacob was wearing better than him and same for wearing her leotard. I think he had the better body, to be honest. I wasn't trying to be petty, but I couldn't help the evil green jealousy that crawled inside of me. I just couldn't let it out. I would only let it out on the ice. To show her that I was the queen.

Logan and I golf clapped, forcing smiles as the Canadian pair slid off the ice. I thought they would go right to their spots with their coach, but instead, Alexis leaned in, putting her arms around me.

A hug? What was this? Was she going to snap my bra or maybe go for a Tonya Harding move and break my knee cap? I saw her thunder thighs; they could easily take me out.

I gingerly hugged her back, and instead of pulling away, Alexis put her lips to my ear. "I should thank Blake for making that bet. See you on the podium…or not."

She pulled away before I could respond and smiled, waving to the crowd then put on her blade guards and headed to the side with Jacob and her coach.

"What was that about?" Logan asked.

I put on my fake smile, waved in Alexis direction, and

whispered to Logan, "It was the fuel this frozen heart needed to melt."

Logan and I got to the center of the ice, and he put his arms around my waist, my back to his stomach. I could feel his heart beating wildly against the side of my cheek.

"Are you ready for this?" I whispered.

He smiled, lifting my chin up to meet his eyes, something that wasn't part of our routine but made a genuine smile cross my face looking at his grin. "We got this," he whispered.

The music started, and we glided together across the ice, every step in sync like we'd done it a million times before. Which we had. But this time was different. This was the last time. Our final competition performance. I wanted to close my eyes and just feel the ice. Feel every movement and ingrain it into my memory forever. But instead, I kept my eyes wide. Looking out into the crowd. I didn't know if there was a dreadlocked man out there, staring back at me, but when Logan and I went into our first jump, I landed flawlessly, basking in the applause from the audience. This was what made me feel free. Feel alive. I'd always been so nervous for competition and kept bottled up. Just focused on my moves, but this time I smiled. I let the applause of the audience fill me and breathed it in. This skate was for us. For me.

I wanted to say that after landing every perfect jump and spin that we made it to gold medal position. But our scores put us just under, and I had to smile and squeeze Logan's hand, standing on the podium with silver around our necks as we watched the Canadian flag lowered with their anthem playing.

Alexis and Jacob smiled as tears streamed down their face, watching their flag waving as the silent crowd watched us all. I wanted to say something smart when their anthem ended, but instead, I hugged the bronze medalist Chinese team in their matching silk kimonos, then turned to Alexis, keeping the smile on my face.

"Great skating you two," I said, shaking Jacob's hand then gingerly hugging Alexis.

"You two. One heck of a comeback," Jacob said, grinning his gap-toothed grin that I was pretty sure was aimed more at Logan's direction than mine. Boy was he barking up the wrong tree.

I smirked. "You know, sometimes it takes a little extra motivation to unthaw something."

Alexis blinked and opened her mouth to say something but before she could, I waved and took Logan's hand. "Come on, Lo. Let's get out of here."

Logan squeezed my hand. "You got it, Elsa."

I laughed, and we skated off the ice to our waiting coach who hugged us both, his arms around our shoulders. "I want you to know that I'm still so proud of both of you. I wish this wasn't our last games."

"Maybe it won't be," Logan sang.

Coach raised an eyebrow then him and Logan both looked at me.

I just shrugged as much as I could. "I guess anything could happen."

I might not have been walking away from my final games with a gold, but I had something better. A new appreciation for life. If I didn't skate forever, or go back for another Games, I knew there was more to my life. Maybe I wouldn't end up in a relationship with a snowboarder, or maybe I'd meet someone in New York.

Either way, I'd been playing The Games for so long that I'd gotten lost in it. I'd lost my heart in it. Having coach talk about the spirit of The Games and leaving my heart on the ice suddenly made it all clearer. I just didn't know what that would mean. My heart was unfrozen, yes, but it was still broken. And I wasn't sure how to fix it.

CHAPTER 17

Blake

"Do you always hang in the shadows? This is getting really creepy." Becca asked, her boots clicking on the cement steps.

"If you're going to try and hit me again, at least let me know where, so I can be prepared. I'm supposed to meet with a protein bar company and would prefer not to have a black and blue face," I said, holding up my hands.

Becca shook her head, walking toward the alcove and the wall I was leaning against. "No hitting this time. Just talking. You know something you should be doing with my sister instead of just trying to make a show for the media."

"This isn't a show. This is what I do. I know your sister is reserved and all, but sometimes you gotta make a statement," I said, crossing my arms over my chest. I expected her to hit me again anyway without warning and I probably deserved it. But I couldn't stay away. I had to watch Kelly. I loved seeing her so entranced with skating. Hell, it had only been a week, but I was starting to love everything the girl did. I would have told her that too if she ever talked to me that is.

"Statements aren't always going to get you the girl. Especially one like my sister. It couldn't hurt you to maybe try and talk to her. Go to our room or something. I don't know. I can message you when she goes to the coffee shop or something. I don't know. I'm not good at this shit."

I groaned. "What do you want me to say, Becca? That I'm going to pull some move like those guys in the movies? Maybe I could be like that long-haired guy from that teen movie who buys the girl a guitar. Though, I don't see your sister as the band type. Maybe I could just get her some new skates. How much do those things cost anyway?"

"Or…you could try talking to her. You know like a real person. Face to face. No jokes. No gimmicks. Just you and my sister," Becca offered.

"Yeah, the key is finding her and getting her to talk to me," I muttered, stuffing my hands in my pockets.

"You know, we're supposed to go to dinner tonight with my parents after this performance. If you happened to show up, I'm sure Mom would invite you to join us," Becca offered.

I raised an eyebrow. "Why are you helping me? I thought you hated me after everything with your sister."

She sighed. "Because it sucks when you like someone and then you mess up in a big way and don't know how to fix it."

"Speaking from personal experience?" I asked.

"I don't think that's any of your business, Dreads."

I shook my head. "Hey, just offering. Since you're helping me out, maybe I can help you."

Becca blew out a big breath, and her shoulders sagged as if she had given up. "Okay. It's a guy I really shouldn't be with, because of how close he is with my..er... family. If things messed up between us, it could go really bad. I thought we were just going to be a hookup for The Games, but...wait, why am I telling you all of these details?"

"This guy wouldn't happen to be your sister's skating partner would he?" I raised my eyebrows, already knowing the answer.

"If I said 'no' would you even believe me?"

I laughed, finally letting the weight off my shoulders since the beginning of our conversation. "I think the guy's pretty into you as well. You should just tell him, 'ey, I like you.' And see where it goes."

"First off, I'm not saying 'ey' because that's really Canadian sounding. And two, that's easier said than done. What if things go bad? Even though this is probably Kelly's last Olympics, I'm sure I'll see him again, and it'll be super awkward. Not that it isn't awkward enough that Kelly walked in on us..."

I shook my head, trying to get the visual of Logan's pasty naked ass out of my head. "Should I even ask what happened with that?"

"I know Kelly wouldn't have walked in on us if you didn't pull that dick move with her finding out she was a bet, so she left your little date or whatever it was early," Becca growled.

I put my hands up. "Okay, fair enough." I sighed, taking a step forward. "Look, Becca, I know you've gotta hate me and you know I like your sister, something I messed up. But I can tell you from experience, if you do really like Logan, tell him. If everything goes wrong, at least you have this time together."

Becca raised an eyebrow. "Are you giving this advice to me or yourself?"

I shrugged. "Maybe both."

The crowd roared with applause behind us, and Becca looked up at the stands, letting out a deep breath. "I'd better go. Hopefully, I get to watch my sister get a medal."

I nodded. "Yeah. Hopefully, it's gold."

Becca smirked. "Not likely, but I'll message you where we're going after this. If she doesn't get a medal, either you're going to cheer her up, or I'm going to have hurt you again."

I smiled in spite of her words. "Sounds like a plan."

Becca messaged me the address of a restaurant downtown Pyeongchang, not far from the bar we went to the first night before the Opening Ceremony.

The guys and I had been living off microwave burritos and Mcdonalds, so I couldn't turn down a chance for local food, and to get to talk to Kelly. Though I had no idea what the hell I was going to say to her. Especially not in front of her parents.

The restaurant was almost completely covered with snow and packed with more Americans than the place had probably ever seen. That was the only way I found the place, because there wasn't much for lights or signs, not that I could read Korean, but the line out the door said it must have been popular.

There was one particular table, crowded in the back, past the smell of sizzling food, that everyone was clamoring to see the girls at that table. Just like everyone else, I was drawn to the blonde in the corner. The one with the megawatt smile that's sparkle matched the silver medal hanging around her neck. A medal that would have been gold if it wasn't for me distracting her. Not that the girl wasn't a distraction to me, but that distraction motivated me. Made me want to push for better. If that's all I ever got from her, I should have been happy and so should have my parents. But I didn't just want her to push me for that one week. I wanted her to push me forever. As stupid as it sounded since I barely knew the girl, I wanted to have her for as long as she'd let me. Maybe it would only be during The Games or a few months after. Or maybe it really would be forever.

My parents had always ground it into me that I had to be the best and work my ass off to get it. But when they pushed, it always made me just want to do the opposite. They had me in fancy ski lessons, and I immediately dropped out when I was in middle school and picked up a board, never stopping. Mom and Dad tried to pretend I never started. I had to save up my own money from tips in at the lodge restaurant to buy my own board and taught myself by watching videos online. When I got the attention of some bigger skiers and snowboarders on the slopes, Mom and Dad finally accepted it as a career then got me a coach to start training me for the Olympics. It took me another thirteen years to make The Games, and each time I didn't qualify, my parents just pushed harder. It wasn't until I went away to train on my own for a few months that I was finally able to make it. I had to be my own motivation.

But with Kelly, everything was different. She made me want to be better. Didn't push, just gave me the inner jolt I needed to board the best I ever had. If only I could go back and not make that bet. Then again, if I didn't agree to it, then I wouldn't have ever met the golden girl.

"Blake, fancy seeing you here," Logan said, standing up and yelling over the crowd. Thank God he changed out of that stupid puffy shirt and vest that made him look like a gay pirate and wore a black sweater and jeans.

I glanced between him and the smiling Becca in her white beanie with wild blonde curls flying out from under it. Then I felt the heat of everyone's eyes on me. Everyone but Kelly who kept her head down, signing a napkin for someone.

Becca and Kelly's mom, Diane, stood up. I loved her bright, warm smile. It was nicer than any expression I'd ever gotten from my parents. "Blake! I feel like it's been forever since we've seen you! I hope you weren't expecting cheese curds since Becca ate them all."

"Damn right I did," Becca said, putting her fist in the air.

Diane took the few steps toward me and enveloped me in a big hug. Her giant American flag sweater smelled like

Korean food and a lot of floral perfume. It smelled like a warm and inviting home. Something I'd been missing out on and didn't know it until I met this American family.

"Hey, Diane, sorry, been busy," I said with a small smile as she let go of me.

"Well join us for dinner! There's always room for one more!" She put her hand on my arm, smiling brightly.

"I'm sure he's busy and has to get back to the slopes, Mom," Kelly said, piping up as she signed one more autograph then the crowd slowly scurried away as if they didn't want to feel her wrath.

She looked so small in the corner of the table in her light blue sweater and blonde hair over her shoulder. Small but fierce. She could give a look that could melt the ice. Or my heart.

I looked up, meeting Kelly's eyes. There was a hint of sadness, but something else to them: hope. At least that's what I wanted it to be. "I don't have any more competitions, so I'm pretty free, if you don't mind me joining," I said cautiously with a shrug.

Kelly pursed her lips. "Not at all."

I walked with Diane the few steps to the empty seat at the table and Kelly's dad, Dwayne, stood up, giving me a handshake that would knock the snot off a moose. He was Country big, towering over me in size and weight with a long gray beard that fell to the middle of his plaid shirt which stretched across his stomach like it was about to burst. "Glad to see you, Blake. That was one hell of a performance you had."

"You saw my slalom?" I asked, taking a seat.

Dwayne laughed, sitting next to me. "Well, when Becca said she had tickets to see something else, I couldn't turn it down. We only got to watch it from the stands and not in the athlete section, but it was still one hell of a show. No offense, Kelly, Skating's nice and all, but it's nice to get out in the snow. You know as long as I'm not driving in it. Or have to be up milking the cows."

"I'm guessing there are some Korean cows if you're getting homesick. Who watches them while you're gone anyway?" I asked.

Dwyane laughed a deep belly laugh, slapping me on the back which almost knocked my teeth out. "You're funny kid."

"Okay?" I asked, not sure how else to respond.

"They have people that work for them to help take care of the cows," Kelly muttered.

Dwayne smiled like a proud Papa. "Yep. That would have never been possible if Kelly, here, wouldn't have become our little golden girl. Hell, if neither one of my girls were Olympic superstars, they'd probably still be my only workers. Never thought I'd be watching them in The Games, or eating food at a hole in the wall in Korea. What do you suppose bulgolgi is anyway? Some kind of fish?" he asked, staring at the menu.

"It says right underneath it, Dad, the one you're looking at is squid and pork belly," Becca said, leaning over him and pointing at the menu.

"Why in the hell would anyone want to eat squid and pork? If you're gonna have pork it better be a pork chop, fried with gravy," Dwayne said with a gruff 'hrmph.' "Have you eaten any of this shit?" he asked, pointing the menu in my direction.

I shook my head. "Can't say that I've gotten a chance to eat much of the local food, sir. It's usually McDonald's or microwaving something in my cabin. The only time I've really had anything decent was with your daughter, but she hasn't let me take her out in a while."

I took a chance and looked up, smiling at Kelly. Instead of her fake smile, she smirked, squinting her eyes.

Diane blinked, looking at her daughter who was sitting next to her. "Well, now that competitions are over and you just have exhibitions, Kelly, maybe you two could get together again. At least before going back to the states. Blake, how far are you from Lake Placid?" Diane turned toward me.

"I'd have to Google it, but it's not a long plane ride, I know," I said, keeping my eyes on Kelly.

She didn't even look at me and put her napkin on the table, standing up and pushing out her chair. "I need to use the restroom. Excuse me."

Kelly didn't wait for a response as she made her way toward the back of the restaurant.

"What the hell was that about? Is she on her period or did you do something really bad to piss her off?" Dwayne asked, watching her walk away.

"Maybe I should go talk to her," Becca offered, but before she could stand, I pushed my chair back, the wooden legs screeching against the linoleum floor.

"Don't worry. I'll go see if she's okay," I said, not waiting for anyone to say something before I left the table and headed in the direction of the two small restrooms.

I guessed that they were one stalls since the restaurant couldn't have been bigger than the tiny cabin I was staying in, so I wouldn't have to worry about anyone else walking in. I just prayed Kelly was actually in there and didn't run away, or lock the door.

With luck, I jiggled the handle, and the door opened easily to a small, white tiled room with a toilet and sink directly in front of me, so close that I practically hit my knee on the toilet when I walked in. Standing in front of the small mirror was Kelly, who as soon as she saw my reflection whirled around, her eyes wide. "What the hell do you think you're doing?"

I closed the door and locked it before turning toward her, and taking the two steps across the floor until I was right in front of her. I put my hands on her cheeks and pulled her lips to mine. I missed her taste. Her touch. I didn't realize how much until I felt her mouth against mine.

She groaned and pulled back, trying to put as much space as she could between us in the tiny bathroom. "You can't just show up at dinner, which I'm sure Logan told you about, and then follow me to the bathroom like some kind of stalker."

"First off, it was Becca that invited me and second off; I'm not a stalker. I just saw how upset you were when you left the table and volunteered to check on you," I said, putting my hands on the sink, resting my palms as close as I could to her sides without touching her, even though I wanted to. I wanted to feel her so bad. It had only been a short while that I'd known her and that I'd been able to touch her, but I missed it. I missed everything about her.

Kelly glared, which should have hurt me, but instead, I couldn't help but smile at how cute she looked when she was mad with her furrowed brow. "You should know why I'm upset."

"I do. I completely understand. You should be enraged. Hitting me. Screaming at me. But instead, you're giving me that look. That absolute look of hatred which guts me, Kelly."

"I'm sure you'll get over it. You have Alexis to keep you warm," she muttered.

"Fuck Alexis. I mean, not literally. But you have to know she's nothing to me."

"Then why was she at your slalom? Why are you doing a sponsorship with her?"

I groaned and craned my neck before meeting Kelly's eyes. "Want me to say 'no' to the sponsorship? Because I'll do it. I was only going to take the damn deal so my parents would get off my back. Now that I have two medals around my neck I can get something better than a pain in the ass shampoo company who wanted to cut off my dreads anyway."

"You were going to cut your dreads?" Kelly asked softly, her hand going up toward my hair that fell on my shoulder. The jolt of electricity between us went straight below my belt just thinking about the feeling of her running her fingers through my hair. Then it was as if she realized what she was doing and shook her head, putting her hand down when she was only millimeters away from touching me.

"I didn't want to, mainly because I knew how much you liked them," I whispered.

"You shouldn't say no to something just because of me. I don't want to be the one to ruin your career," she said softly.

I moved my hands slowly up to her sides. Her body melting into my hands. "Kelly, you've done the exact opposite. You've inspired me to do better. To be better. Without you at these Games, I'd probably still be a punk ass snowboarder who people only believed finally got here because his parents paid off some officials. It may have been a bet that got me talking to you, but if I had to do it all over again, I'd still take that bet."

Kelly narrowed her eyes, but before she could speak, I leaned in closer, wrapping my arms around her waist and pulling her warm body against mine. "You're the best thing that's come into my life. Ever. You challenge me to do better. You make me feel something I've never felt before. That stupid bet may have been the reason I started talking, but damn I'm glad I did. Because I've gotten to know the girl labeled the ice queen and found out she's anything but. She's the queen of the ice. The one who commands the snow and everything else around her. You've commanded my heart, Kelly."

I put one hand on my chest between us. "You have to know that this started out as a bet, but it's always been you. You've controlled this since the beginning, and in the end, I may have won a stupid bet, but I truly lost if I can't have you."

Kelly swallowed hard, tears brimming her eyes that she held back. "I don't know what you want me to say, Blake. I'm hurt. I'm really fucking hurt."

I licked my lips. "I know. And I wish I wasn't the one to hurt you. If there were a way I could take away all the hurt, I would."

She sucked in a deep breath. "I need time, Blake."

"How much time?"

She shrugged. "I don't know, but I need that time and space. I know you mean well, but the more you keep shoving it in my face, the harder it is for me. I just need to think, okay? Can you give me that?"

I sighed. " I don't want to, Kelly. I don't fucking want to because I'm afraid if I do, you're just going to freeze me out forever, no pun intended."

She blinked, a single tear falling down her cheek. "Then you're just going to have to hope that you truly unfroze my heart."

CHAPTER 18

Kelly

I wasn't a crier. I didn't cry after finding out Joe had a fiancée back home in Colorado and I didn't cry the first time I didn't get gold at competition. But Blake Tremblay constantly had me on the verge of tears, and I didn't know how to handle it. How to be this girl that was so used to putting her feelings in check and now couldn't hold anything back.

I told Blake I wanted space and that was exactly what he gave me. He left the restaurant as soon as I told him to. My parents nor Becca or Logan asked where he went and I was okay not to have to discuss it.

But I wasn't okay with not seeing him. The Games were coming to a close, and I kept expecting him to show up at my dorm or see him at a coffee shop or restaurant. But he did just what he said he would do and gave me space. Space that I thought I needed.

But the truth was, by having space I realized how much I missed having him in my life. It was only a short time we were really together, but he changed me so much for the better. He made me realize I didn't need the angst or to ice everyone out to be the best. That I could have emotions and those emotions could push me further.

"Looking for someone dreadlocked in the crowd?" Logan whispered, his sequined suit hitting my cheek.

The exhibition would be our final performance, so we decided to have some fun with a more rock and roll routine. Logan wore the suit and an equally sparkly hat, and I had on a crystal encrusted red dress, wearing my hair down for the first time in competition. The tight updo was my signature, but like other ice queens, it was time for me to let it go. Just like my hatred of Blake, that is if I ever saw him again.

I'd scrolled through his social media on more than one occasion and thought maybe I'd even go to his cabin. But I didn't I was selfish, and I was a coward. And because of that, I could never see the guy again who turned my world upside down.

"Like you're looking for my sister?" I asked, raising an eyebrow as I looked at him over my shoulder.

Logan looked down at the ice. "She's probably out celebrating her gold," he muttered.

I wanted to know what was going on with them. They'd been so hot and cold. One minute they were laughing up a storm and the next they were avoiding each other. When the USA women's hockey team won gold, Logan cheered in the stands alongside my parents and me. He was there for every moment with us, but when we invited him out for a celebratory dinner, he turned it down. Said he was tired or something.

Instead of asking anything further on the subject I just smiled at my partner. "I think she'll be here. She wouldn't miss our last performance."

Logan's eyes slowly met mine. "Same with Blake."

Alexis Cote and Jacob Roy spun to their last position, smiling and waving to the crowd. I hadn't seen the brunette bitch since the free skate and had no intention of seeing her again after these games. Of course, she had to stop and see me, going in for a hug before she walked to her seat.

I darted backward, avoiding her arms and she glared. "What? No good luck hug?"

"Fuck off, Alexis," I spat.

Alexis, Jacob, and Logan's eyes all widened.

"Well, that was rude," Alexis stuttered.

"What's rude is you trying to falter me. We're professionals, or at least I am, and I wouldn't go for as many low blows as you have."

Alexis smirked. "Look who finally got some balls. Borrow those from Blake? Oh no, wait, you two aren't together. Never really were."

"Next up we have American skaters, Kelly Johnson and Logan Smith," the announcer boomed followed by applause filling the arena.

I forced a fake smile in Alexis' direction. "I'd rather be known as Blake Tremblay's bet than the bitch of the ice. Have a fun career with that, Alexis."

Before she could respond, I took Logan's hand, and we made our way to the center of the ice.

"That was awesome," Logan whispered in my ear as he placed his hands on my side and we got to our starting position.

"Gotta try something new every once in a while," I whispered.

"Maybe after this, we can both try something new. Head over to Blake's place so you can makeup and I'll find your sister?" he whispered.

I sighed. "Maybe."

It was what I needed to do. I needed to stop being such a bitch and just let all of this go. Tell him how I felt and if he rejected me in the end, then so be it. But for now, I had to put all of that worry and those feelings away. I had to think with my heart and put all those thoughts of love and lust for Blake into our routine instead of focusing on the bad.

The music started slowly, and we skated side by side then the tempo picked up, Logan grabbing my sides and tossed me in the air. This time I wasn't looking around to see who was watching but living in the moment. Every spin, every jump, it was my last of The Games.

Last.

These would be the last games I'd see Blake. That time in the bathroom might have been the last time I'd ever see him. Tears again pricked my eyes, and I pushed them back, getting ready to move into double triple axels alongside Logan.

When I heard the crowd gasp collectively. I looked over, wondering if Logan fell, but instead, I saw his eyes trailing toward the stand, so I followed all the way up to the glass that separated the seats from us.

The stadium was packed, but instead of everyone watching us, they were staring at the dreadlocked Canadian in a suit, singing along to the music at the top of his lungs and holding up a sign that said "Unfreeze my heart, Kelly. #Klake4eva."

I skated to a stop and stared as a security crew darted down the stairway. Blake glanced behind him then jumped on an empty chair next to him, waving the sign frantically in my direction. Before the guards could get to him, he ran in front of the guests in their seats, causing a roar of laughter to go through the crowd.

"What the hell is he doing?" Logan asked, skating to my side.

I watched as Blake zigged and zagged through the crowd, smiling and laughing until another set of security guards came, and they ended up cornering him, practically dragging him out of the stands.

Without thinking what I was doing, I skated toward the entrance of the rink that we just came in from and Coach was still standing at.

"Where are you going?" Logan yelled.

I opened the door and grabbed my skate guards. Coach opened his mouth to say something and bolted toward me, but I was faster and ran past him, and the camera crew pointed right at me.

I ran through the double doors and up the stairs until I was out in the lobby where more camera crews were focused on a large circle of guards.

I pushed past everyone until I heard his voice.

"Hey, guys, I was just having some fun. No need to get all handsy!"

I stopped, seeing Blake's smiling face with his hands up and a torn poster at his feet. I grabbed the poster and slowly stepped forward. "I think this is yours," I whispered.

The guards and camera crew stopped and stared at us, but I didn't care at that moment. All I cared about was the set of blue eyes on me.

"It's actually yours. Well for you. I had to pay way too much to buy that poster board at a convenience store. I was about to trade in my medal for it," Blake said with a single laugh, but there was no humor to it.

"You could have just messaged me," I said quietly.

"You wanted your space. And I gave it to you, but your space was killing me. I thought maybe I could just sit in the stands, but I think you know that I can't go without making a scene."

I laughed in spite of everything and a large grin spread across my face. "I know. I love that about you."

Blake stepped forward, closing the space between us as he put his hand to my cheek. "And I love everything about you. Frozen heart and all he whispered before pressing his lips to mine."

This time I didn't pull away or fight it. I wrapped my arms around his neck and kissed him fiercely, letting all my worries melt away as the camera crew and guards around us cheered.

I broke the kiss and put my forehead to Blake's. "Did you lose a bet? Is that really why you're here?"

He smiled, kissing me again. "No. I think I won one, without even knowing the game I was playing."

Before I could respond, I heard Logan yell through the crowd. I turned to see him pushing past the camera crew and guards. "Kelly! I saw this on the screen. Way to steal our moment."

I laughed. "Sorry about that. I'm sure we can still finish the routine. It's our last one, after all."

Logan shook his head. "I don't know. The crowd was cheering 2022. Think you can make it back for another Games?"

I turned toward Blake. "What do you think, Blake, wanna go for another Games?"

Blake grinned. "Wanna bet on making it again?"

I laughed, shaking my head. "I think I'm done with betting. Probably The Games too."

He put his hand on my cheek. "I'm not. You were the best bet I ever made."

I smiled in spite of all of the craziness. "And you're the best game I ever played."

He raised an eyebrow. "Are you going to let me win?"

I leaned in and kissed him slowly before whispering. "We'll see about that."

EPILOGUE

Six Months Later
Blake

The Games were a whirlwind, but my time after The Games, from buying a house to moving into that house then having Kelly move in with me was an even bigger rush.

We moved into the Adirondack style house with its own swimming pond that seemed like it was frozen most of the time and looked out over the mountains so we could both keep up with our sports.

Kelly hadn't formally announced anything, but she was definitely going back for The Games in 2022, and I was pretty sure she could convince me to do the same as long as I didn't break one of my old man knees as one of the oldest guys out there.

I just got done boarding for the day and came inside. Shaking the snow out of my dreads, I slipped my boots off on the back deck then went inside to see my phone blinking from the counter. I'd ruined enough of those things or lost them in the snow and had to go hunting in the mountains to know I wasn't going to bring it with me when I was on the board.

Picking up my phone, I unlocked and scrolled through the messages. Mostly from Kelly. It had been six months since I first met the girl and just seeing her name could still make me smile. The girl that started out as a bet had become so much more. And even though we'd only been together for six months, I was ready for that something more.

Kelly: Practicing later than I thought. I'll heat up something for dinner when I get home so don't wait up.

I frowned and looked at our stainless steel fridge. The galley kitchen was small but had a great view of the mountains. And it's not like we did much cooking since Kelly and I were both sponsored by a meal prep company who hooked us up. I was starting to get used to all of the chicken and healthy eating. Maybe I would be in shape for the next Games as the old man. Maybe.

Without thinking of what I was typing, I put in a quick reply to Kelly then went to the fridge, grabbing two of the pre-packed chicken, sweet potato, and green beans meals before throwing them in a plastic bag.

The girl practiced too damn much. She was always so dedicated to everything, and a little break for dinner with her favorite snowboarder probably couldn't hurt.

Kelly and I were regulars at the training center. It was like our own little town where everybody knew our name.

I knew every building and training area like the back of my hand, so it didn't take long to get to the ice rink, which was surprisingly empty.

"What the hell?" I muttered, looking over the freshly zambonied ice.

"Looking for Kelly?" A gruff voice bellowed.

I looked to the stands where Kelly's coach sauntered toward me. He was a burly man with a graying mustache and balding head. He looked like all the coaches I'd always seen on cheesy movies, complete with the permanent scowl. That or the guy still blamed me for Kelly and Logan not getting gold in The Games.

"Yeah. Brought her dinner so she wouldn't get hungry during practice," I said, holding up the plastic bag.

"Hmmm." Coach crossed his arms over his chest. "Her and Logan finished up a few minutes ago. She said she had plans with you."

"With me?" I asked, raising an eyebrow.

Coach sighed, rubbing his forehead. "That's what she told me. She went to the locker room, and I haven't seen her. You can wait for her down that hallway."

I nodded, not sure what else to say. "Okay, thanks, Coach."

I started in the other direction and Coach yelled after me,

"Don't screw up her concentration for practices if you find a surprise you don't like!"

I wasn't sure what any of that meant so I just waved and jogged toward the locker room.

Since the place was empty, with it mostly being summer athletes in to train, and they were all at dinner, I thought the girl's locker room would be empty. And I was right. There wasn't anyone near the first or second set of lockers, and it wasn't until I got toward the back of the room that I heard faint rustling. Slowly I approached the last set and then peered around the corner.

Kelly stood leaned over the bench with her perfect ass toward me. She was wearing nothing but a pair of black satin panties and bra. The sight of all of her creamy white skin already had me rock hard.

She didn't notice me or hear me, so I slowly walked to where she was standing and leaned over, pressing my lips to her ear. "Practicing late?"

She gasped and whirled around, fully standing upright. Damn if I thought the back was a sight, seeing her toned stomach and perky breasts spilling out the top of her bra was enough to get me off right there.

It didn't matter how many times I'd seen her like this; I couldn't get enough of her. She was all mine, and I loved it. I didn't need a bet or anything else. Just us. No secrets. No bets.

"What are you doing here?" She asked, crossing her arms over her chest.

I frowned and held up the bag. "I brought you dinner since you said you were practicing late. I thought I'd surprise you, but you must have had other plans since you're wearing those panties I've never seen."

Anger suddenly boiled up inside of me. Did she tell me she was practicing late so she could meet up with someone else? Would I have to go and kick some blue haired swimmer's ass?

Kelly huffed and rolled her eyes. "No, you hoser, I was going to surprise you and come home early to show you this new set that came in, and now you ruined the surprise."

I grinned, setting the bag down. "Did you just call me a hoser?"

She put her hand on her hip. "Yeah, that's your Canadian slang for an idiot, right?"

I laughed then leaped forward, wrapping my arms around her waist and pulling her tight little body against me. "I love it when you talk Canadian to me."

"Blake!" She squealed. "We're in a locker room! We can do this when we get home!"

"Why?" I asked, sliding my hands down to cup her ass. "Nobody else is here, and you've been saying you need other hobbies," I said as I moved my lips to her supple neck and kissed down to the spot where it met her shoulders.

She moaned, squirming against me, but her core dug right into my bulge. "Blake, by hobbies I didn't mean sex in a locker room," she cooed.

"We don't have to have sex, there are other ways I can make you move," I murmured into her neck, sliding my hand to the waist band of her panties before slowly dipping my fingers to her soft flesh.

"Blake," she whispered.

I didn't know if she said my name for me to keep going or to stop, so I just took it as the former and hooked a finger inside of her. She gasped, her pussy clenching around my finger as I added my thumb, swirling it around her swollen clit.

"Oh, fuck, Blake," she moaned, rocking her hips against my hand.

"I thought you didn't want to do anything in the locker room," I smirked, feeling her clench around my finger.

She moaned her head bowing as she rode out her orgasm. "You can't ask me these types of questions mid-climax, and you can't start something without finishing it."

Before I could ask what she meant by that, her hands were at the waistband of my jeans, unbuttoning, unzipping, and tugging them down.

My dick sprang out of my boxers like it was ready and waiting for her.

"Do you have a condom?" Kelly asked breathlessly.

I froze. "Uh, you know, I'm not sure, but you're on the pill now so why don't we go without? Let me feel all of you," I whispered, regaining my composure and sliding down her bra straps, kissing her shoulders.

"Pulling a sexy move isn't going to make me forget protection, Blake," she murmured, moving her hands to my back pockets.

Before I could stop her, she pulled out the black velvet box. She stepped back, holding the box in her hands.

"Blake…is this…?"

I smirked and grabbed the box from her, opening it up to reveal the sparkling Princess cut diamond ring that I seriously thought about trading in my medal to afford. Luckily, we got a sponsorship the day after I bought the ring. Sure it was soon to think about marriage, but I was more than sure about her.

"Well, Kelly, I was planning this romantic moment with sharing a picnic with you in the stands and telling you how it may be early in our relationship but I've known for a while that you were the only one that I'm supposed to be with."

Kelly stared at me wide-eyed as I got down on my knees, holding the box to her. "But of course, my queen is impatient and had to find the box before I got a chance. So, I guess there's no better way to ask you than now. Kelly Johnson, will you make me the tallest guy on the mountain and be my partner? In The Games, in sponsorships, and as my wife?"

Kelly put her hands to her lips, a small gasp escaping her mouth as tears pricked her eyes.

"Please don't tell me you're gonna say no when I'm here on my knees with my dick out."

She shook her head a small smile crossing her lips as she moved her head down. "No…the answer is definitely not no."

"So it's a yes?" I raised an eyebrow.

"It's a definite yes," she squeaked.

The grin spread across my face, and I put the ring on her finger before standing up and taking her hands. "Now that you interrupted me, and I had to propose with my junk out, we're gonna have to finish."

"But what if I just want to stare at my ring?" Kelly asked with a smile, holding the sparkly diamond glimmering off her ring finger.

I smirked and pulled her to me. "Then we'll have to go for a position that you can do both."

She gasped as I turned her around and pressed her back to my front. Pushing her against the lockers, her hand flattened against the metal doors as I slowly pulled down her black satin panties and she stepped out of them.

"Now spread those beautiful legs, fiancée," I commanded, putting my hand between her thighs as she moved them apart.

"Yes, fiancé," she practically moaned as she lifted her perfectly round ass up.

Since Kelly was a bit shorter than me, I had to lean down, pressing my lips to her shoulder as I moved her hips up, and slowly inched her wet entrance over my cock. She moaned as I filled her up to the hilt and she pushed her ass into me.

"Damn, you always feel so good," I murmured rocking into her. This was the first time we'd gone without a condom, and I could feel all of her.

"You do," she whimpered, circling her hips against me.

I kept one hand on her waist and the other on her braid, pulling on it as I kissed her shoulders, moving in and out of her in a delicately slow rhythm.

"Blake, I'm gonna, I'm gonna," she moaned, her body clenching around me as she writhed against my back.

I moved my hand from her hair and wrapped both arms around her waist, rocking faster in her.

She moaned, her body clenching around me again and I knew I wouldn't last long, so I moved one hand from my waist to her stomach and slid my thumb to her clit, circling it as we moved.

She screamed out her orgasm as I came along side her.

We both stood there, leaning against the cool metal lockers, breathing heavily together.

"You think anyone heard us?" I whispered, kissing just below her earlobe.

"Do we care if they did?" she asked with a laugh.

"Hey, you're the Olympic golden girl."

She held up her hand. "And fiancée of snowboarding world record holder, Blake Tremblay. Think this is going to start a US and Canadian war?"

"I don' t know. Wanna make a bet on it?" I asked.

She laughed. "I think we're both done with bets, though I'm going to have to tell Becca she won."

I raised an eyebrow even though she couldn't see me. "What kind of bet was that? That we'd have sex in the locker room."

Kelly leaned against my back and looked up, her sparkly blue eyes meeting mine. "No, Becca said we'd be engaged within six months. I told her I didn't think so, so we made a bet. I lost."

I smiled, shaking my head. "Technically, when you think about it, you won because you're the one engaged, though I should squeeze you for making a bet about me."

She smiled. "I learned from the best."

I kissed her. Despite everything that happened with us, if I had to go back in time I'd still make the stupid bet because in the end, it led me to something better than a gold medal or The Games: the love of my life.

The End. For Now.

Magan Vernon has been living off of reader tears since she wrote her first short story in 2004. She now spends her time killing off fictional characters, pretending to plot while she really just watches Netflix, and she tries to do this all while her two young children run amok around her Texas ranch.

Website: www.maganvernon.com

Goodreads: www.goodreads.com/maganvernon

Facebook Page: www.facebook.com/authormaganvernon

Twitter: www.twitter.com/maganvernon

Newsletter: http://eepurl.com/qIJA5

Magan's Minions (Reader Group): http://on.fb.me/1lVsZEo